PRAISE FOR **M**

Top 10 Romance of 201.

— BOOKLIS_ _ _ NIGHT IS MINE, HOT POINT, HEART STRIKE

One of our favorite authors.

— RT BOOK REVIEWS

Buchman has catapulted his way to the top tier of my favorite authors.

— FRESH FICTION

A favorite author of mine. I'll read anything that carries his name, no questions asked. Meet your new favorite author!

— THE SASSY BOOKSTER, FLASH OF FIRE

M.L. Buchman is guaranteed to get me lost in a good story.

— THE READING CAFE, WAY OF THE WARRIOR: NSDQ

I love Buchman's writing. His vivid descriptions bring everything to life in an unforgettable way.

— PURE JONEL, HOT POINT

MIDNIGHT TRUST

A DELTA FORCE ROMANCE

M. L. BUCHMAN

Buchman Bookworks

SIGN UP FOR M. L. BUCHMAN'S
NEWSLETTER TODAY

and receive:
Release News
Free Short Stories
a Free book

Do it today. Do it now.
http://free-book.mlbuchman.com

Other works by M. L. Buchman:

$\mathcal{I}$t wasn't his sniper rifle, but Chad could easily be talked into having an M134 minigun of his own to play with now and then.

He short-bursted just two to three seconds at a time—which at four thousand rounds per minute was a daunting couple hundred rounds each time he hit the trigger. When he was on the hustle with his combat rifle, he might shoot a round or two per second. With his sniper rifle, he only ever had to fire it once per target. The minigun might not hit with every round the way he did—Delta Force training wasn't about wasting ammunition —but...

"Hoo-ee doggies! Just lay down now, dudes. Daddy's got a brand new toy."

"Easy, hotshot," Carmen, the way-cute redhead on the big Chinook helicopter's other gun practically laughed.

"Suppressive fire. That's what I'm talking about! Suppressive, hell. This thing is a shredder."

The twin-rotor helicopter was making its second pickup of the night.

He'd been the first: out doing solo recon deep in the

Colombian jungle. Just before sunset, the Night Stalkers' MH-47G helo had swooped in, he'd strolled up the rear ramp, and twenty tons of twin-rotor helo had flitted away with no one the wiser. A couple of other helos had circled high above on guard duty but weren't needed.

Their second pickup—in the last of the failing dusk—wasn't going so hot. Masses of groundfire ripped through the humid, cloying air. One of the joys of the jungle: a man got wetter just standing still than he did running around in most other places.

On the "even worse" side of the list, the Chinook's starboard gunner had just taken a hit right through the gunner's window. It had to be pure luck—put enough lead in the air and you're bound to hit something—their current enemy's rather boring tactic. Had to be, because none of these cocaine-running Colombian hillbillies could shoot that well on purpose.

No fountains of blood sprouted from the gunner's upper arm, which meant the dude's arteries were still flowing in the right direction. Chad had slapped a compression badge on the arm, then tossed it in a sling when it was clear that the bone had been shattered. "Better have someone look at that when you get back to base."

"Ruddy hell *yeah!*" The guy agreed weakly with a posh British accent.

Then Chad had stepped up to the swivel-mounted, six-barrel Gatling Minigun himself and patched in to the intercom before giving it a try.

Su-weet!

He'd never fired an M134D except during weapons familiarization on the Fort Bragg range—certainly not from the vantage of a hovering helo. This weapon delivered a whole new level of hurt to the bad guys.

The extract being run by the 160th Night Stalkers was a textbook setup. Hover at the edge of a steep canyon with sixty feet and twenty tons of monster, twin-rotor helo hanging over a whole lot of nothing. Lower the three-meter-wide rear ramp onto the edge of the cliff, and wait for the cavalry to come trotting out of the jungle. Just to add some spice, the pilots were facing out over the canyon and couldn't see shit behind them, but they were Night Stalkers and had it nailed.

Pure textbook.

Except just like all such scenarios, Chad knew full well *why* they ended up in textbooks…because they always went wrong. This time proved to be no exception.

The jungle ended a hundred meters away, except for just a few scattered trees. Those had forced the helo to hover out at the cliff edge to avoid catching a rotor blade on some wax palm or giant mahogany with helo-crashing in mind.

The good guys had appeared at one end of the clearing while the bad guys were shooting madly from the other.

And from the side.

And from behind the friendlies—which was very unfriendly of them.

Normally an MH-47G Chinook didn't fight—it was the cargo van of Special Operations Forces. They left the dirty work up to the big hammer of the Black Hawks. Except there was so much going on tonight, the two Hawks they'd brought with them were too busy to defend the Chinook as well.

So, Chad leaned out as far as the gun would go and blasted showers of lead back into the jungle's verge. The Minigun did a good job of making would-be shooters keep their heads down. Thankfully, these guys weren't exactly quick learners and he kept picking them off in groups of two and three.

"If I was on the other end of this, I'd be diggin' a hole."

"Wouldn't stop me from finding you," Carmen called back as she, too, blasted away. She wore a ring, but maybe it was one of those phony "Keep Away" signs that a guy could sometimes talk his way around.

"I dunno. When I dig down, I go *deep.*"

Didn't earn him the right kind of laugh, so maybe the ring was real.

He picked off someone with a heavy machine gun and his ammo monkey. Good to have that out of play. The 5.56 mm ammo was a pain—all most of these guys were throwing. But the .50 cal stuff could really hurt—punching holes in people and helicopters—until it suddenly wasn't anymore because he'd blasted it out of existence.

The friendlies were approaching in an MRZR. The four-person military ATV was fast, but not fast enough—they were getting hammered on the long crossing through the sparse trees.

Chad went to unleash his new toy on another section of the unfriendly types.

Pull trigger. Electric motor spins the barrels up to seven hundred RPM, and it starts throwing an impressive line of 7.62 mm rounds into the night. Every fifth one a tracer that shows up brilliant green in his night-vision goggles. It was the strange half-light at end of day where his NVGs were better than nothing, but not by much.

Might as well be firing blind.

For half a second, sweep right.

At a full second, shift and sweep left.

Second and a half—a hellacious grinding noise from the machine and the ammunition belt just stopped moving. The barrels still spun, but the comforting buzz-saw roar of sixty-six supersonic rounds per second wasn't happening.

He let the electric motor spin down.

When he grabbed the barrels and gave them a test spin, they moved just fine. Hot as hell, but he wore gloves, so it was okay. Hot barrels were normal on a Minigun.

He looked down at the wounded Brit leaning with his back against the hull.

"Sounds like you sheared the pin in the delinker. Two-dollar part, but takes ten minutes to replace it."

"We've got, like, thirty seconds."

The guy shrugged, and even in the NVGs, Chad could see him wince at the pain in his arm.

"Got a jam here. Starboard side. Not clearable," Chad reported over the intercom.

"Shit!" Carmen was not happy. "Damn Delta Force operator comes aboard and breaks my hundred-thousand-dollar weapon system."

"This 'damn Delta Force operator' didn't do it to you out of spite."

"Like I'm gonna believe that shit." Too bad she was taken—woman had a mouth on her and kept her sense of humor even when things got bad.

Without comment, the pilots twisted the big helo on its tail. They kept the ramp on the ground and rotated the nose around until Carmen's weapon had almost a full sweep of the jungle, which meant she had to work twice as hard.

"You guys are so damn good," he called out to the pilots as he unlimbered his HK416 rifle. Twenty-round magazine and he only had two spares on him. He'd just gone from a loaded four-thousand-round kicker-case bolted to the deck…to sixty.

As the view on his side was now over the night-shrouded canyon, he strode over to join Carmen. Maybe he could get some shots out the edge of her gun window.

He was halfway across the eight-foot-wide cargo bay when it hit him.

Literally.

The MRZR raced aboard, shot up the length of the cargo bay—and slammed into him.

He heard a scream and a curse, but he wasn't sure which one was his as he was thrown forward.

Chad landed on his back between the two pilot seats and his helmet smacked hard against the main console.

"Nice one, cowboy." Captain Roberts looked down at him. "You just shattered our central screen with your head. Haven't you broken enough already?"

"Guess not," Chad managed to admit and wondered about his own body. Was he in shock? He wasn't feeling any pain. Had his body armor saved him…or not? Experience told him that if he was hurt, he would be feeling it soon enough.

"Well, it's not getting any better. They just knocked out one of our engines." While Roberts flew, the copilot's hands were moving fast. First he pulled the engine fire T-handle and then did more of whatever it was helo copilots did during a crisis.

Chad lay on the radio console that ran between the pilot seats and wondered if he should try getting up. It seemed as if perhaps he should.

He raised his head first. Good sign, his neck still worked.

He could see his left foot was caught between the MRZR's bull-bar bumper and its winch.

He could feel his foot! Another good sign, implying that his spine had remained intact. Attempting to twist his foot free transmitted loud and clear that there was nothing wrong with the nerves in his knee. *Ow!*

The driver was looking at him in some surprise.

Even being dressed like a Spec Ops solider—in armored vest, helmet, and enough weaponry to suppress a riot—couldn't hide that the driver was seriously female.

Woman drivers.

THE MRZR's brakes had worked before Tanya had entered the battle, but she hadn't used them much since then.

Either they were shot out on the crossing or her impact with the side of the Chinook's rear ramp had killed them. The helicopter had twisted just as she'd been racing for the ramp, wanting nothing more than out of the hellhole they'd entered.

At least two of her team were injured—one had nearly blown out her eardrum with a scream as the MRZR slammed to a halt.

Worse, their jungle target had been a dry hole. The senior leaders of the drug lab who were supposed to be there had left an hour before her team struck, but they'd left plenty of cartel troops in place.

The guy she'd hit raised his head to look at her with the twinned cyborg eyes of night-vision goggles. She heard the helo laboring as it struggled to pull back from the cliff. It went nose high—not a good sign.

And the MRZR began rolling backward. She slammed it into first gear—with the engine stopped, that should have been her parking brake. But the helo deck's angle was increasing and it wasn't enough. No chains in place yet to tie it to the deck.

"Out! Out! Out!" Tanya yelled at her crew.

First she stiff-armed Marta beside her, knocking her out of the passenger seat and onto the cargo deck. Then Tanya jumped out and pulled on Carl's shoulder to drag him out of the rear seat as Max jumped out the other side. Carl flopped down to the deck like a bag of steaming dogshit as the MRZR continued rolling backward. She snapped a monkey line onto his vest's lifting ring so that he didn't slide away before she was ready to bandage him up.

"You gotta be kidding me!" The man she'd hit was being dragged by the vehicle as it continued rolling backward down the steeply slanted cargo bay. His foot was caught in the front bumper. A glance showed that the rear cargo ramp was still down, filled with yawning darkness.

She grabbed his hand, but it was too little, too late. In moments they were both sliding along the steel deck. Shouts followed them, but no hands were quick enough.

If she was being smart, she'd let go.

She wasn't being smart.

And his grip on her wrist was so powerful, it wouldn't matter if she did let go—because he didn't.

He kicked free of the MRZR just as they bumped over the rear ramp hinge. She almost got hold of a load tie-down ring, but their momentum ripped it out of her fingertips.

They were launched out of the rear of the helicopter, falling through the night, down into the dark shadows of the jungle-lined canyon.

———————

THE PLUNGE into warm water so far below made Chad feel like *Butch Cassidy and the Sundance Kid.* The Wild West, where men looked like Robert Redford and women looked like Katharine Ross. Of course the jungles of Colombia weren't exactly arid American Wild West.

But any sense of a cute movie-scene-moment was fast replaced by a desperate need to breathe. Chad struggled to the surface in time to see the Chinook regain some degree of control and limp away, trailing black smoke thick enough to blot out the first of the stars.

It was far too dark to see if there was anyone on the tail ramp looking for him. His NVGs were gone along with his helmet. Both were probably at the bottom of the river staring at a brook trout. Fishing with night vision—there was an idea he hadn't thought of. Spear gun and a snorkel—he'd be set.

He hoped it was a trout. Piranha were only in the Amazon, right?

Hopefully *someone* on board had noted his abrupt departure from the aircraft. Maybe even some sympathy points from the redhead.

A short, sharp explosion on some rocks, which were rapidly disappearing astern as the river raced him downstream, told him of the MRZR's final resting place. And good riddance to it. Damned machine. Though it wasn't the machine's fault. It was that damned woman dri—

A Black Hawk rushed down into the canyon. So they *had* missed him. That was gratifying. Along with apparent survival and no obvious crippling injury from being run over while inside a helicopter, it wasn't such a bad night after all.

The river narrowed, picking up even more speed, and raced

him under overhanging trees. The Black Hawk pulled up sharply and disappeared from view. The exotic leaves—that were way bigger than he was—blocked all sign of the searching helo. No chance they'd find him anytime soon.

That's when he remembered that he wasn't alone. The female driver had fallen with him, their hands clasped together until the fall began.

"Hello!"

"Keep your voice down. We do not know who is to be listening." The woman's voice came from close behind him. Her voice was slightly stilted American—fluent enough, but as a second language, with a background accent he didn't recognize. German…ish.

He twisted around enough to face her as the river rushed them along, but there wasn't much to see in the darkness.

"We should be getting out of this river." Woman driver or not, she had the dead calm of a Spec Ops soldier no matter what the danger.

"Perhaps we should wait." There was just enough starlight to see quite how fast they were rushing by the rocks and trees of the narrow canyon. It was going to hurt if they tried to get out of the water here.

"Waiting for what?"

"Wait for—" Then he heard the roar. Not the roar of an incoming rocket. No helicopter sounded like that, American or otherwise. No. It was the roar of—

"Hang on!"

They grabbed each other just as the waterfall flipped them out into space and they began the long fall down to an unseen pool.

---

2

*T*anya lay on the shore of the waterfall's pool. She didn't care that it was lumpy with river-pounded stone, she was simply glad to be out of the rushing water. And breathing.

"Well, that was an exhilarating ride, wasn't it?" The man lay beside her.

She could only laugh. It had been. And if she never had to do it again, it would be much too soon. But it would make a very good story now that she'd lived to tell it. Not that she had anyone to tell it to.

It was too dark to see anything except the stars in the narrow slice of black sky exposed by the jungle river. She checked for her light pack, but it was gone so no NVGs.

"You are, okay?" She had to shout to be heard over the waterfall.

"And now who is raising their voice inappropriately? The damn woman driver who got me into this mess?"

"Maybe I should inappropriate you once in the nose."

" '...one in the nose...' is the idiom you're after. And don't you think that running me over was enough abuse for one evening?"

"And what of you dragging me out of the nice dry helicopter? This was *not* so very nice. I do not know why I even bothered trying to save such a lout. There I was, safely aboard the helicopter, right where I wanted to be, and you go falling out of it and taking me with you. I definitely owe in the nose two."

"Twice."

She could see by his outline moving against the stars that he'd eased to an upright position. She sat up as well.

"Sorry," she actually did feel bad about running him over. "Though I would not have hit you if my brakes had still worked. But they failed. Why did you step all of a sudden into the middle of the lane? All I was going to hit were some steel dividers behind the pilots."

"To test your driving skills, of course. They suck, by the way. And I'll just mention that your 'middle of the lane' was the middle of a helicopter."

"I have already apologized and now I'm done. Maybe the next time, I will be hitting you harder. No easing off the gas."

"Real nice."

"Just like you," Tanya snapped back. None of this was how her quiet night was supposed to have gone. No kingpin leaders taken out. Two people on her crew shot. And now she lay half-drowned along a roaring jungle with a macho jerk.

That earned her an unexpected laugh, "You got that straight, lady. Nice is something I'm very *not* good at. Not one little bit."

"You are a bad man?" There was something familiar about him. His easy banter. His voice.

"Can be if you want me to. I can be very bad," he whispered close beside her ear.

She almost had it. Several years back. Over the border in Bolivia? No! "Venezuela. Hostages on the top floor of a—"

Suddenly a massive hand had a tight chokehold around her throat.

She tried to breathe, but couldn't.

"How do you know about that?"

He didn't ease up enough to let her speak. She pinched the nerve cluster behind his thumb. He grunted as she peeled his hand back, then took a breath.

His punch headed for her kidneys, which she barely blocked in time. That wasn't Spec Ops training, it was street fighting. Then she knew.

"Cut it out, Chad!"

HE FROZE. Not all that many people outside of Delta Force knew his real name. And even fewer of those were women. "Clive" worked well for him when on the prowl—a contrast with his corn-fed, Iowa-farm-boy looks that made him more intriguing to women. He'd tried Dominic, like Vin Diesel's hard-ass character in the *Fast and Furious* movies, but he couldn't seem to get traction with it. Clive, like Mr. Chill Clive Owen, did the trick. And he always made a point of memorizing the local number for Chinese take-out in case the woman wanted solace when she tried to call him for another passage at arms. He'd always considered that to be a kind touch.

This time he reached out into the dark more slowly and brushed a hand over her hair. Fine enough that it was probably blonde. Smooth, with a sharp jawline cut that looked cute on a lot of women.

A kiss. He could always remember a woman by her kiss, but that didn't seem like the right next step. She'd blocked his kidney punch, which only a top soldier could do.

A top soldier with her England-English slightly fractured by a vaguely German accent should be a clue, but it wasn't. And it wasn't exactly German either. He recalled a long time ago when his teammate Richie—their geek and linguist—identified just this accent as…Israeli. It couldn't be!

"Say something. In Spanish."

"*No habla Español,*" she denied with a perfect accent. Her Spanish had always been flawless.

"Tanya Zimmer!" He remembered a lightning-filled sky on Venezuela's Lake Maracaibo. A lake where… "You bitch! You walked away from me. We were doing so good, then just like that…" He tried to snap his fingers, but they were too wet. "Shit, woman!"

"No, I *drove* away in a stolen police boat."

"We had something."

"We did," her voice was unaccountably soft, but he knew all of the tricks women used and that was definitely one of them.

"Well, you're not getting me back that easily."

"As if I'd want you," she didn't even have the decency to hesitate in her answer.

He'd thought about her a lot since then. Nothing serious of course—she was just another woman, after all. But he'd casually watched for her when they were undercover in some crowd, taking down a cocaine lab, or something else that left him time to look around.

He never, ever missed a woman, but…

Shit, man!

"Do you have a radio?" Tanya needed to change the topic and change it fast. People in their line of work couldn't afford attachments. They weren't ever real anyway. Definitely not with a man like Chad or, she had to admit, with a woman like her. Being an operative for Israel's Mossad elite counterterrorism unit, Kidon, didn't exactly make for a predictable homelife—as if she'd want such a thing.

She shifted her butt, trying to find a comfortable position on the river rock without luck. Thankfully the night was warm, so the river water evaporating out of her clothes was only a little chilly.

But happy homelife was what most guys saw in her for reasons she could never fathom. They took one look at her blonde hair and bright blue eyes, then decided she'd make the perfect housewife. Not a chance. Guys might think she was the fantasy lover with the secret family—like Vera Farmiga in *Up in the Air*—which she really had to see someday as so many people thought that's who she was. So very not.

She wouldn't fit in with some family of her own any more than she'd ever fit in the one with her dark-haired, brown-eyed parents. And her father had certainly never forgiven her or her mother for wherever Mom had gone to find those blonde-and-blue genes. Not that she blamed Mom. Dad had been an abusive asshole, very expressive with his fists, right up until the moment he'd "accidentally" stumbled off the sidewalk in front of a truck. She still couldn't find it in her to feel bad about that. Their lives had improved for a little while until Mom found another man just like the last one. It made no sense. That's when Tanya had given up and moved out. She'd finished her last three years of high school while living in the corner of an abandoned Tel Aviv warehouse with some other like-minded teens.

After a brief silence, Chad responded, "Feels as if my radio was smashed against some rocks. Of course, so do I, so I can totally empathize with it. How about you?"

"Mine was smashed in the face of a drug lab's guard just before I breaked his neck. But we should be moving away from this waterfall," the mist in her face was thick and was finally chilling her despite the warm night in central Colombia.

She rose to her feet, but all that came from Chad beside her was some tumbling of small rocks and then a low curse that sounded like pain.

"Are you okay? You said you were okay."

"Apparently my knee has other ideas. A sprain, I think. But I won't enjoy walking on it."

Tanya listened to the sound of the water rushing through the rocks close by their feet. The river was still moving fast. Rapids or maybe another waterfall lay ahead. She had studied all of the escape routes before her mission, but she hadn't bothered to learn the river a mile downstream from the pickup point, two miles from the drug lab. A mistake she wouldn't make again.

"I am certainly not going to be swimming anymore." She reached out until she found his shoulder and tapped twice. At her gesture, he offered a hand and she helped him to his feet.

They slipped their arms around each other's waists. He felt strong and gloriously familiar. There had never been any doubt about the explosion-hot sex between them, but she knew that explosions never lasted past the initial heat.

"You Delta are far more trouble than you are being worth."

"Says the woman with the driving problem."

She loosened her grip as if she was going to dump him to the ground. He hung on a little tighter. By his hard lurches and ragged breath, his injury was much worse than he was letting on. No less than she'd expect from him.

"So, what trouble have you been up to lately?" Chad asked kindly enough, then finished it off with a low curse as she stumbled badly.

"Nothing good," she thought bitterly of her latest mission. "Parts of this country have improved wonderfully since the crushing of the worst of the cartels. Other parts... *Oy vey!* How about you?"

"Well, there's this nice pair of restaurants I could take you to in Medellín. Right up in the *barrios* of *Comuna 13* that might give you some hope. Amazing food. We swept the streets a little while I was there." Meaning that some drug gang or cartel was hurting bad if they'd drawn the attention of Chad's Delta Force team.

"Are you guys still together?"

"Lot of changes since you rode with us, but, yeah, the core team is the same. Kyle and Carla, of course."

"Of course." The team leader and the Wild Woman—wholly unpredictable in a very good way. Tanya had been almost as sorry to leave her behind as she'd been sorry to leave Chad. Interesting that Kyle and Carla were still a couple and yet continuing to serve in the same unit. It didn't sound like the American military—who were as prudish as their Puritan roots—but it did sound very like Kyle and Carla.

"Richie and Duane have both gone down." They hobbled under the cover of a large oak. By the sound of it, the river had widened and slowed, but she still wasn't willing to get back in the water.

"How were they killed?" A shame. She'd liked them, what little she'd known of them.

"*Killed?*" Chad lurched hard to one side as a rock clattered aside and tumbled down the step bank to *plonk* into the rushing river. It seemed to echo off the canyon walls despite the thick jungle to either side. She barely kept them both from going down. "Never said killed. They both fell for that happily-ever-after crap."

"Spec Ops and a civilian. Since when has that ever worked?"

"Never," Chad agreed. "But their ladies are both on the team. Not sure I'd dare mess with either of them any more than with Carla. They're not like her—but they're both dangerous in their own way. And the three of them together are just fucking lethal."

"What about you?"

"Oh, like I believe in that marriage bullshit. Gotta stop and rest. Maybe find a crutch or a passing ambulance."

She helped ease him down at the base of the first tree, a ceiba by the feel of the great flat vertical planes of the roots.

At least they agreed on the nonsense of marriage. She'd take a lover any day, especially one as fantastic as Chad. But long term? He'd said it right—pure bullshit.

CHAD SPOTTED a familiar shape against the stars. Reaching out, he touched a banana. A bunch of them pulled away easily without mushing. He handed a couple to Tanya and they chowed down together.

He missed the feeling of her against his side. Despite all of her heavy gear, Tanya Zimmer was a whole lot of woman. Slender and built. Sexy and lethal.

But he was in no condition to take advantage of it even if she was offering—which, he was chagrined to notice, she wasn't. He'd been awake for four days, not daring to sleep so close to the drug smugglers' camp. And with each minute he didn't report in, his hard-won information was aging. They could have changed patrol strategies, added new booby traps on the approaches, or even have pulled camp and already be on the move.

Being on the verge of the staggers and hallucinations from sleep deprivation wasn't being helped by his knee stinging like a mess of bees each time he took a step. The hallucinations he could deal with—at this point just distant gunfire. He often dreamed of that anyway. Sometimes echoing down the Detroit back alleys of his childhood, sometimes the soft spit of his sniper rifle. As long as they were distant, he didn't care if they were real or just in his sleep-deprived imagination. What he cared about was his heartbeat counting out the seconds one by one— each one aging his knowledge toward a colossal waste of time.

A hot woman like Tanya was beyond anything he could deal with right now. Some women were easy to keep happy. A little foreplay, some hot action, and then let them snuggle to their heart's content afterward, dreaming of long-term shit that was never going to happen.

Some women required more attention.

Tanya had required his *full* attention. Her body and the woman who lived inside that lovely skin had *demanded* it like no one else before her. He'd be glad to drift off if it meant hallucinating a few more things about her.

He banged the back of his head against the tree trunk a few times. It hurt. That was good. It staved off the sleep his body so desperately craved for another few minutes.

3

"*A*we. Aren't you two just the sweetest thing? Too bad neither of you can keep watch for shit and you're both dead now."

"I would suggest great care about the next words you utter, they could be your last." Tanya had spotted the lone man prowling along the river's edge ten minutes ago. She and Chad were barely hidden by the ceiba's buttress-root shadow in the morning light, so it had seemed ill-advised to wake him and try to move. The morning sun was to the newcomer's back, so she couldn't see his face.

"What are you talking about, sweetheart?"

She shifted her hand to reveal the Uzi Pro she'd had zeroed on his face since the moment he came into range. The weapon was based on a Micro Uzi and could unleash 9 mm submachine gun hell from the two-kilo weapon that fit under her arm. At this range, she couldn't miss if she tried.

"I told you he'd be fine," a lovely woman with a soft Spanish accent stepped around the towering buttress root from the other side. Her own Glock 19 Compact sidearm appeared to be lazily held, but its silencer was centered at Tanya's heart.

Tanya flinched. She couldn't help it, the woman had approached from behind with no warning. It took an immense amount of fieldcraft to fool Tanya's training.

"Oh, hey." Chad woke and raised his head from where he'd spent the night slumped against her.

If he hadn't mumbled something about being on solo recon, she might have shoved him off to the other side. But solo recon was tough. She'd done there and been that—it was her usual mode of operation.

Been there and done that? Being around Chad, she could feel the weakness of her American idiom and didn't like that at all. She'd had little opportunity to polish it, serving undercover in South America for the last five years.

She knew what solo recon took out of a person when you didn't dare sleep for a couple of days. Besides, it had been nice having him sleep on her shoulder as if he trusted her. It was a mistake; people in their line of work couldn't afford to trust anyone. But still, it was…nice.

"How you doing, Sofia?" Chad's familiar greeting didn't cause her aim to waver from Tanya's heart in the least.

"I'm good, now that we've found you. Tell your friend to stop pointing her gun at my husband's face."

"Chill, Tanya."

"Tanya?" The man startled. "Shit, didn't recognize you in all the gear and with Sleeping Beauty napping on your shoulder like the little princess he is."

"Go to hell, Duane."

"After you, dude."

Tanya, in turn, hadn't recognized Duane. Three years and a lot of hard missions had gone by since they'd fought on the same team, but it wasn't like her to miss recognizing a man's gait, even with the sun behind him. There was something else. Duane and the lovely Latina Sofia…

"Marriage looks like good clothes on you, Duane," Tanya re-slung her weapon that she'd instinctively hung on to during the double fall last night. She was pleased to see that Chad didn't have his rifle, though his sidearm was still in its holster at the center of his gut.

"…fits you well," Chad mumbled in her ear.

Tanya ignored him. Had marriage changed Duane somehow? He'd always had Delta level fieldcraft, but he'd moved differently. As if…

Scheisse!

She should have seen it. He hadn't *only* been searching for them. He'd also been keeping a careful eye on his wife in the background without seeming to. Tanya should have spotted that he was watching someone behind her and Chad's position, but his craft was good enough that she hadn't caught on.

"It agrees with me." He slung his rifle over his shoulder with a negligent shrug.

"It is a good thing that you say that," Sofia kept her weapon loose but did shift its aim to Tanya's leg instead of her chest. "Now who are you?"

"Chad's one that got away," Duane explained.

"No I'm not." Tanya wasn't anyone's anything.

"So are, babe."

"Watch who you call 'babe', bro," Chad's growl actually sounded for real.

"Or you may find yourself sleeping alone tonight." Sofia agreed as she squatted on the soil near Chad's feet and finally holstered her weapon.

She seemed too slight to be a Delta Force operative. The American unit's selection practices didn't particularly favor size, but it was hard to believe that this slip of a woman could possibly deliver the level of endurance needed. And there was something odd about her attitude, as if weapons weren't her primary tool.

"Tell me." And in that instant, the woman shifted. A quiet intensity slid over her.

Chad started in, but not about the fall that should have

killed them both nor the flight over a jungle waterfall—which she could now see towering in the distance by the light of day and there is no way they should have survived. Instead, he was breaking down a series of observations about a drug smugglers' camp, somewhere different than the lab that had been the focus of her team's failed attack. Patrol timings, perimeter defenses, even delivery schedules.

"How long were you out there?"

"Four days," he barely interrupted the flow of his debrief to answer Tanya's question.

She'd forgotten how much she liked that about Chad. He might appear the chuckleheaded, laughing-boy American, but his mind was pure Special Operations. He'd missed nothing. He even had the timings of nighttime patrols—all in his head, all crosschecked over multiple nights. To do that for four days on solo recon, no wonder he'd slept like the dead on her shoulder.

And this Sofia simply squatted and listened while Chad talked and Duane continued a slow patrol around the area. From her small pack, Sofia pulled out a tablet computer and selected an image, before handing it to Chad.

"Again."

And Chad repeated it all, this time placing markers on the drone's view image, but finding little new to add to his narrative.

Tanya recognized the methods, if not the person. Long ago, a Night Stalkers team had nearly died because of a mole in the Intelligence Support Activity—the most elite intel group in the entire US military, specifically servicing Special Operations. Sofia must have been recruited from some top-level military intelligence to Delta Force—which meant she had amazing skills in two areas.

When he was done, Sofia tipped her head in the characteristic move of someone listening to a radio call. She must be wearing an earbud under her long dark hair.

"Carla wants to know if you're up for this?" Sofia asked.

"Sure," Chad pulled down some more bananas and tossed a couple to her for breakfast. "Want ta come play, Tanya?"

"Your knee."

He flexed his leg. "Still sore. I'll just chew some ibuprofen or something; shouldn't be an issue."

Last night he had hung on to her like it was broken. *Need a crutch or an ambulance?* She'd give him a crutch right across his head.

"You just wanted an excuse to hang all on me."

"An awesome bonus," Chad winked.

And she'd fallen for it. Well, that wasn't going to happen again. She turned to Sofia, who was watching them closely.

"Just give me something to shoot."

Sofia smiled, "I think we can do that."

"Oh," Chad signaled for Sofia to wait a moment. "Ask Richie to find out what happened to Tanya's people. She came aboard the helo with three of them last night. One dead, one alive, but I was sort of moving fast and couldn't slow down enough to see about the third."

Sofia didn't even bother to repeat the question. So, Chad's entire debrief had been broadcast to the whole group. As usual with this team, everyone knew everything from the first moment —except her.

Carl was dead. *Crap!* She'd known it, even as she'd snapped the monkey line on his chest. And this was Chad's other side. A fine sniper, and a soldier who always kept his wits and his sense of humor. But he'd also shown a thoughtful side that was wholly unexpected from a man who projected macho jerk so effectively.

As Kidon, she was far more used to operating alone. Integrating with the UN security team—that had dissolved so catastrophically last night—hadn't been her usual mode.

"The guy is fine—they're giving him a new section of bone in his arm. The woman is just out of surgery, but will keep the leg." Sofia echoed the information coming in over her radio.

Well, compared to the dead third member, that was some very good news.

Still, she had a few thoughts about what to do to Chad's other knee.

4

"*D*idn't think I'd be back here so soon." Chad had seen far too much of this camp over the four long days of scouting it. Now, less than thirty hours after slipping away and ten hours after waking with his head on Tanya's shoulder, he was back, sweating in the late afternoon heat.

A pair of Black Hawks had delivered the full team and a pair of Zodiac boats twenty klicks upriver—no waterfalls in the way, he'd checked first. Apparently the Night Stalkers didn't have any spare Chinooks hanging around Colombia. The one from last night was offshore somewhere being rebuilt.

Not a word from Tanya, lying in the brush close along his right side.

"At least there are no waterfalls this time." They'd raced the Zodiacs northward down the river to a mile above the camp, then hidden the boats and continued overland, half of the team on either shore.

Nothing.

"Gotta talk to me at some point, sweetheart."

"No, I don't. I'm with you because Kyle said I have to follow you."

"Not what's pissing you off, woman." They lay together beneath a clump of thorny bougainvillea that hid them well. The thick sweep of vibrant purple fooled the observer's eye about any colors that didn't belong. There was a slight rise here that offered an unimpeded view of ferry and loading operations. The camp itself was a hundred meters back into the jungle. He'd spent two of his four days on recon—most of it laid up right here. The drugs traveled overland to this camp at the eastern edge of Colombia. They were then ferried across the Orinoco River into Venezuela, where small prop planes waited with bundles of cash to send back the other way. The Colombian side of the river was too rough to cut in an airstrip, so the border was the transfer point.

"You and your fake knee injury."

Chad couldn't help grinning. The knee had really hurt, but some rest and Vicodin had knocked the pain down to bearable. But that combined with the lack of sleep—it hadn't been a ploy that he needed help to traverse the river stones in the dark. But if getting it backward pissed off Tanya, he was good with that.

A lot of things about her that he was good with. It was why he'd chosen this hide for them—it was *very* small. They were forced to squeeze in together, touching foot, thigh, hip, and shooting arms. He'd switched his rifle to leftie so that it wasn't between them.

"You are a small man, Chad Hawkins, if that is how you find your humors."

"Laughs. And you *know* that isn't true."

It almost earned him a smile. Sometimes a man and woman were just the right size for each other, when their bodies simply fit together so perfectly. His and Tanya's bodies had absolutely done that on that mission years before. Her breasts had been as custom-formed as his sniper rifle's stock with his big hands in mind. And when buried all the way into the woman's hips, they were—

The memories were giving him trouble as they lay together

through the last of the hot sweaty afternoon. Since when had memories of a woman even stuck with him? And filled his mind with ideas of what he'd like to do with her again given half the chance? Not once that he could recall.

"Okay, there's the first sign." He tipped his sniper rifle to show the direction he was watching. It really wasn't much yet, but it gave him something to talk about. "I call her Renata."

Renata—as he'd dubbed the curvaceous Latina who walked like she could tame crocodiles in between drug runs—stepped out of the trees to scan up and down the river. They watched her through their scopes. If there was so much as a floating branch she didn't like, she'd sic a patrol on it.

"She's pretty," Tanya remarked with a tone that far too carefully had no tone.

That was a massive understatement. Colombia was typically ranked top five for "most beautiful women." If they were using this Renata for calibration, they'd set the ranking way too low.

Chad couldn't resist the bait of that neutral comment.

"If she let go another button on that shirt, she'd be even prettier." Renata had an awe-inspiring cleavage and wasn't above using it to control the men who worked for her. She acted as if she didn't care what others thought of her, which made her appear even more impressive.

She wore her jungle khaki with a nice snug fit. Army boots laced up to midcalf.

Renata also sported a Colombian Cordova .38 [mm handgun, an American M4A1 rifle, and a machete in a sheath that ran down her spine and placed the handle conveniently above her left shoulder. Southpaw, like Tanya. Somehow that added a bit of spice too.

"I watched her slice off a man's balls before she slit his throat and dumped his body in the river just two days back. She did it herself, with a three-inch blade. So short that she got plenty bloody in the process." He'd been hiding in a red palm wrapped by a strangler fig making it easy to climb, close enough to hear her joking that she had to use such a small knife because the guy's dick was too small for a bigger blade. His own empathetic twitch with the guy's screams as she sawed them off almost gave away his position.

"So, she's not the squeamish sort. What did he do to deserve that?"

"Got me. Maybe tried to shill a couple hundred bucks off a half-mil payment bundle? Tried to jump ahead in the chow line? No idea, but it was seriously nasty."

"Maybe he tried to have his way with this Renata."

"Could be."

"Sounds like just your type."

"Not him. Like my women willing." But Renata sure was. "Always had a thing for dangerous women." He'd bedded more than his fair share of Renatas. Some were his passage into a camp when he was operating undercover. Or back out. Or a little mutual entertainment somewhere in between. Women like that knew that life was short and made love with a certain wild abandon that never failed to crank him up. Women like Tanya Zimmer. Except none of them were like Tanya.

Deciding the river was clear, Renata turned slowly to inspect the trees and sky. He and Tanya both shook a flap of burlap over their rifle scopes so that they didn't catch a sun reflection even though the angle was wrong for that to happen.

Finally satisfied, Renata disappeared back into the jungle.

"Now what?"

"Now we wait another twenty minutes before she makes a final check."

He spent the next twenty minutes trying to think about Renata's cleavage as a distraction, but all he could think about was that after three years, he was lying beside Tanya once more. A hot, sweaty, angry Tanya in the middle of a thorn bush, who probably wasn't thinking at all along the lines he was. He'd never picked back up with a former lover before, and had no idea how to go about it.

Tanya had been with a few "Renatas" when the mission left no other option, but she'd certainly had her fair share of "Romeros." She doubted that Chad could say the same thing in the other direction—he was far too alpha-bull male.

Five years she'd been working the South American problem. Israeli youth were certainly obtaining their drugs easily enough, and a lot of their supply started in the coca fields of Bolivia and Colombia. She'd been solo for most of those years, but that was becoming more and more problematic. There were so many situations where a small team was necessary. Missions like this one would be impossible by herself. Even a mash-up team—like the one she'd run for four weeks but had ended in disaster last night—had its shortcomings.

Chad's Delta Force team was something other. There was such a degree of cohesion that any comment was always known by the whole team. Any idea traveled as instantly as if they were a single being. But they were Delta, so they were all also highly intelligent and deeply individualistic.

They'd all teased Chad about being Sleeping Beauty and offered to buy him a ball gown. But Sofia and the blonde Melissa—the two additions since Tanya had fought beside this team—had watched her every move carefully each time she came anywhere close to Chad.

Protective. Intensely so.

They backed off some after Carla greeted her with a kind hug, but not by much.

Despite being so protective and being top fighters, the Deltas were also incredibly cooperative. Richie barely had to hold out a hand before Melissa slapped a spare radio into his palm. He'd stepped over and wired it for Tanya without comment. Richie had always been the team's geek—belonging, but just a little to the outside. No longer. It was as if marrying Melissa had at last fully integrated him into operations.

With Sofia leading the discussion, they'd formulated an attack plan in minutes. That explained Sofia's role. She was an intelligence analyst first and a Delta operator second. Carla had always been the wild card, leaping to crazy solutions as if on a whim. But that consistently worked for Carla because she backed it up with equally intense action and immense skill. Sofia was the big picture gal and the whole team listened to her plans carefully. Some variations, but they were ready to implement it quickly and had spent most of the last six hours getting into position.

It was a pleasure to watch. Being a part of this team had its own special charge. The surprising part was that it was just as powerful a feeling as her memory had said it was. And that had seemed unlikely whenever she'd thought about it.

"Here we go," Chad pointed to the east where a trio of small planes came in low over the treetops on the Venezuela side of the river, catching the last of the sunset.

Tanya considered pointing out that they had nowhere to land. The narrow dirt airstrip hacked into the jungle had been blocked at midfield by the fall of a towering wax palm—massive in its demise: thicker than Chad was tall and over fifty meters long on the ground. Chad didn't seem to think this was an issue, so she waited and watched.

A low thunder sounded over the distant airplanes' propeller buzz. It took her a moment to spot the large diesel bulldozer on the far side of the airfield—it had been painted in camouflage and was parked deep in the trees. It lurched forward, then jolted to a stop. The low thunder of the engine now roared to life and the massive log was dragged off the field. How they had managed to move a bulldozer to this trackless bit of jungle in the first place was a different question that didn't concern her. To any aerial inspection, this airfield would be unusable— except for the brief moments like this one when the tree was dragged aside. An anti-drug patrol with any sense would cross this runway off their map and never look at it again.

The instant the runway was clear, the three airplanes swooped in to land.

Renata had again appeared from the wall of jungle, this time so close below them that Tanya didn't need her scope to see the woman clearly. She carried her M4A1 and enough spare magazines for an extended firefight. Her small emasculating knife wasn't in evidence, but a large field knife was sheathed along her thigh and the machete still angled across her shoulders.

Again the careful survey. Twice her eyes swept over their hiding position, but they didn't appear to hesitate. She almost turned once more in their direction, but shrugged it off like an itch.

"Clean?" Tanya whispered.

She could feel Chad's shrug against her shoulder. Even if they weren't, there should be enough distractions soon from the other team members. She knew where they were and that they, too, were watching the planes and Renata, but they hadn't spoken a single word about the mission since the end of the planning session in Medellín. Stone cold radio silence was one of their operating standards even with encryption-enabled equipment. They were the silent warriors and didn't need to speak. Tanya had been through Medellín a dozen times over the last three years and never once caught the least hint that this Delta team was operating in the city.

Yet as they'd waited for the Black Hawks to fetch them from the river's edge below the waterfall, the three Deltas had talked about where to have dinner when they got back to Medellín after the mission. Restaurants that she'd never heard of in various *communes* that implied a deep knowledge of the city.

Once aboard, Chad and Duane did what any Spec Ops soldier did on a flight: they fell asleep almost instantly. Sofia had sat with her back to the rear cargo net and stared forward as if intently watching the two crew chiefs at their Miniguns and the back of the two pilots' heads even though there was nothing to see.

"We hunted narco submarines together. Chad and I, and the others." Tanya didn't know quite why she'd felt it necessary to start a conversation or to explain herself.

Sofia nodded. "I should have recognized you from the Negev Desert fiasco."

"No one—" Tanya stopped. The only people who had seen her in that entire operation were select members of the Night Stalkers 5th Battalion D Company, mostly Kara Moretti and Justin Roberts, and also Delta Force commander Michael Gibson. Them and… "You're Activity."

Sofia nodded. "Former Activity. I was recruited to Delta during a mission last year."

Tanya had been called in from the field to uncover a mole in The Activity's operation. One who had threatened the entire Israeli-American alliance.

"The Activity"—short for the Army Intelligence Support Activity—was the intel group built for only one reason: to provide the best information to Delta, SEAL Team 6, and the Air Force 24th STS combat controllers. In the global landscape of military intelligence, they were the uncontested pinnacle. No surprise at all that Sofia had done the planning for this mission. The Activity only recruited the very best—and now this Delta team had that skill embedded right in its core. That was a fantastic asset.

Tanya had thought it was a once-in-a-lifetime opportunity to work with The Activity. And now here it was again.

For the rest of the flight from the Rio Saldaña to the Orinoco River, they had quietly discussed Sofia's plans. She'd been staying awake considering moves and countermoves. Tanya had done her best to play demon's advocate for her. When Tanya had finally succeeded in causing a small alteration in Sofia's plan, she felt a sense of real accomplishment—Sofia was just as staggering as one would expect from a former Activity agent turned Delta.

That single alteration had been mentioned to Carla as they were loading into the Zodiacs on the Orinoco. Carla had raised an eyebrow, Sofia had tipped her head toward Tanya, and that had earned her one of Carla's radiant smiles. Melissa spotted the brief smile and stared at Tanya for a long second as its recipient, then shrugged that maybe, *just* maybe, Tanya was okay—all without any of them slowing down for a second. Or the men noticing a thing.

Tanya had had a problem seeing how anything could go wrong with this mission. That in itself was always a bad sign in planning.

She actually felt better now that the first thing had gone wrong.

Renata, or whatever her name was, was supposed to be down by the ferryboat to watch over the transfer. Instead, she was less than thirty meters away from their hideout, sitting on a log and watching the drug transfer from a distance. This close, Chad would barely need a scope to stare down the woman's cleavage.

SHIT! She'd never done that. Renata was always in the middle of all operations. This close, even their flash suppressors wouldn't wholly hide their fire. The dusk would reveal some of the muzzle flare. Puffs of dust kicked up by the muzzle brake's blowback would be recognizable. And there was no way to hide the supersonic crack of the bullets. The distances of this operation were too big to use subsonic rounds that would attract so much less attention.

Maybe if he was patient, she'd move.

Everything else was playing out normally. The dozen guards moved out of the jungle's edge with their rifles at the ready. It hadn't been clear in the two other times he'd watched this operation whether they were being cautious about defense or if they were merely threatening the next group to appear. The drug mules—peasants used as slaves by the drug runners—began hauling the heavy boxes of processed and packaged cocaine out of the trees and over to the small ferryboat.

On the far side of the river, the airplane pilots remained in their planes as the Venezuelan contingent of the operation began shifting heavy bales of money out of the planes and down to the shore. Here in the Colombian jungle, finished cocaine was going for about four thousand USD a kilo.

This side of the river represented the "New FARC" who had refused to lay down arms along with the FARC revolutionary army. Drug running and kidnapping for ransom was too profitable. Now that it was no longer even tentatively connected to political ideals, it had become an even uglier business.

That's what the Delta team was banking on.

Once the boat was loaded, the drug mules huddled beneath the verge of the jungle. Six of the armed guards climbed onto the boat, their weight dropping it almost to the gunwales. But the river was calm here and posed little threat as they motored across.

He could feel Tanya glancing over at him, then down at Renata. The woman hadn't moved from her log. It was up to him to call the abort. Everything was in place except for that one woman.

"Alpha out," he whispered quietly over the radio. His was the "Alpha" position of Sofia's plan. Calling themselves as compromised hurt, but it was the safest move.

A second later, just as the boat was grinding into the shallows on the far side of the river, the two Delta teams on the Venezuelan side opened fire. They were far back in the trees and well shielded. It would appear as if their fire was coming from the Venezuelans and striking the ferryboat's crew. In moments, the six guards on the boat were down without a shot fired by either side—it had all been Delta.

However, the Colombian contingent, still guarding the cowering drug mules, assumed that it was the Venezuelans' doing. Exactly as Sofia had expected, a hail of gunfire was aimed across the river. Soon, magazine after magazine was being emptied back and forth across the river.

Duane should be using his sniper rifle from vantage on this side, to make sure that the Venezuelans were actually going down. He and Tanya were supposed to be adding to the idea that it was a cross-river war, but still Renata didn't move.

"What the hell is she waiting for?" Tanya whispered.

Chad didn't know, but he didn't like it.

They couldn't risk shooting her in the back. It would be obvious to anyone who found her that she'd been shot from this side of the river.

Besides, Sofia had said that they had to leave her alive if they wanted to break the trust and interrupt this supply chain. By creating a border war among the drug smugglers, they'd waste time fighting each other rather than suspecting intervention by some "Drug War" team. Sofia's plan called for letting her escape, if possible, to spread word of the Venezuelans' "betrayal."

Finally, Renata stood and simply walked away into the woods as if going for a Sunday stroll.

Tanya was up and on the move half a heartbeat later.

"Tan—" no point in whispering, she was already gone. Cursing to himself, he moved out after her. It would make sense if she was pulling back. Perhaps Renata had uncovered their position earlier, in which case getting away from here before Renata could sneak around behind them was a good idea.

Instead Tanya was angling down the hill to intercept Renata under the trees.

He slipped along behind her. In the jungle, the evening was already full night. Pulling on his night-vision goggles, he plunged into a world of green heat signatures. Tanya prowled ahead with the lithe moves of a jungle cat. The woman was hot even in NVGs and he wasn't talking about her infrared signature.

What did he really know about her? They'd fought one battle together three years ago.

Had she somehow tipped off Renata to save her from what was about to go down?

A lot of money flowed along the cocaine trail and maybe they'd found Tanya's price. Half of her team had gone down last night—one dead and one badly wounded. Plus the Chinook gunner and his helo being badly shot up. It was rare for someone to get the drop on the Night Stalkers.

Really rare.

Majorly not a good sign.

He slung his sniper rifle and pulled out his silenced Glock 17. It was better for close-in work among the dense trees.

Be a real shame to mess up such a fine-looking woman with a hole in her head, but if that's what was called for… *Shit, man!*

LATELY, Tanya had heard rumors of the rise of *la Capitana*. As significant a player in the Colombian drug world as the Torres sisters were in Mexico's Sinaloa cartel. The rumors also said that, unlike Luisa Marie and Marisol, *la Capitana* didn't run her operation from behind the scenes. But neither was she some social media slut like Claudia Ochoa Félix who posted lewd images of herself and her hot pink AK-47 lying on a giant mound of hundred-dollar bills.

Most had said *la Capitana* was actually a man, hiding his identity behind a female *nom de plume*. The woman striding away through the jungle might be working for such a man.

But what if she actually was a female who wasn't going to hide her gender under any lousy male identity like *El Capitan* even if it would decrease the risk? What if she *was* the true leader? It would offend Tanya's own sense of righteousness to have to hide behind some male's name. Maybe this woman felt the same.

If Renata really was The Captain, it would be the first confirmed sighting—ever. *La Capitana* was a rumor, a ghost who Tanya had crossed the trail of in the unlikeliest of places—a trail that had always been too cold to follow very far. Was she part of some massive operation like Pablo Escobar had been? Was she a loner like the "Expediter" who had abruptly disappeared two years ago and not been heard from since?

Three years. Three long years she'd followed the Expediter's trail only to have it go up in smoke right in front of her face. Literally.

She almost stumbled on an arching root. The Expediter had worked for a kingpin who'd been burned alive in a massive explosion at a jungle processing camp. Tanya had been less than five miles away when a massive explosion had blown so high and hard that it had formed a mushroom cloud. The camp had been deserted, with little more than charcoal left by the time she'd reached the destroyed airstrip in the jungle. Pederson's corpse—the purported male leader—had barely been recognizable.

There hadn't been a single peep anywhere of the Expediter since that time.

Had this team been the one to clear them out—if that's what had happened? If so, it was a major event that was still rippling over the drug cartel landscape. They'd left a huge hole in smuggling operations that still hadn't been healed.

Not her concern at the moment.

Any normal Renata could be allowed to escape, but *la Capitana* was far too important to let go. She had to be taken, or taken down.

Tanya caught up with her just as the woman kicked a Yamaha 250 dirt bike to life. Spotting Tanya at the last moment, she popped the clutch hard with full throttle. That explained how she'd gotten here without any roads—she didn't seem the sort to move at pack mule speeds. The thin red dirt of the jungle floor bloomed into an impenetrable cloud even as the rear wheel peppered Tanya with flying detritus.

Two other bikes were parked close by. She jumped on one and, cranking the throttle to full herself, shot off into the darkness following *la Capitana's* dust trail. As she wound around a ceiba and ducked under a palm frond, a branch or something caught at her shoulder, snapped loudly, and let her go.

CHAD ONLY MANAGED the one shot and it had been mostly blind through the dust.

He could hear Tanya shift up another gear, so it was a miss.

"She bolted. With Renata. I'm in pursuit," Chad reported over the radio.

Carla's soft, "You're kidding," was backed up by the sharp clack of the bolt working on her rifle as she continued implementing the on-going operation.

"I wish." But he didn't bother transmitting his reply.

He turned for the third bike and just barely caught the heat signature of some asshole rushing at him with a knife blade. Two rounds to the face and one to the heart, the guy dropped like the sack of shit he was. NVGs really had crappy peripheral vision, but they were better than being night blind.

"Never bring a knife to a gun fight, bro," he told the stupid corpse who had an AK-47 hanging over his shoulder.

At least the drug runners kept their getaway machines in good shape. The bike kicked to life on the second try.

Damn the woman to hell! She'd strolled back into his world and played him for a complete sucker. Gotten a signal to Renata to keep her safely out of the game. And now he was out of the game as well, not keeping up his part of the plan. His job was to put holes in a pair of the airplanes and their pilots—from the Colombian side of the river. One would be allowed to slip away —without the money or the drugs. Because someone had to take the news of the Colombians' "betrayal" back into the heart of Venezuela.

Instead he was out here trying to follow a fast-fading dust trail. With his own engine running, he could no longer hear Renata's or Tanya's bike. The dust and dirt showed only as a dimming of the forest. He finally spotted what he needed; his NVGs revealed the heat plume of the bikes' exhaust as they left a hazy trail that wound around trees, ducked under branches, and jumped off logs.

He'd stolen his first motorcycle at thirteen and showed his first time a good time with a fast ride out into the countryside north of Detroit—they'd done it in some weekender's master bedroom while half-snorked on his Crown Royal. Chad was a late bloomer; she'd already been working the Street for a year by the time she hit that age. She hadn't even charged him until he'd run out of gas halfway back to the city. It had been a long, cold-shouldered walk back to the Dale in the heart of the city. He'd always watched the gas gauge carefully ever since.

Talk about cold-shouldered bitches, this one—

He twisted aside. He'd almost ridden between two towering ceiba root walls, which would have plowed him head-on into the trunk. One exhaust trail had led around the north side of the tree and the other around the south, making it look as if they'd gone straight through.

Tanya hadn't even had the decency to fuck him before she, well, fucked him.

He'd give her credit for one thing, the woman could really ride. Half a dozen places he almost ate it, only to spot at the last instant how Tanya had avoided disaster.

The heat plume of her exhaust was getting brighter in his NVGs. Finally, he caught sight of a flicker of taillight. With their tracks as guidance, he was able to gain ground faster than they were making it.

The two bikes wove and twisted like the women were playing with each other.

Two bitches. Bitches on bikes.

Well, one of them was going down.

They were climbing a ridge fast. Once over the ridge, who knew where they'd end up. No way to catch them before they crested it.

He chose his spot.

At a slight rise of the trail, there was a clear view of the ridge ahead.

He dumped the bike, hit the ground in a roll, and came up with the butt of his Mk 21 sniper rifle against his shoulder.

The first bike cleared the ridge and was gone.

He timed it for the second one, waited for his heartbeat, then fired.

---

5

*T*anya catapulted to the ground. With no helmet, she tucked and rolled. Bouncing over rib-bruising rocks, she finally slammed back-first against a particularly stout palm tree. Her NVGs flew aside and disappeared into the brush.

Too dazed to figure out what had happened, she lay still for a long moment. She'd been chasing someone. A ghost. A mirage.

La Capitana!

She tried not to groan as she rolled to her feet and fought her way through the thinning jungle to the top of the ridge—she'd lost any trace of the switchbacked track they'd been racing along. She'd been less than twenty meters behind the woman. With no way to free up a hand to shoot—not over such challenging terrain—she'd still have been close enough in another minute for Tanya to pull alongside *la Capitana* and simply ram her.

Tanya collapsed at the top of the ridge and looked down.

Nothing…

Nothing…

There!

The trail had cut sharply north as it descended back into the trees on the other side. Tanya yanked out her HK416, which remained strapped to her through the fall. Her shoulder hurt like hell—it had been getting worse the longer she rode since that branch had gouged her—but she ignored it.

She lined the rifle up on the headlight dancing off into the distance.

Her eyes were still tearing from the pain of the fall and the massive blowback of *la Capitana's* dust she'd been riding in.

No time to wipe them.

She blinked hard, ignoring the grit-filled scratchiness, and sighted through the scope. The glass was badly fractured.

She tried firing blind, but all she heard was a dull click. Somewhere along the way, she'd hit the magazine release and the weapon was empty.

A blinding light shone in her face. She raised an arm to block it.

"Don't move." She couldn't see who was behind the motorcycle's headlight, but there was no mistaking the voice.

"Chad. Thank god." She twisted to look over the ridge, but *la Capitana* was long gone.

"I said don't move!"

"Why? Am I hurt?" She had walked the last few steps to lie prone atop the ridge, hadn't she? She checked…and quickly centered on her shoulder. "Ow!" It was a long slice and her fingers came away hot and wet.

"So, I didn't miss," he sounded smug as he killed his bike's engine and stepped off the machine without dousing the blinding headlight. He pulled aside his NVGs.

"You…"

Her shoulder hadn't been caught by a branch?

He'd *shot* her?

"Got a lot to answer for, Zimmer."

She struggled to her feet. *She* had a lot to answer for?

Chad had shot her. In the shoulder.

She could see his smile in the backwash of the motorcycle's headlamp.

Giving it everything her father and Kidon had ever taught her, she smashed her fist into Chad's face. The surprise of it slipped past all of his defenses.

He fell backward over his motorcycle and collapsed in a heap.

"Never bring a gun to a fistfighting!"

"Fistfight," he groaned.

She kicked the sole of his boot for good measure.

Her shoulder now truly hurt like hell, but she was feeling much better.

"Aww, what happened to Sleeping Beauty's pretty face?"

Chad considered giving Duane a demonstration, but decided against it.

"That eye is really something," Melissa was unrolling a med kit.

"Leave me the hell alone."

"It's not for you. It's for her." Melissa pulled out the shears and cut away a section of Tanya's blouse. "It's a clean graze, mostly just sliced the skin. I'll hit it with antiseptic and glue it for you. Should heal fine."

"Don't bother. We're gonna question the bitch, then bury her." Chad took the water-soaked kerchief that Duane handed him and placed it gingerly over his eye. Which stung like a son of a bitch. Probably be a day or two before he could even open that eye again. Woman had a hell of a punch.

Tanya's bike had been a write-off—he'd punched a round into the transmission. When he'd fallen backward over his bike, a rock had snagged the chain and snapped it.

It had been a long and very silent walk back to the agreed rendezvous point. A little too reminiscent of his long, silent walk at thirteen after running out of gas—with none of the good parts beforehand.

"Why did you shoot me?" Tanya glared at him over the shoulder Melissa was fixing.

"Why did you warn off Renata?"

"I didn't."

"Trust me," he looked at the others of his team gathered around. "She did. When I was on recon, I could set my watch by Renata's schedule. Suddenly, she changes everything? She's always been on the boat. She *always* does the transaction herself."

"Not this time."

"Yeah, right. And what made you think you could escape with her?"

"I was chasing her, you idiot."

Chad opened his mouth, then hesitated. "No. We agreed to let her go."

Tanya sighed.

Everyone else was quiet. Even Melissa, kneeling close behind Tanya, was no longer moving. Melissa had passed off her weapons to Sofia before approaching Tanya to avoid having them grabbed—at least he wasn't the only one treating her with caution. Chad had marched her back in at gunpoint—even one-eyed he could take her down at five paces. Duane now raised his weapon quietly so that it was centered on the back of Tanya's head.

"Yes," Tanya sounded exhausted. "That was a good idea, until I figured out who she must be."

"And who's that?"

"*Mierda!*" Sofia cursed softly.

"What?"

But Sofia wasn't watching him, she was watching Tanya. "Really?"

Tanya shrugged, then cursed, *"Scheisse!"* She brushed her fingers over her wounded shoulder.

"It fits," Sofia was nodding.

Chad had learned that when Sofia used that tone, there was no point arguing because she always turned out to be right. But right about what?

"Who is she?" Carla asked.

He felt a little better that Carla hadn't figured it out either.

"*La Capitana,*" Tanya and Sofia said in unison.

Carla cursed just as Sofia had.

Chad glanced at Duane, who gave him back an infinitesimal shrug. Neither Melissa nor Kyle knew who she was either, which made him feel a little better. Richie was too busy fixing Tanya's rifle to pay attention.

Still, no way was he going to be the one to ask who The Captain was.

6

"*O*h, you people. You always bring me the best and the worst news." Fred Smith practically crowed with delight.

Tanya glanced at Carla, who shrugged amiably as if a garrulous CIA agent was somehow normal. She'd found most of them to be taciturn, misogynistic bastards with crappy ideas of what international cooperation with an ally was supposed to look like. That no mere CIA agent—outside their black ops Special Operations Group—could even understand, never mind match her level of training didn't seem to dent their American air of superiority. And the SOG was so dark and dirty that even she didn't want to mess with them.

After trekking back upriver to the boats and calling for a pickup by the Night Stalkers, their team worked their way back to Medellín. At least she assumed they were a team again—in their minds. Being shot twice in the same day, once in the shoulder and once in the motorcycle transmission, made her feel less friendly than she had been.

Kyle led them to a suite high on the hills overlooking Medellín. It was in one of the new high rises that were popping up faster than bamboo all over the area. The city was growing by a quarter of a million or more per decade and had been doing it since the 1950s. With the smashing of the big cartels in the 1990s, it was a much quieter and safer city and developers were pouring in capital.

The safe house was the top, third floor of an apartment building perched on the edge of *Comuna 13*. This particular *barrio* had been the worst neighborhood of the *Comuna*, which meant of the entire city. It had been owned by the gangs until very recently. The outside was only moderately rundown and its walls were covered in brilliantly creative blue-and-gold graffiti.

Inside, she could have been in her King David Tower condo in Tel Aviv overlooking the Bograshov beach. It had been a long time since she'd been there. Perhaps too long, but the work in South America never seemed to stop.

She leaned back in the armchair and tried not to groan when her shoulder rested against the back cushion. Every muscle was sore from the last thirty-six hours. The shootout, the waterfall, infiltrating into position was much harder work than it sounded, and then, of course, Chad forcing her to crash into the rocks.

After three days awake, she felt a little empathy for Chad—who groaned just as deeply as he eased onto one of the couches—but not much. If he was a little closer, she'd kick him again, but he was smart enough to keep his distance.

The voluble CIA guy had spread out a proper Colombian breakfast. *Arepas de choclo*—corn cakes with soft white cheese, a breakfast that she'd taken a long time to become used to, but now missed when she was out of the country—along with massive cups of rich Colombian hot chocolate. There were also spicy chorizo sausage tamales with red and green bell pepper, onion, an egg, and almost enough zing to wake her up.

"You bring me the first-ever confirmed siting of *la Capitana*," Fred Smith sighed happily. He looked like on over-tall cherub with brilliant red hair. "No one, but no one has ever positively identified her. When we processed Chad's surveillance photos from his recon, all we got when we ran her ID was 'female unknown.' Isn't that amazing?"

It was amazing that this was a CIA guy. Clearly not a field agent, but he appeared to be the one running this team's assignments, which said something of his credentials if not his manner.

"I never said I was confirmed it," Tanya finally found the brief gap in his words to insert her own.

"Seriously? *Seriously?*" Smith didn't appear to be the least bit less excited. "The instincts of a Mossad field agent aren't wrong that often."

Tanya's glance at Carla revealed only a tiny shake of her head. Good, she wouldn't like the CIA knowing who she really was. Oddly, she'd always been comfortable with Carla knowing. And what Carla knew, the rest of the team did. Then why had Chad shot her?

He'd already explained his reasoning on that. Renata's changed routine. Tanya racing off close behind her. Maybe she'd have made the same assumption if she was in his boots, but maybe not. Like her, he was suspicious of absolutely everyone. Unlike her, he was part of a team that he trusted and protected. A very different frame of reference—to Chad, you were either on the team or you were suspect. Her life was much simpler: everyone was suspect.

Perhaps she'd forgive him…in a lifetime when her shoulder didn't hurt so much.

"And Sofia, you confirmed it," Fred continued.

Sofia shook her head, "I only said that it made sense. It was a good guess, perhaps even a valid one. It fits what little is known about her."

"You realize that is a better, clearer lead than our entire history on her. Everything else is rumor and innuendo. We only last month managed to confirm some such person existing at all."

"So," Chad leaned in for another tamale, then grunted and raised a hand tenderly to his face. She'd really landed it—the black and blue spread all over that side of his face. *Good!*

"Two Face." That's what he looked like and it was hard not to laugh in his wounded face.

"Two Face?" Richie's attention zeroed in on Chad said he was suddenly surprised by the thought.

"Always wanted to be a Batman villain," Chad grinned at him then winced as that pulled on his purpling cheek.

"You know, Tanya, if you dyed your hair dark and wore a trench coat and hat, you could pass for Harvey Dent's girlfriend and aide, Renee Montoya." Richie began painting a picture with wide hand gestures.

"Who's Harvey Dent?"

Richie merely looked at her aghast.

"Batman villain," Melissa whispered to her as she patted Richie's knee to console him.

Tanya had never read or seen this Batman. She'd meant to refer to Janus, the two-faced Roman god of beginnings and endings. Or even the thespian masks of comedy and tragedy. To one side the easygoing blond funny man, always so buddy-buddy with his teammates. And to the other, the lethal Spec Ops soldier revealed by his garish battle wound purpling around his swollen-shut eye. She flexed her hand into a fist and, more slowly, back out. *Scheisse* but he had a hard head. Tanya let him have his moment, but didn't smile back.

"So," this time he moved much slower as he completed the gesture to fetch his tamale from the low coffee table between them. "What do we know about this bitch?" His tone sounded like he was talking about *la Capitana*. But the free hand he laid gently on his face and the half smile he aimed her way said that he was pleased to be aiming at two targets for the price of one.

Tanya gave him the finger, which, she could see with her two good eyes, he took completely the wrong way with his one bad one.

CHAD SMILED at the gesture and ignored the sting that caused.

He'd been feeling pretty shitty about shooting Tanya now that he'd found out what she'd really been doing. But if she was willing to tease him by flipping him off, she must have decided to take it in stride.

Carla rolled her eyes at him. Everyone else except Duane was watching the big-screen TV as Smith turned it on and connected his laptop.

"What?" He mouthed at her, but Carla just looked away.

"Aw, dude," Duane mouthed back with pity. Chad didn't like that somehow Duane knew something he was missing. If it was so obvious, why wasn't he seeing it?

"First, some background you already know." Fred Smith loved his little lectures and they'd all learned there was no turning him aside. He kept them interesting, and always delivered stuff even Sofia didn't know, which was pretty impressive.

Chad chomped down on his tamale and ignored the pain of chewing. Tanya was very studiously not looking at him. *What the hell was up with the woman?* He'd *barely* shot her and she'd landed a punch as sweet as he'd ever seen—nobody except Tanya was good enough to get so far past his guard. They were even, weren't they?

"Colombia was a small mess before we sent General Yarborough here back in 1962 to turn it into a big mess."

The general glared at them out of the TV. Looked like a major sourpuss—actually a General Sourpuss. Though maybe that was how Yarborough looked each time he thought about the mess he'd caused in the name of democracy.

"The Colombian government was fighting communist guerillas with little success. But with our help, the military set up and funded a lot of paramilitary groups to fight 'the communist threat.' What had started as a friendly little battle for social ideals rapidly became a screwed-up disaster. The guerillas were now under real pressure for the first time, so they needed another avenue of income. Drugs, kidnapping, and extortion rose rapidly in the back country."

"The blame-it-on-the-commies era," Duane commented.

"We were always good at that," Chad added, but his heart wasn't in their normal back-and-forth ribbing.

"Americans. You do it everywheres," Tanya sounded actively disgusted, which killed even the little bit of fun they usually found heckling the CIA agent.

"Everywhere," Chad whispered to her. For a second he thought she was going to pummel the other side of his face. Maybe he should just back off for a moment. Too bad he so rarely followed his own good advice.

"Then," Fred continued as unperturbed as always, "the pressure caused the communists to form into the two revolutionary armies—the FARC and the ELN. To combat them, the paramilitaries started financing themselves in a similar fashion while the military studiously looked the other way— anything that pressured the commies was good in their eyes. The rural folks got sandwiched between the two. For aiding the communists, they were slaughtered. For defying the brutal paramilitaries who now wanted their own plantations for coca cultivation, they were driven out or also slaughtered." He flicked through slides of the Alto Naya and Betoyes massacres along with others, revealing chainsaw executed bodies, peasants digging their own mass graves, and so on.

"Hence the DTOs," Sofia was never one to be outdone by a mere CIA guy.

"Right. The birth of the drug trafficking organizations," Fred took no offense even though he was meant to.

Why couldn't Tanya be more like that? It wasn't like he'd killed her or anything.

"The paramilitaries went vertical and built massive organizations. The DTOs—reaching their pinnacle in the Cali and Medellín cartels—built empires that controlled everything from coca growth to processing and shipment, even end-market distribution in the US and Europe."

"And Israel," Tanya added in her sourest tone yet. She glared at him as if it was his fault.

"Until we killed their asses," Chad wasn't going to just sit here and take shit from everyone. Delta had been there for the Escobar takedown and a whole list of others. Neither Duane nor Sofia picked up the cue to add something.

Tanya just clamped her mouth shut.

To hell with you too, lady.

"Until we killed their asses," Fred agreed, flicking to a slide of Pablo Escobar shot dead on the roof he'd been attempting to escape across. The terra cotta curved Spanish tiles dripping from the neat double headshot that had taken him down.

Too neat to have been done by the local forces who'd bothered to show up. *Go Delta!* Chad cheered quietly to himself.

"The neo-paramilitaries have never achieved the huge power of the old DTOs, but they've gotten even dirtier. No longer claiming any ideals, they're just living for the drug trafficking with a little kidnapping on the side."

"And the gold," Chad wasn't a slouch either. "Don't forget all that pretty gold they're stripping the country for."

"Major issue," Smith agreed. "More money than cocaine for some operations. Their methods have continued to drive the massive exodus from the countryside to the cities."

"Colombia does have the second highest rate of internally displaced population after The Sudan," Richie offered one of his endless supply of factoids.

"Like our buddies along the jungle river, who we just set up to kill each other." Except he hadn't been there to do his part. Instead, he'd been off in the jungle chasing a woman who was chasing a ghost. "What does all this have to do with this *Capitana*?"

"Almost there," Fred flashed up a photo of Daniel Rendón

Herrera's ugly mug taken shortly after his arrest. His people had abandoned him to live like a squatter in the jungle after being one of the wealthiest post-Escobar leaders.

"So much for loyalty."

"He had it coming, bro." At least Duane was back on board.

"*El Clan del Golfo*, formerly *Los Urabeños*, is the most successful of the neo-paramilitary organizations. They use strict military discipline and structure, which makes for a minimum of infighting and a resiliency of operational structure. They subcontract hit men, informers, and distributors. And they pay well."

"Maybe when we're done with Delta we should sign up, bro," Chad tried to wink at Duane and then wished that some bitch hadn't punched him in the eye.

"Got me some wine waiting," Duane winked back and draped his arm around Sofia's shoulders. Sofia was a major wine heiress before she turned Activity then Delta; her sister was running the outfit until Sofia retired. Suddenly his best friend had this whole future staked out: lounging in the Oregon hills and tending damned grape vines. Be a nice change after the Loony Tunes attacking coca fields guarded with claymore mines and machine guns, but it just didn't seem right.

Next thing he knew, the women would all get pregnant, the guys would retire to "less dangerous circumstances," and he'd be left to dangle in the wind with Tanya Punch-you-in-the-face Thank-you-so-much Zimmer. He'd seen it happen before in the Rangers—good guys, tough fighters, giving it all up to become family men. Of course the guys who stayed in didn't seem to have the best answer either. Typically their family lives imploded. Soon they were worrying about alimony and the kid they only got to see while supervised on weekends until they became such basket cases that they got sloppy and stepped in front of a round or on a mine and solved everyone's problems.

Not him. No how. No way. Growing up on the Detroit streets had taught him just what civilian life was all about. He was in this until they put him six feet under. So, time to pay some attention.

"You saying that *la Capitana* is one of the three aliased leaders of the Gulf Clan?"

Fred shook his head and put up his next slide.

Everyone leaned forward to read the flyer there. It was hard to read through all of the blood stains.

"We took this off a bounty hunter. One who'd lost his head moments before we arrived. Machete, by the look of it."

Four men were pictured on the bloodied flyer. There were names under each picture. The print across the top said simply, "$10M US—each." One had a large red X over his face—Herrera. There was nothing else, except for the three gold stars of a Colombian captain's rank clustered at the bottom.

"The guy on the left is Otoniel, their Number One—the leader of *el Clan del Golfo.* Numbers Two and Three went down sometime after this flyer was issued—the latter practically turned himself in to get away from the bounty. We had never seen them before, but once we ran profiles on them, it fit."

"We're going after Otoniel," Chad was more than ready.

"You were. But now I think that he is best left to the bounty hunters. He's recruiting new leadership, but the price on their heads is apparently causing him problems. There's a reason I showed you this flyer. Did you notice the three clustered gold stars across the bottom? They're distinctively shaped—the rank symbol of a Colombian military captain. *La Capitana* appears to have declared war on *el Clan del Golfo.* It is the first proof we've ever had that there even is a *la Capitana* though we've heard rumors for two years now. She came out of nowhere and, if real, is fast becoming the most powerful player in all of South America."

The silence in the room was echoing. So quiet that for the first time he noted the distant sound of the city wafting in through the open balcony door.

Then Fred flashed to Chad's surveillance photos, including

the one he'd had the sense to snap when she was so close to where he and Tanya had been laid up.

Duane let out a low whistle, "Damn, dude. She's hot." Then he appeared to choke when Sofia glared at him.

"You should go for her, Chad," Richie totally missed the dynamic. "*La Capitana* and Sleeping Beauty—like one of those romance novels but with a gender role reversal."

The room burst out laughing. Only after everyone was howling did Richie get what he'd just said—calling Chad a little girl. It was a good moment and Chad just cuffed him on the back of the head, careful not to jar Melissa, who was kissing Richie on the temple.

Chad turned back to inspect the photos as the predictable round of "Chad the Princess" ran around the room.

"You know, Colombia allows same sex marriage between the two little girls." "Which one of them do you think would wear the pants in the family?" "Gotta see you in a princess dress, dude. Though I'd have to burn out my eyes afterward."

Yeah, yeah. Whatever.

Renata *was* a serious piece of work. At least five-ten, with a damn serious chest. The knotted tails of her jungle-green blouse revealed flat abs and that her smoky-dark skin went all the way down. Her hair was a teasingly dark tangle that brushed over her shoulders and always seemed to hide her face. She probably did that on purpose, along with the highly distracting cleavage reveal. If he hadn't watched her for four days, he'd be hard-pressed to describe her face.

He remembered the Expediter—Analie Sala. Her face had been narrow, as slender as the woman herself. The few times she removed her sunglasses, her eyes had seemed as narrow and dark as she was. She'd ended up as shark food a hundred miles off Panama, and if he hadn't seen the body himself, he'd have wondered which would win. The battle seemed fairly even.

In sharp contrast, Renata's face—if it was ever revealed all at once—would be as open as her blouse: broad cheeks, wide eyes that could suck a man into their dark depths until he could never swim free. There was a smooth beauty of confidence and a shapely chin. Imagining what it would be like to bed such a woman was part of how he'd kept himself awake on the long watches. Now he suspected it would be a fast way to end up dead.

Male drug runners were lethal, amoral, vicious bastards. He'd met more than a few—typically in the last minutes of their lives—and it was like walking into a meat freezer. The chill that came off those guys was nasty. Even a chill bitch like Analie hadn't radiated that kind of cold.

Renata, on the other hand, had seemed so warm and open. He'd watched from a distance as she drank and joked with the others around the campfire. Had watched as she'd taken one of the men off into the trees and had listened to the friendly catcalls that had followed them each night. Most of those men were dead now. He flashed on the image of the man who had come at him with a knife as Chad had taken the last motorcycle. *La Capitana's* lover of previous nights—down and dead.

He wondered if it pissed her off to know her lover was dead? Or was he just some random *hombre* she'd used to soothe that awesome body?

That was the thing about women that was so different from the male drug runners. Men got even. They might be vicious, but by comparison the women were downright nasty. Women waited and then did something truly horrid—the guy losing his balls before being fed to the Orinoco crocodiles. Men tried to win. Women were all about getting even—bad enough to count in this life *and* the next.

"Anything you want to be telling me?" he asked Tanya as the last of the jokes rattled about the group.

She didn't say a word.

Way too chill.

7

Tanya glanced around the suite.

Chad's room was obvious by the beautiful Mk 21 sniper rifle he'd leaned inside the door. Not wanting to separate the man from his weapon, she set it outside before closing and locking the door.

The room had its own bath. Not American large, but generous by Colombian standards—not that she cared. She used Chad's toothbrush. She considered swirling it in the toilet before putting it back on the counter, but she might need it again later. Her own gear was—she couldn't even remember where at this point.

She stripped slowly. Partly because every muscle was stiff and sore. Partly because she hadn't slept in long enough that she didn't want to risk losing her balance accidently and ending up in the toilet herself. The failed attack on the drug lab had been two days ago or three? She couldn't straighten it out. Adding "staying up all night to keep watch while Chad slept" to her grudge list didn't help her mood.

She'd definitely need to borrow a blouse. The bloody-stained hole that Melissa had hacked out of the shoulder to fix Chad's gunshot wound wouldn't go well out in public. Carla had the figure, but was about eight inches too short. Melissa was tall enough, but was so slender that there wasn't a chance of her clothes fitting. Sofia landed halfway in between on both counts, but appeared to favor tighter clothes—her black t-shirt had certainly clung enough to show her fine physique.

Clawing out of her khakis—which were only disgustingly dirty, not bloody or torn, so she'd deal with them later—she managed to drag herself into the glass shower enclosure.

Hot.

She ran the water hot and let it drag all the frustration, trail dust, and grime out of her hair. The soap stung like murder on her shoulder, but she scrubbed at it until the caked and dried blood stopped coloring the shower water at her feet. After she washed herself head to toe twice more, she decided that she wasn't going to get any cleaner on the outside.

Cranking the heat a little closer to full steam, she let it pound down upon her neck and back as she leaned her head against the stall's wall.

She needed to think.

La Capitana taking on *el Clan del Golfo*...that had meaning. Somehow it tied into the delivery that Delta Force had interrupted at the ferry crossing. And somehow Chad had stepped back into her life.

Tanya wasn't big on regrets. Her father's "fall" from the sidewalk. Leaving her mother and lecherous stepfather to rot in their homemade hell together. Each of the steps that had led her from the year of mandatory Army service into Mossad, and finally Kidon, had served her well. Her life as a counterterrorism assassin in defense of the homeland had left a trail of bodies behind her. Few of those bothered her either.

Removing the Iranian nuclear scientists thankfully hadn't been hers to do. That one had seemed borderline—they were scientists, not combatants or criminals or former Nazis.

She'd spent most of her career in South America. Her father

had been an Argentine Jew—though not a religious one before or after "moving back to the homeland." He'd insisted that Tanya only speak Spanish at home, despite living in Tel Aviv. It had made her a loner in the neighborhood and became a true burden when she reached school. In vengeance, she'd learned German, Hebrew, Yiddish, and English—though the last was her weakest as Chad kept pointing out. She'd also learned how to win her own fights—which Chad might learn soon if he wasn't careful.

Yet in a life of so few regrets, she'd regretted leaving this team in the midst of a massive storm on Lake Maracaibo, Venezuela. For those three brief days, and one battle-filled night, she'd belonged.

She shouldn't miss that.

It was weak.

Tanya Zimmer was never weak. She'd spent a lifetime building the woman who was never weak. And she wouldn't be weak now.

When everyone was asleep, she would slide out and find a way to pick up *la Capitana's* trail on her own. She was strong, but she was also very patient. If it took a year to track down her target, she'd do it, now that the woman was in her sights. She had a face, a very memorable one. That was more than anyone before had ever had.

A hard slap, which she'd like to place on the other side of Chad's face, turned off the water. She shoved open the glass door and confronted the large towel being held out in front of her.

"Goddamn it, Chad!" If the bathroom was a little bigger, she'd place a roundhouse kick into that smug face. Of course a cheap door lock wouldn't even slow down a Delta operator.

"I stopped him halfway through the door." Carla sat on the counter, almost bringing her to eye level with Tanya.

"You probably just saved his life," Tanya took the towel and began drying her hair as the steam swirled thickly about the small room. The white-and-blue tile walls were streaked with tears of condensation.

"I would appreciate it if you didn't kill any of my teammates. At least not without checking with me first." Carla's smile was always a surprise on the rare occasions when she let it out.

"Fair enough. I shall give you warning on anyone other than Chad."

"Guess that'll do."

"It is the best I will be giving you." Since Carla didn't show any signs of leaving, Tanya continued drying herself off.

"Other than shooting you, what have you got against him?" Carla leaned back against the mirror and folded her hands in her lap as if she was some little girl, not a beautiful and lethal Delta operator. The first one to ever fight her way in through the full Delta Selection and Operator Training Course.

"Other than shooting me?"

"Uh-huh."

Tanya kicked down the lid and sat on the toilet. The small room was still too hot and steamy to cover herself with the thick towel. "That isn't enough?"

"I know when I see a woman who is really pissed off. I've got a mirror after all." She gestured to her own face and shook her head. "Not enough."

Carla had never been one to pull her punches, verbal or otherwise. They had the latter in common, but Tanya had often found the subtle approach more sustainable. Not so Carla.

"Long time ago you called me 'sister,' Tanya."

"To confuse a hotel maid who had the very hots for both of us and much information we needed."

Carla smiled briefly at the memory, so briefly that it evaporated even faster than the last of the steam.

Tanya casually draped the towel over her good shoulder and let it cascade down her front.

"I never had a sister," Carla's tone was almost wistful. Once they'd stopped mistrusting each other, they *had* functioned with a near-sibling level of *sympatico*.

"I haven't had much luck with sisters. Mine killed herself when she was fourteen." Then Tanya choked. She'd never told anyone about Jimena. She did her best to never think about her. And she wouldn't now either. Wouldn't think about the massive drug overdose that had removed her older sister from her life. Or about how Father had "accidentally killed himself" stumbling off the sidewalk on the day of Jimena's funeral. His abuse had driven Jimena to her addiction and her intentional overdose—Tanya had been the one to find the body and the note (a note she'd never shown to anyone).

Carla nodded as if she'd said nothing unusual while Tanya tried to remember how to breathe. "I joined because of a dead brother. Shot in the head during a black ops mission."

"How did you do that?"

"Do what? Join the Army?"

"No, how did you just speak of him without wanting to cry?"

Carla's smile was sad this time. "Who says I did?"

"Can one of you explain women to me?"

Richie and Melissa were crouched over a laptop trying to composite together enough slices of Renata's face into a single image to send off for recognition analysis—left eye from one image, nose and right eye from another but at a different angle. Kyle and Fred were online back to CIA headquarters in Langley, Virginia, working to trace back the drug path they'd interrupted last night. Maybe, if they could figure out where the drugs originated, they could trace some link to *la Capitana*.

Carla had slammed his own bedroom door in his face, and who knew what the hell she and Tanya were talking about. Carla read him the riot act—without saying a word. All he'd been planning to do was go talk to Tanya. Instead Carla had delivered a sound lambasting with a single, long, fulminating look and a stony silence. Shit but that woman was scary when she was on about something.

Duane and Sofia had taken the last of their breakfast out onto the balcony. Chad had followed them out and they all sat looking at the vista of Medellín.

The city fell away almost vertically below them. The core of the city had long since filled the narrow river valley. The poor had rapidly covered the surrounding hills, building *barrios* whose poverty became more and more staggering with each layer out from the city. And where there was abject poverty, the drug culture dug in its talons. *Comuna 13*, where the team now sat, had once contained the most violent *barrios* of any city anywhere —including Detroit. It was healing now, but Chad wasn't heading back to Detroit anytime soon to see how they were doing.

Their suite looked down on one of the signs of that change. It was a real oddity—the first of its kind anywhere. A thirty-story outdoor escalator wound its way up the face of the hillside. What had been a painful, hour-long commute along twisting, one-lane roads across the face of the steep hillside between the poor *barrio* and the promise of wealthy jobs below was now nine minutes on the escalator. With the new connections had come new developers. As workers flowed down the hill during the day, money had flowed up the hill each night, pushing back the drugs. It drove the violence outward, into the poorest and newest slums surrounding the city, but in another decade or so, perhaps they too would be as connected.

If the city was healing itself, then what the hell was wrong with him?

"You always said you knew everything about women, dude. Now you're asking for advice?" Duane lay back in his lounger with a mug of chili-pepper hot chocolate in one hand and Sofia's hand in the other.

"Life made a shitload more sense back in the Green Berets, man." Back then, men had been men and women had been available. Now?

"Wouldn't know. I was a Ranger."

"Pansy," Chad accused him, but didn't put any heat behind it. Duane was weirdly defensive about his old unit.

They stared in silence out at the city as the morning sun warmed the night air from the typical low of sixties slowly toward the average midday seventies. Five thousand feet up in the Andes and six degrees off the equator, it never became too hot or too cold. He could see settling here. There'd be gangs to fight back for years to come. The food was such a far cry from the fare of Detroit—the one place on the entire planet he never intended to go back to. The nightclubs here were filled with hot music and hotter women who—

"Would you like a woman's opinion?" Sofia said softly.

"Don't bother," Duane closed his eyes as if getting ready for a nap. "He already knows everything about women, just ask him."

He didn't like it, but didn't see any way around it. "Okay, hit me."

"I think Tanya already has done that." Sofia was in her absolutely logical intel analyst mode. Why didn't that sound good?

"Try me anyway."

"It's not women who are confusing you. It is one woman."

Crap! He'd been right. It wasn't good.

CARLA HANDED Chad's comb to her.

Tanya took it with a sigh and began working at the snarls in her hair. Each stroke and the resultant twinge in her shoulder reminded her that he'd shot her, and each released snarl emphasized that wasn't the problem.

"He couldn't make you so angry just by being himself."

"Sure he could."

Carla grimaced. "I suppose. But he isn't often a real asshole unless he's doing it intentionally."

"How can you tell with him?"

"I never figured that out. He just knows that I can be much more of an asshole than he can, so he doesn't mess with me."

"No sane person would mess with you." Carla's size had nothing to do with her intense competence. Also, she hadn't picked up the nickname Wild Woman by being calm and predictable. Her fighting style reflected the same chaos—she was even more wholly unpredictable to her opponents than to her teammates.

"Good. I like it that way. So does Chad, just in case you're wondering."

"He likes being scary?"

"He grew up on the streets. That's all he's ever told anyone about his past—not even Duane, as far as I know. Never once said a word about his parents."

Neither had she about hers. How had she not known that they shared the Street in common?

"So, now what's really bothering you about him?"

"I'd prefer any other topic, which I'm guessing…"

"Is off the table. There was no one to corner me on my shit, so I figure it's the least I can do for my friends."

"*Are* we friends, Carla? That is definitely not something I have experience with."

"I have six." Carla nodded toward the rest of the suite. "Total. And I'm married to one of them."

"What about Fred Smith?"

Carla sighed. "Never imagined being friends with a CIA agent, but he's a good guy. But would I trust him with my life?"

A measure that sounded about right to Tanya.

"Guess I have, a couple dozen times over the years. Okay, six friends and one husband. There's also this woman who once called me sister," Carla nodded to indicate her. "Melissa and Sofia can barely use my name without stumbling over themselves. They're awesome, but treat me as something 'other'."

"Because you scare the shit out of anyone who is sane?"

Carla shrugged.

"Good thing I'm *loco.*"

"Good thing," and once again that softer version of Carla showed through for an instant. "So, *sister,* you do know how far gone Chad is on you?"

"Of course. So much that he shot me."

Carla's look told her that was irrelevant. Chad's loyalty was never in question, even if he'd doubted hers.

"Not that he knows it either, but guess again, *sister.*"

Was Carla saying that she expected to actually become related to Tanya by the connection of team—which for her would be far deeper than blood?

Chad's comb caught a snarl so badly that it almost sliced off Tanya's ear when it let go.

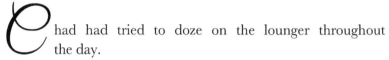 had had tried to doze on the lounger throughout the day.

When Carla had strolled out of his bedroom—offering one of her unreadable (but thankfully not overtly hostile) looks—she'd made a show of closing the bedroom door solidly behind her.

Tanya did not follow her out of the room.

The "Do Not Enter" was clear, but there was no indicator of what the hell had happened behind that closed door. Or where he was supposed to sleep. Clearly not on Tanya's shoulder —he was still pissed that he'd simply passed out on that prime real estate yet didn't remember any of it.

The problem was that the couches in this place were about a foot shorter than he was. Great for lovebirds like Richie and Melissa—who had eventually retreated into their room to sleep away the day just as the others had.

Sucked for him.

He liked taking up his man-space when he slept. If there was something warm and soft to curl up in his arms while he was doing that, he never had any complaints about sharing—as long as he could stretch out.

That sure like fuck wasn't what was happening here. The lounger was built for Colombian natives—maybe miniature versions of them. His feet stuck off the end and every time his arms came uncrossed, they slipped off the sides and he smacked his knuckles on the concrete. Even lying out here on the balcony, he could feel the ever-so-happy couples sleeping together behind him.

At first he'd thought it was kind of cool that, for their one team, the military was looking the other way. No question about the leadership team Kyle and Carla made together. He'd never served with better and never expected to again. Each day with them was something special. No way was the military dumb enough to break up something so successful.

Richie the Nerd had needed a woman bad. When Melissa the Cat had prowled into his life, it was like nerddom on steroids. He'd made her a better nerd and she'd made him an even better fighter. Couldn't wish a better match for him.

His buddy Duane going down had been tough to swallow. But Sofia was such a freaking dynamo, it was damned hard to complain—dangerous too. The analytic brain she stowed inside that pretty head of hers was such an asset that it was hard to argue. As an unexpected bonus, instead of getting pushed out of his friendship with Duane, they'd gotten closer. He loved hanging with the two of them. And Sofia always added a quick beat to any teasing going back and forth. He sometimes wondered how different things would have been if he'd been the one sent into the human trafficking camp that Sofia had uncovered rather than Duane. But you didn't envy your best friend's woman no matter how hot she was.

He was cool with each of the couples individually. Never bothered him being a fifth wheel...or a seventh as in this case. Their team was a monster truck with duallies: Kyle and Carla steering, the other two couples as the dually power wheels, and him hanging out as rearguard. Sometimes he found a ride-along, but never for long.

But something about this sucked today and he half-wished the military hadn't decided to test the functionality of fraternization between team members on their team. He wouldn't wish away a single member, but it sucked to not quite belong either.

Especially because he'd been chased out of his own goddamn bedroom.

It was midsummer, so having a balcony that faced due north didn't help either. The sun was fifteen degrees *north* of overhead in Medellín. It meant that it had been burning in under the edge of the awning and broiling him from the knees down all day without him really noticing. Shorts. Why the hell had he opted for shorts?

From the nose over, his punched face was angry purple. And now from the knees down, his legs were even angrier red. And inside he was goddamn *green!*

Since when was he ever envious of someone having a woman? Jealousy? Him?

Shit, Chad. Get your fucking act together.

He sat up and ignored the painful stretchiness in his calves and the sudden pounding of his pulse in his face.

Maybe if he just went and took the woman down but good. He knew they'd both enjoy it. One good round and they'd clear the air. Even if they were done after that, no question it would be good. Their stolen moments on the Maracaibo mission had proved that there was nothing other than incredible going on between them.

He pushed to his feet, ignoring the big white palm prints he left on his red knees. The wind shifted slightly with the evening. The flavors of Medellín wafted across the balcony. Grilling beef for *carne asada.* Frying onion. Poblano chili peppers being charred to remove the skin and sweet roast the insides.

Not just woman, woman and food. The evening was looking better already.

He stepped into the suite's shared living room just as Fred Smith let himself in through the front door.

"Chad! Good. Roust the others, would you. We've got a small side mission while Langley chews on the data about *la Capitana.*"

"Food first." Now why did he choose that one? Because saying, "Must get laid first," wouldn't exactly improve the conversation. He could feel his merry tumble with Tanya slipping out of his fingers.

"Got it all set up downstairs. *Bandeja Paisa.* Ten minutes."

Chad's stomach growled audibly, sealing his fate. Should he knock on his own door to roust Tanya first or last? Ten minutes, they could have a quickie at least. He thumped a hinge-rattling fist on Duane's and Richie's rooms, calling out "Ten minutes. Food." Across the suite, he did the same thing on Kyle's.

As he moved to his own door—no knock, he was just gonna go in; his room, after all—Tanya opened it and stepped into the living room.

Chad couldn't seem to process what he was seeing. It had been three years since he'd seen Tanya out of battle gear; she'd still been wearing her shredded and bloodied battle shirt at breakfast. He liked her scuffed up and muddy—all snarled up and ready for action. But now she was wearing fresh-washed jeans, a t-shirt that was nicely tight and too short by several inches of perfectly toned midriff, and her sleek blonde hair shone almost as brightly as her brilliant blue eyes.

"Damn, woman!" He barely managed to gasp it out.

Tanya laughed in his face.

———

SHE COULDN'T HELP IT.

Chad looked like he'd slept in a tumble dryer and only lately escaped. He was wide-eyed and rumpled. His face was already shifting from blue-purple to yellow-and-green. And his pale legs —even lighter than her own—were as electric red as a neon beer sign—a sunburnt beer sign.

"You better go shower."

"Hoping you'd scrub my back," he offered her a wolfish grin. Lopsided, because of the stiffer side of his face.

She stepped around him and gave him a shove on the shoulders. He limped as he went, and it didn't look like a sympathy limp. His knee must still be hurting no matter what he'd been pretending yesterday. Pretending he hadn't been hurt after getting so much of her sympathy the night before? Had he changed his story just to keep her off balance?

No. He'd been pretending it was less than it had been so that he wouldn't get cut out of the operation. Then he'd chased her on a motorcycle over the brutal terrain, which must have him hurting as much as her shoulder. *Good!*

Carla stepped into the suite just in time to see Tanya close the door behind Chad. She raised a single eyebrow.

"Go to hell, *little* sister." Carla was over six inches shorter than she was, after all.

"Not saying a word."

"About what?" Melissa eased up with the loose-hipped walk of a recently very happy woman.

Carla made a show of locking her lips and tossing away the key.

"I surmise," Sofia was still brushing her long dark hair to a shimmer as she joined them. "That Carla's unspoken words are because Tanya is not presently in with Chad humping his brains out. I've observed that Carla has an exceptionally one-track mind. Sex fixes everything in her world view."

"No. It screws everything up, but since that's nothing new, I figure I might as well have fun while everything is being a mess." Then Carla slapped her hands back over her mouth before tossing away another imaginary key.

All three women turned to look at her. As if Tanya hadn't spent the first half of the day (that was supposed to be her night) wondering why Chad didn't come into the room and the second half (when she still only slept in starts and fits), wondering if she should go fetch him.

"I think that you are all having a one-track mind on this subject. Who didn't have sex last night?"

"Oh, I like this conversation," Duane called out to Kyle as he took the brush from Sofia's hands and continued brushing her hair for her.

"It's quite simple," Richie remarked as he stepped up and took Melissa's hand. "Guys, raise your hands if you can't imagine keeping your hands off your wife."

All three guys raised their hands.

"I am hating all of you." Tanya's body had a clear preference. Men were pleasant and forgettable—wholly forgettable. Chad was…not.

Carla mumbled something, but kept her lips clamped as if they were still locked.

"She says, 'So, have some sex.' I'd second that vote," Melissa added cheerfully.

"Mm-hm," Carla mumbled.

"Wild sex," Melissa corrected.

"So, are we almost ready?" Fred came over from where he'd been talking on his phone.

CHAD STEPPED out of the bedroom behind Tanya.

Every single face in the suite turned to look at him. Most of them were grinning like love-sated fools.

"What?"

Tanya's back was to him. She alone didn't turn. It would be so easy to reach out and stroke a hand over her hair and down that lovely back. The tight shirt revealed the muscle definition of her shoulders. The neck scooped a few inches below her hair, showing the tan of a woman who lived mostly outdoors that was echoed in the narrow slice of the gap between her shirt and jeans. The curve at her spine, bridged by her jeans, invited his hand to slip down the gap and see just how well he remembered the feel of her exceptional butt against his palm.

He tore his attention back to the group.

Carla's jaw was firmly clamped shut, or just maybe she was smiling.

"Hello? Food?" Fred rang the Pavlovian bell and Chad's stomach grumbled again, which broke up the group far more than it should have. Duane slapped a hand onto Chad's back hard enough to sting as he howled with laughter. Sofia and Melissa actually leaned on each other's shoulders they were giggling so hard.

"What?...No!" Chad didn't want to know. "Never mind." Ever! "Food. Now! C'mon Fred," the only person as in the dark as he was. "Let's get away from these loons." He stepped around Tanya without even tracing a finger over a long knife scar on her biceps that hadn't been there three years ago. The scar didn't bother him, it was part of their trade. But that he didn't know its origin, hadn't been there to murder the man who gave it to her…that bothered him.

He really was losing it.

He didn't wait for Fred to lead the way out the door and down the stairs onto the street.

The restaurant, less than two blocks from their suite, was a recent favorite: *Paisan Comida*—literally "Medellín Native Food" or "Local Food." It was as unpretentious as its name. The concrete frontage had been painted a brilliant sea blue as part of a block-long mural. The mayor had given the *Comuna 13* youths thousands of gallons of paint to beautify their neighborhood as they saw fit. Some parts of town were wild graffiti, others were actual building-by-building paint jobs. This area was halfway in between. No matter what, that single mayoral act had been the beginning of the turnaround for the area.

Inside, the owner's hand had taken over, painting with broad strokes in warm oranges and reds. Traditional art hung haphazardly on one wall, lit by twinkle lights. It wasn't arranged by some plan, but rather by three generations of women who had run the place. Wide-brimmed hats of woven black-and-white straw hung next to a grinning mask tattooed in more-vibrant-than-Crayola colors. A rug that might have been a neon stork delivering a baby in swaddling clothes, or perhaps a toucan delivering a banana, hung next to a Flower Festival basket filled with a brilliant bouquet of irises and gladioli.

"My boys!" Estela greeted them with a happy cry as they came in. She waddled out from behind the counter.

"How did you get even more pregnant than last week?" Chad bent down to hug her.

"I'm bigger than a horse. Soon I will be too big to fit inside my own restaurant. I will have to have you kill my husband for doing this to me." Her liquid Spanish was as beautiful as she was. Her face glowed gloriously bright as she hugged Duane as well. He and Chad had extracted one of the last drug-gang leaders from the neighborhood, arriving almost too late to save Estela's and Ramiro's lives. The very quiet trip that Jesús Rivera had taken on an unmarked DEA plane back to the States had solved that problem. There the coward had spilled his guts about every supplier, enforcer, and runner he had—without even being offered leniency. Two judges and twenty police officers had also been taken out of circulation—including two second lieutenants who had not gone so quietly into the night.

She'd pushed her two biggest tables together, which meant that the back half of the tiny restaurant was theirs. Several of the locals came up to greet them as well.

Estela drifted back to her small kitchen and the food was soon flowing outward in platter-loads big enough to make up for his last week in the jungle.

Fred made several failed attempts to divert attention to their mission, but the distraction of Estela's *Bandeja Paisa* completely outclassed him. The meal nestled around the base of a small cast iron pot of Colombian beans mixed with pork hocks and green plantain. A generous mound of sticky white rice and a corn *arepo* cake for some carbs. Pork cracklings and powdered pork—shredded so fine it almost did look powdered—were kept company by a chorizo sausage because a growing boy could never get enough meat. A baked plantain for sweetness, a pair of fried eggs for color, and an avocado for the hell of it.

"A warrior's lunch." Duane chortled as he dug in. "And it's everywhere in Colombia. I'm in heaven."

"At Estela's it is a glorious mountain to conquer," Chad couldn't agree more.

"You're both oafs. You must tell the cook that it is the best you've ever eaten," Sofia teased them, then raised her voice to do exactly that.

"I could bathe in this hogao sauce," Duane dredged up more of the sharp salsa.

"You smell like it. Your stink reaches all the way over here, bro."

Sofia leaned over to sniff at Duane's shoulder. He took the opportunity to kiss her soundly. Very soundly, continuing until Kyle scoffed, "Newlyweds."

"Hmm," Sofia hummed happily, then ended the kiss. "He doesn't smell like hogao, but he certainly tastes of it. Only better."

Duane, the dog, just smiled.

Chad couldn't help but glance at Tanya. She'd ended up across the table from him, between Carla and Richie. He tried sliding a foot over to rub against her ankle, but when Richie looked up in surprise and scanned the table, Chad slowly withdrew his foot.

CHAD'S FOOT sliding against her ankle had sent a warm tingle of surprise up Tanya's spine.

She didn't want Chad's warm tingles.

Under the table, she managed to kick Richie's shin from a slightly unexpected angle. Richie startled and Chad's foot instantly slid off her ankle.

Why was she resisting him?

He was an exceptional lover—unless he'd gotten even better over the intervening years.

He was very pretty, especially out of his clothes. He could pass for a Greek god with that body.

She even liked him.

And *there* was the problem. She *did* like Chad. With only a few memorable exceptions, she'd "liked" all the men she'd slept with, but that was all.

She liked Chad…a great deal.

Not acceptable! Not in her world—not anywhere in her life.

Focusing on her food wasn't sufficient distraction. Even at this table of America's super warriors, Chad stood out. He wasn't the leader or the brains. Richie and Duane were the tech guy and explosives guy. But in a group of incredible sharpshooters—you had to be or you weren't part of Delta— Chad was their top sniper and weapons specialist.

She'd used her looks and her brains to survive, even thrive in this clandestine game of international conflict fought with drugs, trafficking, subterfuge, and great scads of money. But she'd started out as a shooter.

The *Tzahal*—the Israeli Defense Forces or IDF—had recognized that quickly. She could tear down a jammed Uzi faster than most grunts could change magazines. She'd made *kala sa'ar* (designated marksman) before she was out of boot camp. The day they'd issued her an IWI Galatz was still one of the most memorable days of her life. Mossad and ultimately Kidon had made sure that she was an expert on a hundred different weapons systems—because you never knew what would best fit the mission in the field. But that old wood-stocked sniper rifle had been her constant companion for two years in the *Tzahal* and her first two in Mossad—Israel's answer to the CIA.

Her mission profiles had somehow slid out of her control since then.

She put down a forkful of homemade chorizo sausage she'd just sliced—it suddenly tasted like sand.

Tanya's life of comfortably carefree solo missions had been broken by three days of service with this team several years ago. It had led her into more and more "cooperative missions" and ad hoc teams that had culminated so horribly just three nights ago with her team suffering a death, a grave injury, and a complete loss of confidence. She was—

"What do you say, Tanya?"

"To what?" She'd completely missed the talk around the table and Smith's question made no sense.

Most of the people around the table were looking at her with a puzzled frown. Carla's expression was blank, assessing. Her eyes didn't need to flicker sideways to Chad to state the core of the question.

Clearly Smith had been laying out some sort of mission. Her inclusion might be simply because she was a handy asset. But Carla would know that the mission wasn't the real question for her.

It was Chad.

Tanya looked at him, without looking at him. Instead, reviewing his expression in memory from when her gaze had flicked around the table. It was…hopeful.

That almost tipped her into the "no way" column. She'd be fine again on her own. No more teams. Just her and the enemy for however long she could last.

But Carla's neutral gaze was unwavering, forcing her to face her own reasons.

A chance to fight once more with this team was attractive.

And if Tanya dodged out because of Chad, she knew that she wouldn't be living up to Carla's standards. Anyone else and she'd tell them to go to hell, but not "sister" Carla. Maybe if Tanya just this once—

"She's in," Carla looked away with no other acknowledgement. Either Carla got tired of waiting, or she read Tanya's answer before she knew it herself. Tanya would wager on the latter.

It was impossible to miss the sigh of relief from Chad.

Her decision had been important to him. More important than just where was he going to next get sex? That was unclear.

More important to her than merely choosing her next lover?

That too was unclear.

9

"*W*eren't we just here?"

Chad glanced over at Tanya as the sunset chased them up the rear ramp on the MH-47G Chinook.

"But if we were, it was going *that* way." He pointed down the ramp in the direction they'd slid and tumbled into the jungle river.

After dinner and a planning session, the team had taken a couple of unremarkable Toyota Corollas to a small clearing deep in the Medellín hills before donning their gear.

They'd scrounged up enough for Tanya. Over that tight t-shirt from Sofia, one of Richie's camo shirts fit her well enough. Melissa had remarkably long legs, which meant her slacks had fit Tanya nicely. Night-vision goggles and a new radio came out of general supplies. They'd all donned Ecuadoran military insignia patches for their collar points. They also had Colombian insignias tucked away in case they needed them.

Damn but she looked good in a full kit. His kind of lethal.

She'd hung onto her Uzi during the river canyon fall as well, but he'd loaned her his second sniper rifle—an HK MSG90 that he'd always liked. Lately he'd carried it less and less in favor of a

Mk 21 PSR—precision sniper rifle. It didn't hurt his ego that his PSR also threw the bigger .338 Lapua round that could reach out and touch someone at almost twice the distance of the MSG's 7.62 mm rounds.

They had been on a Chinook just two days ago…briefly.

He checked the loadmaster. Seriously cute redhead. Same bird ruling the roost meant they were on the same bird. Man, they'd gotten this bolted back together fast.

"Yeah," Chad looked around as if mildly surprised. "We *were* just here. At least *I* was until *you* ran me over."

"And *I* was until *you* dragged me out of the helo teakettle over ass."

"Other way around, sweetheart."

She thumped him in the kidneys with the butt of her rifle hard enough to hurt even through his vest. "Not your sweetheart. And I did not drag you out, you dragged me out when I tried to save you. Stop trying to change the truth."

"No. I—Never mind." Maybe things would go better if he stopped pointing out Tanya's idiomatic peculiarities. He checked in with the redhead, partly to find out how the wounded gunner was doing and partly to irritate Tanya. The Brit was out of surgery and the prognosis was good—a chunk of his arm would be titanium from now on, but full recovery. They traded fist-to-shoulder thumps and the woman headed off to take care of other things.

Which left him to face Tanya again. The rest of the team were already involved in other things. Sofia, Richie, and Kyle on the action plan. Carla, Melissa, and Duane going over their weapons and restocking from supplies the Chinook had brought along. Tanya was sitting in one of the jump seats by herself and staring blankly into space.

"Hey," he dropped down next to her. He considered stripping his rifle for something to do. Not that it needed it, he'd only taken the one shot with it last night to bring down Tanya's bike.

He'd forgotten about that during the long slow day of kinda snoozing and sunburning the crap out of his shins.

Chad popped the magazine, fished inside a pouch, and restocked the missing round so he'd have a full mag.

"Go to hell, Chad."

"Look, I'm sorry about your shoulder and shooting your bike out from under you."

"You shot me *twice?*" Tanya didn't look at him, instead she looked at the cargo bay's ceiling and muttered, "*Putz.*"

"Well, you once and your bike once." Right, he'd shot the bike with his rifle, but he'd grazed her shoulder with his Glock handgun. Better top off that mag as well.

"But you were aiming for me."

"Moving target and all…" Maybe it was time to keep his mouth shut. Should have said he was aiming for the bike, but he hadn't been. In the half second of travel time for the round, the trail she'd been on must have gotten abruptly steeper, lifting her the crucial half meter out of danger.

"Where were you?"

"That hump in the trail just past where you and *la Capitana* circled opposite sides of a monster ceiba. Dumped the bike and did a dive and roll. One-knee shot. Call it four-hundred-plus meters and you were upslope."

"Nice," was all she said after a moment's silent consideration. "I took a shot like that once standing in the rear of a Range Rover in the hills above Valencia. Driver was doing seventy down one of those laughable dirt stretches the Venezuelans call a road. I was actually bounced into the air and took the shot while floating—far steadier than being in the Rover. Only three hundred meters though."

"Get him?"

"Closer than you. Chest, not head—off-center to his right side so he was still breathing. Took care of that when we got closer."

"When were you in Valencia?"

"Last October."

"Shit! We were in Caracas then, could have met up."

"Caracas." Tanya was staring at the ceiling again.

The line of her neck against the last of the sunset filling the sky beyond the open rear ramp teased him to nibble on it, but some survival instinct told him better not to. The jungle was now racing by below them as the crew flew south.

"The SEBIN takedown?" Tanya didn't turn to face him. "That was your team? I should have known. It was too damn perfect."

"That was just the distraction. We tapped their secret police's entire communications network so that it's beamed straight to us. Sofia's first major op with us—she likes her data. It was really her doing."

Tanya looked toward Sofia for a moment as if reassessing her based on the news. She still hadn't looked at him.

"Look. Tanya. I—"

"I'm here for the fight, Chad. That's all." Tanya needed to make that perfectly clear. To him. To herself.

"What did I do so wrong?"

"Other than shooting me? Twice?"

"Right. Other than that."

She clamped her mouth shut. Other than that, he hadn't done anything wrong.

Except for being himself.

"Leave me alone."

She could feel him squinting at her in the fading light. Knew what would happen if she turned to him, and she wasn't ready for that. Then, very quietly, he rose to his feet and took a step over to join the others. A step like he had his tail between his legs. Ninety kilos and more than one-eighty centimeters of sad-puppy warrior.

She waited until he lifted his other foot, which would place him slightly off balance. Then she snagged the back of his belt and gave it a yank. He landed back in the seat beside her with something of a crash. She ignored the looks from the rest of the team.

"Stop being such a pain in the ass, Chad."

"Thought I was being nice. Leaving you alone when you asked."

"You were. So cut it out."

"You're not makin' a whole lotta sense there, Zimmer."

Tell her about it. "Just sit there and be quiet for a minute."

"I can do that." And just to irritate her even more, that's what he did.

"Asshole," she muttered.

"Takes one to know one." He began cleaning his rifle as if he had nothing better to do. As if reloading the rounds *he'd shot her with* hadn't been enough of a slap. He just had to make a point about where he thought the power lay in their relationship —no matter how misguided that view was.

The jungle had now disappeared into the darkness. The dull red of the night-operations light now filled the helo's cargo bay with ghoulish shadows.

Their relationship? They didn't have a relationship. All they had was this twisted…thing between them. Next they'd be stripping down right here on the cargo deck and comparing battle scars. Of course it would have to be only the recent ones, as they'd done exactly that three years ago. Why the hell had *that* been a turn on? Surely she was a collection of more than her battle injuries…wasn't she?

Of course if she was, then he must be too. Wasn't he?

Her thoughts were looping and there was no way out of it.

"Say something."

Rather than speak, he traced a finger down the scar that ran the length of her biceps.

A shiver slid up her spine.

"Tell me that, before you killed him, you tortured the bastard who did this to you."

And there he was again, both meeting and completely confusing her expectations.

"Look—" he had to swallow hard to stop the "babe" that most women seemed to think was sweet, but Tanya certainly didn't. "—Lady Sniper. You're the sexiest goddamn thing I've ever seen on two legs."

"Got a thing for four-legged critters?" she shot right back at him.

"Not what I meant. And no. What I've got is a thing for a gorgeous woman who shoots *almost* as well as I do."

She scowled at him just as he'd intended and he couldn't keep back the laugh. That earned him a grimace of acknowledgement that she'd fallen for his trap.

"But Tanya, if you think I've got any idea what's going on here, you got another guess coming."

"We're going on a takedown mission to cut off a cocaine export route running out through Ecuador."

"No, I meant…" And now he'd fallen for her straight line. He rested his fingers on her thigh. When he went to rub a thumb along the side, he ended up stroking the sheath for her Ari B'Lilah tactical knife. If nothing else defined her as Israeli elite Specials Operations, that custom knife certainly did. "You ever want to work out a trade, I've got a nice Strider SMF blade from the Marine Corps."

"Stripping dead bodies?" Tanya teased him.

"Wish I had a better story about it. Wild poker. Sex with a hot lieutenant. Something. But no, I did a training mission with Marine Corps Detachment One—me and Richie training them. Trust me, it wasn't the other way round. Gave us each a blade as thanks."

"Well," Tanya traced her hand down her blade and over his thumb. "Nobody gets an Ari B'Lilah that easy." Her touch was as light as her tone. Just enough louder than the beating rotor blades to understand, but soft enough that he had to lean in to be sure of her words. She smelled of combat gear and gun oil— so damn sweet.

"So, what do I have to do to get one? I'm guessing being a good boy isn't enough." Her fingers lingered on the back of his hand, sending shock waves into his system.

"Being a bad boy isn't going to get you there either." Then she casually twisted his pinkie backward until he had to kneel on the steel deck to relieve the pressure, but she didn't ease off—just as he wouldn't have.

"What will?" He managed to keep his voice steady despite the line of pain he could feel running right through his elbow joint.

She let him go and he made a show of *not* rubbing away the pain.

"Seriously." It surprised him, but he really did want to know. He was careful not to put any pressure on that arm as he again sat beside her. Flexing his fingers slowly eased down the pain.

"Seriously?" She scowled out into the darkness.

Even the blood-red operations nightlight looked good on her. Rather than going splotchy, she looked like some sexy demoness of temptation the preachers were always going on about—her blonde hair gone deep red and her light blue eyes seeming to glow with fire. He'd sat in the back pew of enough churches during bitter Detroit winters to know the liturgy better than most of the priests. Knew their fire and brimstone as well as the seven mortal sins. Not one of the seven ever sounded half as good as Tanya looked.

"In truth, I have less idea than one of your four-footed friends."

Chad regathered the parts of his cleaning kit that had scattered to the decking when she'd folded back his finger. He coiled up the BoreSnake and tucked it into a pocket along with the little squeeze bottle of oil.

They sat in silence for a couple kilometers as the helo continued to climb. They were doing a high jump tonight.

He wanted Tanya. That was a given. What sane man wouldn't? Especially because he'd had a taste of that three years ago and knew just what she brought to the game.

"Truth?" He muttered it for himself, but Tanya must have heard between one rotor beat and the next for she turned to him.

Truth wasn't something he spoke often to women. They didn't want to hear that he was only there for the sex. They didn't like that the moment he redeployed (which, being Delta, happened often and usually on zero notice), they were never going to see him again. And no way did they want to know that most of them had half the skill of the teenage whore who took his virginity on someone else's silk sheets and that he would never think of them again.

Except Tanya had spent three years tap dancing around the back of his thoughts. Sex with her wasn't memorable—it was the kind of thing epic movies were written about. And he'd…

"I missed you."

Tanya didn't even blink. Instead she nodded slowly as if agreeing. Agreeing that *she* had missed *him* and that feeling didn't fit any better in her world than it did in his.

"I—"

"Out of time, dude." Carla dropped a parachute rig into his lap. "Should have kissed her while you still had the chance." The look she gave Tanya was unreadable as she plopped a second rig in Tanya's lap.

TANYA STUCK her tongue out at Carla, which earned her a bark of laughter and then a view of Carla's backside as she strode up the length of the helo's cargo bay to don her own rig. The others in the crew were at various stages of prepping their gear. No rush, but being Delta efficient.

She straightened out the harness.

"Um, you *are* jump qualified, *babe?*" Chad was once again being Chad. Their moment was gone, slipping back behind the curtain of the normal. That was fine with her. Truth was overrated anyway.

With a clean flip, she slid the harness into place. Standing, she shot her hips forward then back, expertly catching the tails of the straps as they swung between her legs. Tanya snapped them onto the hip rings. Holding the half squat, she yanked the adjusters to cinch the leg straps. Four more motions latched and adjusted waist and chest straps. One more slung the long sniper rifle safely out of the way.

Chad had stood when she did, but hadn't moved a single muscle to put on his harness, instead just watching her as if he'd gone numb.

Grabbing the front of his shirt, she jerked him closer and kissed him.

She'd show the bastard just exactly who was competent.

But she could feel his smile grow as they kissed. What she'd intended as a short vengeful drive at him, opened and expanded. Kissing Chad wasn't like kissing other men. For some, it was a control thing. For others it was some level of friendly gesture like "Thanks for the good fuck" or "Let's fuck, soon!"

Chad could turn a kiss into a whole sexual act of its own.

Rather than clamping an arm around her to keep her in place, he trusted to her hold on him to take care of that. Instead, he ran his hand over her waist, down the leg strap that circled her buttock, and then brushed his fingertips along her Ari B'Lilah knife, tracing the outline of the sheath on her thigh. Acknowledging the jumper and fighter along with the woman currently devouring his lips. Her memory hadn't failed her on what an exceptional kisser he was.

"You jumping with us, Chad?" Carla again.

Tanya opened one eye; she hadn't remembered closing them. The rest of the team was fully harnessed and lining up at the helo's lowered rear ramp. Three tough men and three lethal women. Gods but she'd missed this.

The adrenaline kept pumping.

Chad went to ease back, but she held him in place. Taking his lower lip between her teeth, she dared him to pull away. If the reserve chute at her belly wasn't holding them apart, she'd have rubbed her hips against his to distract him.

She *wanted* to rub her hips against him. Rub her entire body!

"Thirty seconds," the female crew chief called out with a laugh.

Tanya kept him pinned for another ten seconds, but his wandering touch was gone—distracted—no longer teasing her leg to wrap around him.

He took a sudden step back, flipped his harness over his head, and seemed to make all of the attachments and adjustments in a single smooth motion. She buddy-checked his harness, but he hadn't missed a thing.

This time she used the chest strap of his harness to pull him back against her. He clamped his hands around her waist and held her as tightly as she was holding him, despite the *two* reserve chutes now between them.

"Ten!"

His kiss kept heating. It asked the question of why she'd even wasted time with other lovers over the last years since they'd been together. And she answered with greedy need that wasn't like her at all.

"Five."

She groaned into the kiss.

"Four."

This shouldn't be possible.

"Three."

Jumping was always *the* massive adrenal charge—with a night jump topping the list. Even better than battle because generally no one was trying to kill her during a night jump.

"Two."

Chad's kiss loomed even bigger—her pulse was pounding so hard that it threatened to punch her heart out through t-shirt, camo blouse, and jump harness.

"One."

She pushed away.

"Jump! Jump! Jump!" The crew chief's shout was only marginally louder than the ringing in Tanya's ears.

The rest of the team was streaming off the rear ramp.

At the edge of the ramp, she turned back to face Chad. He still hadn't moved.

"Don't forget your rifle!" Tanya shouted at him.

He swore and turned for his weapon as she leaned backward and tumbled off the rear ramp and into the night close behind Carla.

She'd made a sniper of Chad's dedication completely forget about his rifle. Tanya unleashed a crow of delight that no one except the wind could hear.

She slapped her night-vision goggles into place. Then, adjusting her arms, she let herself roll through a pair of backward somersaults. Popping her chute, she steered into her slot in the jump group.

There were times when being a woman was the best feeling on the planet.

10

---

*C*had did a full flail and twist as he hit the airstream and the crew chief's laugh followed him down. To hell with her. He didn't need a married Night Stalker crew chief, no matter how goddamn cute and red-headed she was. Not when Tanya Zimmer was falling through the sky ahead of him.

He finally managed to get his rifle stowed securely enough for a drop. By the time he stabilized his flight and shifted his NVGs into place, he'd fallen an extra eight seconds and was gonna be stuck a thousand feet below the team for the rest of the flight.

He popped his chute and grunted as the leg straps caught him sharply in the balls—not enough attention to adjusting them properly. He and his balls had been busy thinking about other things.

It was only the autonomic skills pounded into his skull by Airborne's relentless trainers that had him buckling the harness at all. Tanya kissed the way a howitzer fired shells—full bore. Her tongue had so scorched a path in his mouth that he could still feel it like a witch's tracery. The hex sign of his everlasting doom.

95

Be a hell of a way to go—sex slave to a blonde demoness.
"Bring it on!"

Somewhere above him he heard a laugh echo through the darkness. He'd forgotten how easily sound carried in the still night air once chutes were deployed. Definitely female, but no way to tell if it was a scoffing Carla or a chortling Tanya. He didn't care if it was the former, but he sure hoped it was the latter. The woman was playing hard to get—because everything with Tanya was just that way. He too knew how to play those games. And sparring with Tanya was the best game he'd ever played with a woman.

Thank god games was all they were...weren't they? It was certainly all that they'd ever been. But now? The landscape was changing under him and he wasn't talking about the sharp peaks and abrupt river valleys as they flew their parachutes over the Andes Mountains.

Who the hell could he ask?

Certainly not Tanya, as that would spoil the play.

But neither could he ask Duane. Ever since he'd fallen for Sofia, his buddy had gotten all strange about women. He and Chad used to cruise together, sweeping the ladies down better than a pair of B-52s on a carpet-bombing run. Not only had Duane married Sofia, but now he acted like there actually could be a single, truly right woman for a guy. No matter how much he liked Sofia, it was just way too weird for Chad's tastes. If he got much worse, Duane was gonna start spouting off about true love and shit like that.

Not this boy.

Focus on the flying.

The oversized Ram-Air chutes were built for distance flying —almost paragliders. The Chinook had lifted them to its upper limit for a light load, around nineteen thousand feet. Which wasn't as much advantage as it sounded because Tulcán, Ecuador, lay at almost ten thousand above sea level.

Yeah. That's why he was feeling lightheaded. Not because of

some woman. It was the altitude, not because of the hottest kiss ever delivered—anywhere. He sucked on some auxiliary oxygen —that he was supposed to have been breathing since they'd crossed fifteen thousand heading upward. Instead of breathing in her…

No more of that shit. He was on a mission and no woman was worth being distracted from a mission.

The Night Stalkers had dumped them out within five miles of Colombia's southern border with Ecuador. They'd kept far enough back to avoid alerting either the Ecuadoran military or any smugglers who might be working the newest cross-border drug route.

Chad shaped his chute for best glide and hoped that the others were sloppy enough to eventually drift down so that he could get into formation. Fat chance. They were Delta and had the same master parachutist jump training he did, with plenty of nighttime combat jumps. The last official "combat jump" by the US military had been into Iraq back in '03, but that didn't count Spec Ops infiltration jumps like this one.

Focus on the mission and forget how it had felt for even a moment to have Tanya back in his arms. Forget how her slightest touch heated his body until it burned more than Estela's hogao sauce or the sunburn still scorching his calves.

Focus on Ecuador.

Ecuador had become a major drug delivery route without anyone noticing until suddenly the Ecuadorian military started capturing a hundred tons of cocaine a year. That eventually got the DEA's attention. Intel—and capturing over a hundred of his henchmen—had led them to Gerald the Boatman. It was the alias of Washington Prado Álava. As the massive drug trafficking organizations had collapsed, Gerald had taken over the Colombia to Mexico and US transport all up the Pacific coast. He knew everyone and had developed a tight and effective business.

The Colombian military sent a "very comely" Colombian

undercover agent who enticed Gerald into a relationship. She'd convinced the modern era's top smuggler to attend a "family party" in Colombia, where they'd arrested his ass and extradited it to the US along with the rest of him.

He'd transshipped two hundred and fifty tons of cocaine right under Ecuador's and the DEA's noses—about a quarter of the yearly global market.

Hello, people! Little slow on the uptake.

With Gerald's demise and the vastly increased attention to the coastal routes that he had been leveraging, much of the trade had moved inland.

Tulcán, Ecuador.

It lay in one of the least convenient places imaginable. The little city of fifty thousand was the highest in all of Ecuador. Its great claim to fame was that of the three highways that crossed the seven hundred kilometer border with Colombia, one was fifteen kilometers from Tulcán and one went through the heart of it. It also had the only real airport for fifty kilometers around in Ecuador, making it a top transfer point. The single runway had been cut into the side of the hill with the city running along one side and a narrow river valley along the other.

Their mission tonight: to interrupt that transfer point. With "Gerald" gone, the amount of cocaine that the Ecuadoran military captured had briefly skyrocketed. Then it had plummeted.

The popular theory was that the capture glut had been because of the loss of Gerald's guiding hand leading to chaos and disorganization, making for easy pickings. The theory also said that the plummet had been the demise of the coastal route without Gerald keeping it alive.

Fred Smith had a different idea. The CIA agent theorized that just as much cocaine was moving as ever, but now it was going by different routes under a different man's plan. It was time to find the new routes and snip them before they were too well established.

The team continued floating in from the northwest. The runway defined the southeast edge of the city, but they couldn't approach from that side. To do so would have placed them directly over the suspected smuggler's route, perhaps raising an alarm.

Instead, they were to fly high across the city, then descend sharply into the airport. There were no airlines flying at night, at least no scheduled ones. The airport should be silent except for their team and whoever was moving the drugs.

There was only one problem…Chad wasn't flying so high. Not only had he opened his chute too low, but he was the heaviest person on the squad. The women weighed nothing. Kyle had Chad's height, but not his breadth of shoulder. Richie was a pencil-neck geek—Delta style. Duane had almost Chad's breadth, but stood a couple inches shorter.

Which meant that he was descending faster than the others. The fact that he was the team's top sniper also had him typically carrying twice the ammo anyone else did. He didn't like the feeling of an empty weapon in his hand. Not one little bit. It was all that had saved his father's life the first time as he beat Chad's mother to death. No real loss—a coke whore who hadn't been straight a day in her life. But when he'd come for Chad on another night, he'd gone down hard. Chad hadn't been without twice the ammo he needed since he'd been six.

Tulcán the city was getting bigger too damn fast. He was coming down less than half a klick shy of the airfield, but he was definitely coming down in the heart of the city. It was night, so no last-second thermal was going to lift him up the extra couple hundred meters he needed.

Out of reprieves, he headed for the only spot with no lights in the whole city—some park right at the center.

TANYA KEPT TWISTING to watch Chad. But each time she did,

she lost a little distance and a little altitude on the rest of the team. At first her eyes had lined up with Sofia's chute. Then with her feet. Soon, Sofia flew several stories above her.

It felt as if Chad was somehow pulling her down to earth. By flying so low, he had snagged her with an invisible shroud line that continually, insidiously, hauled her in a direction she didn't want to go. Bit by little bit, she was being hauled toward him. She did *not* like the metaphor at all, but couldn't seem to shake it.

Why had she even come on tonight's mission? All it had made her do was kiss Chad—which he'd rapidly proved to be the dumbest thing a girl could ever do. The man was a bone-melter...and knew it. She didn't need her bones melted; she liked them just fine the way they were.

Yet during her inattention, she slid a little lower. Perhaps she still had enough lift to reach the airport, but it was clear that Chad didn't. He was going down alone in a strange city.

She'd done that enough times in her life. So had he, probably. But that had been the failure of her UN team of just a few nights ago. She'd gone off on recon, and returned at the back of a hostile patrol that had somehow located the hideout of the other three members of her team.

Coming from the jungle behind the hostiles, Tanya had walked into the wrong end of a firefight. She'd used her wilderness skills to slip up behind the drug runners and dispatch them one by one from behind without the others noticing. However, it was slow going and her team had taken the brunt of it even as she had eased and ultimately erased the threat.

Would they all still be alive if she'd been with them?

Or would they all be dead because she hadn't been there to pick off the bad guys from behind?

She hated those kinds of questions—the kinds that never had a right answer and to which the answer could never be known.

The order was for radio silence. And the others were

preparing for their final approach on the airport. They all flew too close above the city's two-story landscape to risk shouting a question.

No one to ask.

"Damn it!"

She hauled on the left toggle and the chute twisted sharply. In moments she was dumping altitude in a steep spiral that swung her well out to the side of the canopy. She could feel Carla watching her, but Tanya didn't have time to look away from her and Chad's descent. As if she'd be able to read Carla's expression from two hundred meters away, at night through NVGs, when she couldn't even read it sitting across from her in a brightly lit bathroom no longer filled with steam.

It was full dark, but not that late. The city lights blasted the NVGs and they kept automatically dimming down so that she couldn't see the details she needed in the shadows. Only by carefully focusing on the sole dark patch did they reveal what she needed to see. The hard spiral dropped her most of the way to Chad just as he was preparing for his landing round out. She had to pay attention to her own line, but aimed to land near him.

Tanya crossed the first dark border fifty feet above the streetlights' glow. She was on the verge of stalling the chute and coming down when she finally made sense of what lay below her.

A graveyard surrounded by a massive hedge.

And the section she was about to land in was closely packed with headstones that looked alarmingly substantial. Any attempt to land here and she'd finish bloody and broken.

She released her toggles, trading her last bit of speed for a moment of lift. Her feet dragged over the tall hedge that separated her from the next section of the cemetery. This one—thankfully, since she had no more choices—hadn't been filled in yet, and she managed a clean land and roll on the lush grass. Grabbing the forward shroud lines, she made quick work of dumping the last of the air, gathering her chute, and dropping her harness. Time to go looking for Chad.

There was something wrong with the cemetery. Everything was distorted and none of the shadowed angles made sense. It was as if she'd become drunk during the flight. Nothing looked right.

An impossible bird, with a head three meters across, glared down at her from atop a square podium. A man who might have been a bear, or a bear who might have been a man, stood five meters tall and appeared to be grinning. Maybe the air was filled with hallucinogens. A giant—

She tipped up her NVGs. By the soft spill of the streetlights, she could see what the latent heat amplified by the NVGs had hidden.

The cemetery was surrounded by a massive topiary hedge. But rather than toucans and jaguars, or even monkeys and crocodiles, the hedges had been carved into wild and fanciful shapes. Cubes, spheres, and pyramids abounded. Squat men, as wide as they were tall, offered grins a double arm-span wide.

No sign of Chad in this section, she ducked into a line of arches so massive and solid that they practically formed a tunnel. She had to touch them to convince herself that they were topiary rather than dark stone.

Nothing in the next section.

She walked beneath something that might have been the Looming Hand of God, or perhaps a fanciful tropical flower, and spotted him.

It had to be the worst landing of his career. At least no one else had been around to see it.

He'd almost been down in a broad green area. At the last moment, his missing gust had appeared from nowhere, finally lifting him when he didn't want to be. He flew three meters up between a pair of what looked like fat canaries roughly the size of VW Beetles. Then a marble statue of the weeping Virgin Mary as she cradled the dead Jesus loomed before him at the last second.

Not wanting to slam his crotch on the Virgin Mother's head, he yanked full strength on his right toggle…except that was the hand that Tanya had nerve-pinched off her thigh.

The hard pull had the toggle slipping out of his still tingling fingers.

He moved his free hand to protect himself as he yanked on the left toggle, hoping to get clearance to the other side.

Instead, he spun backward and the Virgin Mary headbutted him in the ass.

He barely had time for a *mea culpa*.

The chute still had air and dragged him backward, completely out of control.

His flail for the lost toggle merely snarled his arms in the risers. Fighting for freedom lost him the second toggle.

The chute cleared a hedge, but he didn't—crashing into it back first. Of course the chute, wherever it was, couldn't just collapse. Oh no, that would be too easy. After failing to find any extra lift for the entire flight, it now tugged and jerked at him hard enough to make the hedge bend and flex, burying him deeper in the branches with each yank.

He was effectively pinned in place two stories off the ground —back to the hedge, his arms pinned by the straining shroud lines. Worse, he'd still forgotten to tighten the harness' leg straps while flying. Each pop and yank by the parachute on the far side of the hedge was an excruciating slam to the nuts.

Then, before he could do anything about it, he looked down and spotted Tanya standing in front of him with her arms crossed. His NVGs had gone who knew where—lost in the hedge until years from now some hedge-trimmer dude would find them and wonder *What the hell?*—but he could feel her scowl even if he couldn't see it.

"I could have predicted that."

"Goddamn it! I know how to fly, woman. Better than you know how to drive!"

"Do you want my help or not?"

"No!" He tried to free one arm with no luck, chance had tied a clove hitch around one wrist and he could feel his hand going numb. The other arm was snarled behind his head and he couldn't get any leverage on it.

Shit!

The parachute released him enough to slide a foot toward the ground—then slammed him back twice as hard.

Ow!

"Yes." He hated asking for help.

In answer, Tanya yanked out her knife and for half a second, he thought that she was going to throw it *at* him.

Instead, she walked directly below his feet and disappeared from view.

"What are you doing?"

"Shh!" was the only answer he got.

Then a line let go and, with its sudden release, the length of it dribbled all over his head. Then another, and three more. His hands were still caught and he couldn't do anything about the rope wig that was gathering about his head and shoulders.

She was slicing his parachute lines.

He hoped that she remembered he was two stories up.

Five more lines slithered down over him.

Then the chute gave up its air all at once and the remaining lines went limp at the same moment.

He fell the two stories, barely managing a tuck and roll to protect himself. His somersault left the lines wound as tightly around him as a netted fish.

Tanya reappeared a moment later, crumpling his chute into a compact bundle.

"Looky what you caught." He went for humor over

humiliation. Actually both. Maybe more of the latter. A whole lot more. But he should get points for trying.

"Is it too late to throw you back?"

He wished he could tell if Tanya was joking. "Just cut me out of this mess."

"You are so polite that maybe I'm not in the mood."

"Impolite," he corrected her. "And if you cut me out, I'd be glad to put you in the mood."

She glared at him for so long, he almost wondered if she'd leave him there. But she didn't.

Finally freed, he rolled over to look up at her, and saw the massive topiary he'd landed against. He'd been pinned like a sacrifice between a woman's monstrous breasts, his shroud lines must have been strung over her goddess-sized shoulders. At least she was smiling about it. Unlike Tanya.

"Oh." That's what she'd found predictable, not that he was a screwup of a parachutist. Still, he didn't like failing in front of her.

As the blood rushed back into his hand, he was even less pleased—it stung like he'd put his fist in a wasp's nest.

"Thanks, I guess."

She threw the parachute in his face.

11

*T*anya should leave him here—snarled up in his own mess. Better yet, she should never have turned back to help him. He was a big boy and could take care of himself.

Except when he was strung twenty feet up in a giant topiary.

If only she'd thought to take a photo. She'd have loved to share that one with the rest of the team—they'd still be laughing come Christmas. Of course, she hadn't thought to take one, because she'd never had someone to share such things with. Normally fine with that thought (one she recognized as only an occasional annoyance), it bothered her tonight. She'd like to have seen Carla with her head thrown back howling at Chad's predicament. Watch Melissa's quiet smile as Sofia teased Chad. It would have been a good moment.

No, she didn't need to belong. And each step she took closer to Chad was just going to make it harder when she left.

What had she been thinking when she kissed him?

Mission. Get back on the mission.

Tanya unslung her rifle and did a fast patrol, leaving Chad to untangle himself. At every turn, topiaries confronted her. Incan heads rose twice her height in a line. A massive mausoleum made of topiary rose in a three-story edifice. Things that might have been snails or hedgehogs watched her as she moved.

She finally found an exit from the bewildering maze. It opened onto a wide green lawn with no gravestones—still hedged in on all sides by the monstrous topiaries. At the far corner was the exit to the surrounding city. Before she could slip across the lawn to peer out at what part of the city they'd have to cross, people began streaming in. Some had lanterns, others flashlights. Within moments, a small band was playing music and people were spreading out blankets and late suppers. No way to tell if it was a religious celebration, a party, or simply dinnertime on whatever day this was.

More people kept coming. Soon, they were expanding beyond the green square of grass. Some people were dancing, others walking arm in arm. Several couples lay curled together more intimately on their blankets while they enjoyed the music. The Latinos were such a demonstrative race. In Israel, holding hands didn't happen at all except among the rebellious teens— and not even very often then. Here it was unusual not to.

Small family groups began wandering the cemetery's pathways.

Tanya faded back fast, retracing her route to Chad.

"We have to hide."

Some things a Special Operations soldier didn't need to be told twice.

In moments they had ducked under the feet of a topiary that might have been a giant Angry Bird...or maybe one of the green pigs they were so angry at.

Either way, it made their hide above the river where they spotted *la Capitana* seem generous. Tanya's leg was crossed over Chad's. Their bodies were pressed together from shoulder to hip. Neither of them could draw their rifles even if they had to. It was dark and smelled richly loamy under the hedge where the air had seemed dry and drawn thin with the altitude in the open.

"Well, this is fun," Chad's whisper had a teasing laugh behind it.

"What is it with you and sex?"

"What's wrong with sex?"

Nothing as far as Tanya was concerned, she just didn't make a joke of it every moment. Maybe if she and Chad had sex— something meaningless and mind-numbing—then they'd be done with all this. Or she'd be hooked worse than some cokehead dope-fiend.

Chad twisted until they lay face to face so smoothly that not a single leaf or branch rustled. Their parachute harnesses were crammed under the edge of a pinch-faced gnome who squatted as the next topiary over. Now, only their clothes separated them —their South American, summer-weight clothes. Her leg, which had been casually hooked over his, was now wrapped around the back of his thighs, drawing them even closer together than the cramped space called for.

Again that breathtakingly light touch of Chad's fingers brushed over her knife, but this time it didn't linger there for long. Instead, it traced a line as smooth as a serpent, tracking over buttock, hip, dipping down around her shoulder before circling back to her breast. Her body leaned into his palm even though she knew it was a mistake.

"Mistakes aren't supposed to feel so good."

The brush of his lips on hers was even lighter than his touch. "Am I a mistake?" His whisper tickled her ear as he nuzzled it.

"In so many ways." Yet, her own traitorous hand began exploring his chest. It was even more well-toned than she remembered. She slid a little deeper into the topiary so that she could lay her face against that chest. It also forced his hand to other places. Of all ludicrous things, he cupped that big hand of his into her hair and held her gently against his chest. Not aggressive or controlling—supportive.

In the stillness she could hear couples chatting softly as they moved along the walkways. A nearby topiary rustled loudly as a woman giggled—a giggle that shifted to a moan of delight. They didn't seem to care who saw or heard them. Tanya tried to imagine the innocence of soul necessary for a woman to giggle. She couldn't. It was too foreign. Sexual play could be erotic, wild, gentle, soothing, but it was never cause for something like that giggle that broke out again into the night.

"Someone's having fun," Chad whispered in her ear.

For half a second she took it as an insult, as if he wasn't. Or maybe it was just Chad's teasing observation—not teasing her, but the other couple.

He wanted fun did he?

Tough!

It was her turn to have fun. Her turn not to be losing teammates, falling out of helicopters, or crashing motorcycles. Her turn not to be the teased.

And nothing sounded better at the moment than torturing Chad.

She let loose a sub-vocalized groan—that wasn't quite as much pretended as she meant it to be—just enough for him to feel it with their bodies pressed so tightly together. Then she slid a hand back down the exact route he'd followed up her body: magnificent pecs, around his shoulder blade, and over hip and buttock. She felt his breathing hitch as she traced her finger around the edge of his knife sheath. Instead of something particularly fancy or nasty, he wore a traditional Ka-Bar knife. An old one by the feel of it.

"What is down with this?" She ran her fingers over it again.

"Up with this."

"Up with this."

"Marine Corps Gunnery Sergeant Wollson." His voice almost went dead.

She left her hand there and waited for him to say something more.

He buried his face in her hair and gave his head the tiniest of negative shakes.

Tanya tapped the knife sheath with her finger hard enough that he'd feel it. She wasn't even sure why she did it. What did she care if the man had secrets? She just wanted to play with his body. Torture him with a little fun.

But she waited.

With his face still nuzzled against the top of her head, he wrapped those big arms around her shoulders and back and pulled her in so tightly that it was difficult to breathe. Then he inhaled, as if he was breathing her in. His chest pressed against hers. His heady scent of pure, well-deserved testosterone-laden maleness reminded her of her original goal. She didn't care about his knife, she cared about his body and just what she could do with it.

She slid her hand once more around the long sheath of his blade, feeling the echo on her own thigh of when he'd done the same around her Ari B'Lilah. As her hand moved away, he reached down and clamped it in place.

Tanya was strong. Far stronger than the average woman. Stronger than most men, even most military men. Against Chad's strength, she couldn't have moved her hand if her life depended on it.

He breathed her in hard once more until his expanding chest threatened to crush her against his encircling arm.

"I stripped his body."

She couldn't read a single emotion in his voice.

"THAT WAR-TORN old bastard kept me alive on the streets back when I was a dumbshit kid. Half his brain was gone. Cracker musta been seventy by the time I met him, and he was still living in the Vietnam jungle in his head. Never came out of it, I guess. I was a skinny waste of space working as a drug runner out of Coleman Airport. Wollson was really old, but still as big as a house. For three years we worked out together every day. Hours of it. He'd tell me we had to be ready when the pajama people came down the trail. Only ever saw one guy in black pajamas—a Latino delivery driver for one of the gangs who didn't know better and thought he was swaggering. Wollson almost beat him to death."

And Chad could feel the darkness of the Street—despite the brilliant light of the woman lying quiet in his arms.

A couple decades back, the area of Detroit between Gratiot and Rosemary was vying for worst neighborhood in America—and doing a fine job of it.

"Three in twenty used to die there every year. Every seventh person. Every year. And don't think I'm forgetting that I'm now seventh man on this team. Not saying I didn't put down my fair share, but I never did anyone that the justice system—if it had worked at all—wouldn't ha' done the same to." He could feel his voice slipping into Street patterns—ones he normally kept buried very deep. He struggled to pull himself back from that. It was an inner darkness that was still far too easy to find.

Tanya lay quiet. Listening. Listening to a story he'd never told. It was weird to be telling it here. Crouched in the darkness fit…too well. But the warm, lithe woman in his arms didn't. The happy, gasping moans nearby. The music pattering across the night air.

"Wollson taught me that they were just using me 'til I was caught or gunned down. Then they'd just find another joeboy. He's the one who kept me straight. Taught me to be smart. And he taught me to fight. I watched the gangs and the drugs chew up a lot of friends."

"As much as the Street even lets you have friends," Tanya's voice whispered with understanding.

"Yeah. As much as." Chad kept his face in her white-blonde

hair. Despite the darkness, he knew it was there, how it caught the wind, how it framed her lovely face.

Maybe that was what gave Tanya such power over him—she was so damn memorable.

"He went down hard. Some up-and-comer chose the wrong old man to harass on the Street, showing off to his friends. Wollson took him down and five more besides. I kept his knife, the only thing he had left other than his pride at being a Marine."

"What about the others?"

"Took me three months to locate and air out the rest of the gang. The last two hid deep, even knowing there was no escape —had to go to Memphis to put them down."

"Why aren't you a Marine?"

Chad could almost laugh about it now, though he'd considered taking down the Marine recruiter at the time. "Wouldn't have me. I was a street shit who lied about my age— never once thinking they'd actually check. No record because Wollson had taught me to be careful, but they didn't want squat to do with me. Still wouldn't touch me at eighteen because they kept a record that I'd lied and they didn't want 'my kind.' Went Green Berets the next day. Thought I was gonna be John Wayne."

"Who?"

"What?"

She clamped a hand over his mouth to keep him quiet.

"Moo mea fuk mif Hon Hayne?" This couldn't be happening. He shoved her hand aside, but kept his voice down. "How can you be the perfect woman if you don't know who John Wayne is?"

TANYA GIGGLED.

She couldn't believe that she was doing it, but she actually giggled—very quietly.

Chad had just spilled out his heart about his past—even worse than hers if you ignored the occasional rape attempts. (Some of which had been close and ended bloody. Twice she'd left corpses behind.) And what he'd gotten upset about was when she pretended to not know about the Duke? How much more charming could the man be?

She'd thought to tease him to the edge of insanity using sex as they lay beneath a topiary in the middle of a crowded cemetery. It was a weapon that had never failed her.

Instead she kissed him. Kissed him until his protests died. Kissed him until he stopped thinking about anything except her.

He may have shot her—twice—but he was such a good man in so many ways. He too had scraped himself up off the Street and made himself who he was today.

There wasn't enough room to undress here; besides, the low branches and ground detritus would prickle when out of their clothes. But that didn't slow down Chad. He teased and enticed her body until all she could hear was her ragged breath and her racing heart. Not once did he break the kiss she'd initiated. She'd locked her arms around his neck and hadn't let go. Not because she wanted to pin him there. She wanted, she *needed* to feel his mouth on her. She clamped onto him because it was the sole anchor in the storm he aroused in her.

When he at long last slid his hand down her front, beneath her underclothes, the heat of his touch burned. It burned and escalated until even the sounds of heart and blood ceased and all that remained was his touch. His kiss. Her need. Her—

Her releases, on the rare occasions when she found them, were soft rides. An easy shudder that smoothed out her thoughts and her nerves.

With Chad, her mind blanked. Her body bucked as if trying to escape. Or get closer, which was impossible. His kiss and his palm against her were all that existed for her until they escalated her past reason.

The Tanya Zimmer she knew never lost control. Ever.

Not even when they'd been lovers three years ago.

Tonight, in the middle of a massive bird topiary, she completely lost it. Her body was no longer hers. Her very breath was no longer hers, it came from Chad as she groaned into his kiss.

The final release, though, that was a hundred percent hers. A bullseye strike from two thousand meters. A .50 cal blow that knocked her out of herself and placed her over a whole new horizon.

Finally breaking the kiss, she buried her face at the base of his neck and did her best to ride it out. Nothing had ever made her so doubt the woman she'd spent so many years carefully fabricating. As the blast's heat continued rolling over her, some tiny part of her mind struggled to classify and categorize, to understand. Pointlessly. Chad had reached down and somehow found an aspect of her inner woman that Tanya knew nothing about.

"Christ, lady," Chad's whisper sounded breathlessly in her ear. "What was that?"

She could only shake her head, rubbing her nose against his collarbone.

She had no idea.

12

*A*n hour later, Chad eased out into the open. Whatever event had brought the locals to the park hadn't lasted but the hour. Tanya had slept, curled up in his arms, her legs clamped so tightly around his hand that he couldn't remove it. He'd been left in silence to consider what had just happened, but he wasn't any wiser for all his thinking.

Some women gave themselves up to the act of sex, but that was the key—the *act* of sex. When he'd been with Tanya before, it had been a glorious romp. They'd used bathroom walls, balcony ledges, even going at it when the other one was driving a car. The best game he'd ever played.

He'd expected a rematch.

Instead Tanya had kissed him like she really meant it, meant it all the way down to her core. And rather than it being about the act of sex, or even real sex, it had taken on some whole other meaning. No woman had so exposed herself to him as Tanya had, unraveling in his arms.

When the coast was clear, he woke her gently.

She offered no reaction for him to read.

He held out a hand to help her from under the topiary—

which she ignored. The Kidon assassin was back. He could respect that. At least he knew what to do with that version of the woman.

"We need to lose the parachutes." She was going to play it a hundred percent practical, then so would he.

He spotted a dug grave, dirt mounded to one side, and a pair of shovels. The grave was deep and empty. Probably a burial first thing in the morning.

No need to tell Tanya to keep watch; she'd know to do that without his telling her.

Dropping down into the hole, he quickly punched down another two feet. She tossed down the chutes and harnesses, and he buried them at the bottom of the hole. Tomorrow they'd be under a coffin and another six feet of soil. Couldn't think of any reason for a corpse to mind and the family would never know. Good enough. He leveraged himself out of the hole.

Tanya handed him a burlap sack she'd scrounged up from somewhere in the garden. Her rifle was already in it. It probably wouldn't be too strange around here if they wore sidearms and knives with their camo, but a pair of four-foot-long sniper rifles was another story. He slid in his own. Then, after a moment's consideration, he swiped one of the shovels and stuck it in the bag as well. Slinging it over his shoulder with the shovel blade sticking up into the air, he figured no one was likely to bother them.

No one remained in the cemetery. At the exit Tanya dropped her NVGs into the bag as well.

As they stepped out onto the street, he pulled Tanya against him and slid his hand into her back pocket. The finest ass in Christendom. He'd always admired that about her. He'd never taken her from behind, but he was looking forward to a chance to do it.

She slid her hand into his back pocket as well, and gave a quick double squeeze like a hug of approval.

The paved street was quiet. The few streetlights lay blocks

away. Most of the buildings were unlit. The occasional light still burned in a second-story bedroom, and the city didn't extend to third stories other than a few apartment blocks and a cathedral that towered several blocks to the west. They passed a couple staggering home from a *taberna* who paid them no attention. A lone car eased by but also didn't hesitate. A dog barked but didn't put much heart into it. It was as easy to walk along the quiet street as the narrow sidewalk.

Six blocks later, they'd crossed the width of the city from one side to the other.

"Gotta love small towns," Chad commented in Spanish as they slipped through the airport fence a hundred meters away from the official entrance. He'd stay in the language for the rest of the mission so that they wouldn't be caught speaking English —the team rarely spoke English outside their suite despite their diverse backgrounds.

"Is that what you want when you're done, a small town?" Tanya slipped their rifles and her NVGs out of the burlap bag.

When he was done?

Done?

If not for Gunnery Sergeant Wollson, he'd have been "done" in the back alley off Gratiot Ave. Walking into Mosul and a few hundred other hellholes with the Green Berets should have stamped "done" on his forehead as well—his unit had certainly shipped home more than their fair share of body bags. And most of his missions with Delta Force had made that Green Beret shit look safe and easy by comparison.

"Never thought about being done, other than six feet under. What about you?" He checked over his Mk 21. Good to go.

Tanya sat with her back to the airport fence and pulled on her NVGs. While she did a wide area inspection, he sighted through his scope, which offered plenty of light amplification but only in a very narrow view. He began inspecting the terminal. It was a low structure, big enough for a couple planes to park in front of but no more.

There were a few hangars and a half dozen light planes parked out in the open at tie-downs. A dark and lonely control tower rose five stories. He spotted two figures lying flat on the roof of the tower. There was a brief blink from an infrared flashlight aimed in his direction—invisible without night vision—flashing long-short-long. The letter K. He sent back a K of his own using the rifle's infrared spotting laser—everything okay on both ends. If anything was going down tonight, it hadn't yet. Good. He'd hate to have missed out on the fun again. He couldn't spot the other four members of the team, but that was no surprise—they were Delta.

"Duane and Sofia atop the tower," he whispered to Tanya.

"Rest of the field looks quiet from here. One of the hangars has a marginally higher heat signature. Could be a fluke, a cooling aircraft engine, or a small team." It was a standard, square metal hangar, the peak two stories up so it could fit moderate planes, but not more than the nose of a big jet.

She tucked away her goggles into the burlap bag and slipped it through a belt loop. Then they rose in unison to go check it out.

"I have a condo in Tel Aviv," Tanya restarted their earlier conversation as they moved down through the sparse trees and crossed the grassy verge. "At least I think I do. I've been in the field a long time."

"Big city gal."

"Maybe," he could sense her shrug as they eased up to the back of the hangar in question. He lay the shovel there and kicked some dirt on it. No one would think anything of it if they stumbled on it.

Chad tried to imagine life "after," but never having thought about it, he couldn't conjure up any clear images. He rested the muzzle of his Glock pistol against the metal wall of the hangar, then pressed his ear to the butt of the handgrip.

"Voices," Tanya whispered. She was doing the same thing he was.

He couldn't distinguish any words, but the discussion sounded idle rather than heated.

"We know one thing," Tanya holstered her sidearm.

"They aren't Delta." Because Delta wouldn't be speaking above a whisper if they had to speak at all. He holstered his own weapon.

Again in effortless unison, they slipped around the back corner of the hangar, just as someone else stepped around the front corner in the process of unzipping his fly.

His reactions were good. Usually, thinking about a full bladder slowed a guy down. Not this *hombre*. His weapon was out almost as fast as his own and Tanya's. Then he unleashed a soft whistle. In moments, they were surrounded.

Chad reholstered his weapon, but kept his hand loosely on the grip.

"You hiring, *mi amigo?*"

Tanya didn't know whether to be shocked or to laugh. It was a brilliant ploy.

She slapped her own weapon into its holster, making it clear that she wasn't going to be the first to shoot but they'd better not try to take it. She and Chad were here as equals.

Still, one of the men came forward, leading with his own pistol aimed at Chad's face. His rifle, like her own, was slung over his shoulder. The man reached out one hand for Chad's holstered weapon.

The fool made the mistake of getting one step too close.

Chad grabbed the man's gun out of his hands, spun it around to aim it point-blank at the guy's face for a long second, then ejected the magazine, dumped the slide, and tossed the pieces back to him. While he was trying to catch the pieces of his weapon, Chad shoved his shoulder enough to make him turn. Tanya's kick to his ass sent him stumbling back toward his comrades.

It earned him a round of derisive laughter that the guy would never live down.

"Heard there was a team in need of *real* skills around here," she addressed the man who'd hung farthest back. His fly might still be open, but his gun was held two-handed and rock steady. No question who was in charge.

At least not until one more figure stepped around the front corner of the hangar.

It took everything Tanya had to not react. Even in silhouette, it was impossible to mistake that figure for anyone else.

La Capitana.

They were hundreds of kilometers from the river crossing, yet here she was—just as they'd seen her two days ago, right down to the machete. Thank God that there was no way for the woman to recognize herself or Chad. She strolled through her men as if they weren't even there until she was standing just two meters away. She casually crossed her arms beneath her breasts.

"*Tu la jefa, señora?*" Chad's Spanish came out smooth and unconcerned—doing his "charming the woman" thing.

Is that what he'd done to her? It didn't feel like it. It couldn't be. They'd had sex under a topiary—in which he'd been in total control and toying with her. Meaningless. All meaningless! Even if it hadn't felt that way at the time, that's what it must have been. And she'd fallen for it. *Dummkopf!*

Chad made it clear that he wasn't looking only at the woman's face.

Tanya was such an idiot. There was a reason she operated best alone. She couldn't wait until she was again. But at the moment, she had a role to play.

La Capitana wasn't falling for any of Chad's games. With the slightest nod, she indicated their rifles.

Chad swung out his Mk 21 PSR. "Beauty, isn't it? Guy was real sad to let it go. So sad that it killed him."

She lifted it from his extended hands, checked the balance, then raised it to her shoulder with a smooth, practiced motion and aimed it toward the horizon. Not, Tanya was thankful to notice, too close to the tower where Duane and Sofia lay. She tossed it back and Chad caught it lightly before slinging it once more over his shoulder.

La Capitana's attention next snagged on Tanya's Ari B'Lilah knife. She shouldn't have worn it, it was too unique. She was in South America. No one ever recognized it…until it was too late. But this woman did.

"Lion of the Night," the woman's voice was soft and husky. Had Chad known the translation of the knife's name? If she knew that, then she knew precisely what it meant. It tagged Tanya as Mossad counterterrorism. The question of *la Capitana's* simple words held death.

"Like the man who 'gave' his rifle to my companion." Her companion? Not for long. "*La Princesa* hated letting go of it."

That snagged both *la Capitana's* and Chad's attention. Over the last four years, Tanya had mostly posed undercover as a journalist "investigating" the drug culture. That had also aided her in building a lethal reputation that had ranged into many strange corners of the drug trafficking world. That's what she'd been doing when she'd hooked up with Chad's team the first time.

Shortly after that mission with Delta, she'd struck on the idea of writing about her own exploits in ways to add mystique and terror to her undercover doings—and also to throw the scent off any trail that led back to her. It had proved very effective and she was gratified that Chad was both impressed and surprised. Now that she (Tanya present tense) laid claim to killing herself (the lethal *la Princesa*), she (Tanya the undercover journalist) would have to think about how to write that up.

"That Israeli bitch messed with the wrong girl. Estevan," the narco-submarine fleet builder, "was very good to me. It took me three years to track her down and pay her back for his death. Now I wear her knife in his honor." Dropping Estevan's name should also buy them some credibility. It was a relief that she was more fluent in Spanish than English—in English she could feel her awkward stumbles and hated each time Chad pointed them out.

La Capitana slid a hand along Chad's cheek as if caressing him.

Do it. Just do it, Chad! Humiliate me with another woman right to my face.

But the woman withdrew her hand and was holding Chad's radio earpiece that had been hidden under the straight fall of his blond hair.

"Say 'Report in'," she instructed Tanya as she listened in on Chad's earpiece.

Tanya did, then listened herself. Not so much as a click or beep from the rest of the team.

Chad offered one of his smarmy grins. "I like whispering suggestive ideas in Tanya's ear."

"He does," Tanya confirmed with a sad sigh.

"Destroy them."

Chad shrugged as if it was no big deal. He yanked the wire, pulled the radio off his belt, then dropped it to the pavement and crushed it with his bootheel.

At a loss for what else to do, Tanya did the same. Now they were cut off from the Delta team. There were still hand signs, but they'd be much less useful if it all became ugly.

"Who were you with last?"

For half a second, Tanya thought *la Capitana* meant Chad. She'd been with Chad…and felt used. Had he enjoyed toying with her to his own satisfaction? She hoped so, because it was the last time it was going to happen.

Oh! Who had she been *fighting for* last? She had no good

answer. A UN team which had been taken down hard? Before that she'd—

"That bitch Expediter," Chad suddenly sounded pissed. "Been odd-jobbing ever since she burned the jungle camp and flew away. Woman left us. We were her top shooters and she fucking left us to rot. Never even gave us a dead letter drop to lead us to her new location."

So, she'd been right about the Delta team taking down the Expediter. But now Chad was pretending that he and Tanya were the inseparable team, even though she hadn't been part of that operation.

He was making it up as he went along.

Did Chad even know what reality was? Did he actually know how deeply he'd affected her? Or was he so disconnected, so used to living the lie with women, that she'd never be able to tell what he thought?

"Prove it," *la Capitana* stated flatly. Her guards, who had slowly relaxed to this point, suddenly snapped back to rigid focus. Nine shooters. There was no way that she and Chad could take down nine. Even if the Delta team began helping with their long rifles, she and Chad were going down and going down hard.

"How? By pointing out that Pederson was her dupe? Shit, everyone knew that."

Tanya hadn't. He'd been the head of the operation and the Expediter had been his right hand...except apparently not.

Chad continued, "That Analie Sala is a cold, narrow-assed bitch who only gets off humping on top of a pallet of kilo bags? Which was easy, as she had thirteen tons of the purest cocaine in the hold of that little luxury jet of hers, with the king-size bed in the back right over it. Thirteen tons! Uncut, that's way over a billion on the street. I had the channels all set up in Detroit. A little cutting and we'd really have cashed in. Coulda moved that in four weeks and retired to some island mansion and screwed our brains out, but the bitch turned it down cold."

So, Chad had even screwed the Expediter. The man had no morals at all. But why should she care? Of course, for the mission, she'd twisted that line a few times herself. Still...the Expediter? Eww!

"Turned *you* down cold," Tanya spoke up. "You never told *me* about that part of the deal." Let *la Capitana* think they weren't above betraying each other for the right price, because it was clear that Chad wasn't.

"Shit!" Chad did a good job of sounding guilty. "Sorry, babe. I woulda taken you along for sure. You're my favorite squeeze. You know that."

"You, me, and Sala? One of your little three-way fantasies? Eat shit, Chad." She let the embarrassment she was feeling spill out as heat. Then Tanya turned to *la Capitana* and reused one of her earlier lines.

"Just give me something to shoot. Or someone!"

She made a point of scowling at Chad.

CHAD COULDN'T BELIEVE how in tune they were. Tanya hadn't missed a single cue. She'd amplified, exaggerated, even been pissed in ways he'd never have thought of.

It was like when he'd had his hands on her. He'd had three years of fantasies about the woman and did his best to deliver on some of them. Even thinking of how she'd responded made him rock hard all over again.

She hadn't mentioned it, but he'd sure heard his own words about her being the "perfect woman."

He'd never said that about anybody.

Never *thought* it.

But with her it was so true. Warrior. Funny. Sexier than Charlize Theron kicking Mad Max's ass. And that was all before she'd given herself to him so unexpectedly. He'd never been able to make a woman feel like that.

It was old Wollson who'd explained women to him. "You make it the best you can for them and they'll do twice that in return—less, of course, if she's a selfish bitch. Then you just take her down and have a good time."

Tanya was no selfish bitch. She'd dedicated herself to battling the worst scourge of the modern age—even going it alone when she had no other option. How could he not respect that?

"You know how to shoot those rifles?" *La Capitana's* question slammed his attention back to the present. Four days of watching her and he'd thought her sexy as hell: beautiful, dangerous, and built like a one-woman porn movie. Standing next to Tanya, he didn't know why he'd ever thought that. There was a deep anger that seemed to radiate from the curvy Latina—an insatiable rage. At close quarters, danger signals flashed from her like sharp spikes. Tanya was as levelheaded as any top operator.

"Can I shoot? Shit, yeah."

La Capitana stepped to the front of the hangar. A person-sized door was open. He barely had a moment to see the big plane parked in there. Loaded or unloaded? Headed where? Where was Richie when you needed a pilot? Somewhere downfield watching this little scene unfold. Probably with his rifle zeroed between the woman's awesome breasts—aimed straight at that cold heart.

"There," the woman pointed at the far end of the runway. "*Pare.* The stop sign."

The runway at Teniente Coronel Luis A. Mantilla International Airport was twenty-four-hundred-meters long. The hangar lay at approximately midfield. Call it twelve hundred meters to the stop sign, warning traffic not to turn onto the active runway without checking for landing air traffic first. Too far to make out that it was octagonal rather than round. Too far to read the bold letters—*PARE*—that must adorn it.

Twelve hundred meters. Two thirds of a mile. A night shot.

Certainly wasn't a standing shot.

He lay down on the cooling pavement and slowly shut out the world.

But Tanya's voice intruded, "Temp is about twenty-seven C. Wind west-north-west at six knots. Dry. And remember we're at ten thousand MSL here."

Right. Tulcán was way above mean sea level. The air was thinner, so the bullet would fly farther than normal.

She was even the perfect spotter, helping him guide his shot onto the target. "Perfect woman" might not be all that far from the truth.

He clicked in the corrections on his scope, then zeroed on the sign—a tiny spec in the scope lit only by the starlight. His pulse was still fast from thinking about Tanya; he consciously slowed that down. His breath was fast because of the thin air—not much he could do about that without a couple days acclimatization.

The shot slowly came into focus. Not through the scope, he already had that. He let his mind's eye visualize the result. The flight of the .338 Lapua, heavier, more foot-pounds than the 7.62. Some instinct had him shifting a fraction down and left. If he missed, there would be no way in the night to determine which side he missed to. And he couldn't appear to be on a fishing expedition. The first strike had to—

Training at some deep instinctual level made him squeeze the trigger. He manipulated the bolt, tipping the hot brass into his palm and closing the chamber on the next round. He pocketed the brass from the sniper's habit of leaving no trace.

One point three seconds later, he thought he saw a dust splash off the metal. Three and a half seconds after that—the speed of sound was less than half the speed of his bullet—the soft sound of a tinny thump reached them in the still night air and told him he'd hit it.

Then he heard the click of a safety coming off. He glanced over to see that Tanya had unlimbered the MSG90 he'd loaned her. This was going to be a much harder shot—it was out near the limits of the 7.62 mm round, no matter what weapon it was fired from.

He offered her the Mk 21, but she was already far enough into the zone to just shake her head tersely.

"Zeroed at five hundred," was all he could think to offer her. She'd already analyzed all of the other elements. Except…what had his instincts corrected for at the last moment? Something. Something…

"You're firing northeast and close to the equator." The Coriolis Effect. Firing eastward, the bullet would rise more than expected and most strongly near the equator.

He saw her make the tiniest shift as she fired.

Chad bent back to his own scope to watch.

One heartbeat. Two. Splash of dust into the darkness. One. Two. Three—

A small ping wandered back down the wind.

"Damn, girl. Now that was a hell of a shot."

Tanya grinned happily at him for a long moment—then her smile snapped out like a shot-out searchlight.

Oh, right.

Chad rolled over to face *la Capitana* as Tanya cleared her brass.

"We know how to shoot."

The woman didn't say anything. Instead, she stared at them for a long moment before turning and walking back through her men again as if they weren't even there.

Chad kept the safety off on his rifle and idly dropped his hand to his knife as if brushing himself off after lying on the ground.

Tanya didn't miss the cue, retucking her blouse placed her hand close beside her holster.

"Let's go," *la Capitana's* voice had a galvanic effect on her men. They all turned and holstered their weapons. All except the one whom they'd surprised with his fly open.

Chad rose and offered a hand to Tanya, which she again ignored.

As they strode past the last remaining guard, he finally holstered his weapon.

Chad thumped a fist on his shoulder. "No hard feelings."

The man merely snarled back a foul curse before finally returning to peeing against the side of the building. His bladder must be killing him by now.

---

13

*T*he man, Silva, wasn't any more pleasant after he returned to the hangar. *La Capitana* drew him aside and they spoke in a whisper. Then Silva, without making any obvious show of it, collected one of his fellow guards and drifted to the far side of the hangar. It left *la Capitana* and seven guards to one side of them, with Silva and his mate ostensibly cleaning weapons to the other. It placed them in the middle of a crossfire pattern—an indefensible position.

"Did it work?" Tanya whispered to Chad as they both made a show of replacing their fired rounds. They sat on the same wooden crate, small enough that they couldn't sit facing the same direction, which worked well—better lines of sight and fire if things didn't go their way.

"Not dead yet. Taking that as a good sign."

"You never did answer the question." Tanya wasn't sure why she bothered. She didn't *really* want to know more about Chad. Where he wanted to live after he retired? Who cared. What made a man like him be…a man like him? None of that. And yet she did.

"Nope, I didn't." Chad rose and wandered over to a cooler

as if he'd always been here and came back with a couple bottles of water. To their right was a twin turboprop plane painted in shining white with the blue TAME of the national airline. It was an ATR-42 forty-passenger plane with a cargo capacity that could move six tons very nicely to anywhere within seven hundred miles. In the back corner were a pair of Beechcraft—one clearly being scrapped for parts to rebuild the other.

The dim lighting revealed a few workbenches, but they looked more meant for the hobbyist than an airline mechanic. A small stack of suitcases filled the corner. Some sprouted bits of bent metal sheathing that must be fuselage panels. Others held headsets in need of repair. One was piled deep with clothes lost by some passenger that had now been used as oily cleanup rags. A bent prop leaned against the wall beside a half-disassembled motorcycle. Several tires—some worn, others threadbare, none new—were scattered about the floor as if a child had been playing with them. The place smelled of grease and rust.

"Didn't see a fuel truck."

She hadn't been looking for one. She supposed that it meant the airport was even less frequented than she'd suspected.

"Vermont or Maine. Maybe Alaska."

For a moment, Tanya couldn't figure out what he was saying, then she realized that he was answering her question at long last.

"Somewhere to get out and about. Do some hunting for the dinner table rather than of things that are trying to kill me. Might be nice having a neighbor who wasn't a coke dealer or a heroin addict."

Tanya could almost picture him there. Not yet. But someday, wearing a ball cap as his blond hair bypassed gray and shifted to white. Perhaps out on a snowmobile or a fishing boat. She too was tired of the heat. The scorching desert of the Negev where she'd done her early training. The sweltering South American jungles.

Maybe she'd—

"I'm not easy to find," *la Capitana* stood in front of them. Up close, she was even more beautiful than she'd looked through the scope.

Tanya knew that she herself was pretty; her looks had served her very well in the field. But this woman was astonishing. More Latina supermodel than drug dealer. Her glossy dark hair flowed back over her shoulders, leaving her smooth, dark cream skin on clear display. Her wide, dark eyes gave her face an amazing depth of character. They were eyes that Tanya recognized in the mirror. Haunted, hunting eyes.

"Weren't looking for you," Chad said easily, but offered a leer that said he was damn glad he'd found her. "Just heard there was a crew passing through and took our chances. Are you somebody we should have been looking for?"

"It depends." The woman did not explain.

"Well, we've had shit for luck lately. Worked the coca fields for a while down in Bolivia, but had no better luck in the country than we did in the city."

"Maybe you are bad luck and I should kill you now."

"Couldn't prove different by me, sister," he heaved a long-suffering sigh. "Weren't for Tanya here, I'd have bagged out long ago. But a man dreams of providing for his wife against all odds."

Then Chad turned to her, all solicitous.

"I'll replace that ring with a big-ass rock to match your lovely blue eyes, honey. That's a promise."

And now they were married? She'd been wondering if she'd survive him for the duration of the operation and now she had no choice?

No. He wasn't playing this game with her.

"You've still got some explaining to do if you don't want it shoved back down your throat." Tanya was surprised at how easy it was to find the anger.

"Is that what happened to your face?" *La Capitana* asked.

Chad hooked a thumb in her direction.

"He can make me so mad sometimes that I don't know why I stay with him." And she didn't, except that was the mission she'd signed up for. "This wasn't even for the big one."

"I told you before," Chad picked right up on the line. "Sala was just a mistake, sweetheart. I figured if I did her, then she might do my Detroit deal and we'd be set for life."

"You and her," bitterness so strong it stung like bile at the back of her throat.

"Aw, sweetie. Wouldn't do that to you. I was going to introduce her to my buddy Wollson. They could've ended up together, you know."

Wollson was dead.

She managed to not bumble the next line. "You think they'd have been happy together?"

"'Til death do us part and all that. I betcha anything."

Tanya decided she'd better drop it until they could speak not in code. Had Chad been willing to sleep with Sala the Expediter to do his deal for a billion-dollar payout? Or had he done it because he didn't mind screwing women he'd been assigned to kill?

CHAD COULDN'T FOLLOW the signals Tanya was sending out now.

Scared? Of what? Didn't sound like her.

Angry? At who? Him? He couldn't think of why.

Acting? Maybe. Damn good if she was.

No way to explain that he'd been sleeping with a British undercover drug agent—without realizing it—during the Analie Sala mission. He hadn't been kidding when he said Sala was a cold bitch. Some people had no soul, just a world of black inside them, and she had been one of those. Couldn't pay him to go anywhere near that kinda head trip.

La Capitana was a different issue. The hurt in those eyes

broadcast pain like a lighthouse. Only by declaring himself married to Tanya could he be sure he wouldn't go messing around there because she was really something. Beautiful, powerful, hurt in some twisted-up vulnerable way that he'd bet she'd kill him if she knew he could see it in her—all *kinds* of attractive things about her.

"Swore my heart to this gal," he told *la Capitana*. "Priest, the whole bit. We were riding high on what Estevan was paying her —I was a hunter for the *Cartel de los Soles* at the time. Did it up in the Basilica of Our Lady of the Rosary of Chiquinquirá in Maracaibo. Estevan gave her away just the week before he died and his daughter stood maid of honor. Really beautiful ceremony. Had some rough patches across the years, but I've been clean and sober since that bitch Analie. Trying to make it up to you, honey." He turned once more to Tanya because he wasn't sure how much more he could layer on without giving himself away. Delta had taken down several key players of the *Cartel de las Soles* and Estevan had tried to murder their whole team. Chad *had* stood best man for Kyle and Carla in that church, even if Tanya was long gone.

"He teach you to shoot?" *la Capitana* turned to Tanya.

Before Chad could open his mouth to proudly take credit, Tanya snapped out two words.

"My father." She hugged herself so hard that he was surprised she didn't break.

What was it with beautiful, dangerous women turning honest all of a sudden? He was being confronted with two ridiculously attractive women who couldn't be more different if they tried. The darkly gorgeous drug dealer and the brilliant golden-girl assassin.

And hounded by enough pain they might have been twins.

La Capitana stared at Tanya in silence for a long time. The women were communing with some secret code invisible to men. He'd seen Carla, Melissa, and Sofia do this sometimes and long since learned to keep his mouth shut and his thoughts to himself when they were doing it. Despite being married to Melissa, Richie got geeked out whenever he noticed it—which was less than half the time. He swore he was going to crack their code, but Chad knew there were some things that a man was never meant to understand.

At long last, *la Capitana* held out her hand to Tanya, who shook it.

"I'm Daniela. Welcome aboard, Tanya."

Tanya looked hard-pressed to not remark on the nickname they weren't supposed to know.

"Any relation to *la Capitana?*" Chad bulldozed straight in, because, what the hell. He could almost hear Tanya's silent groan. Maybe it was a bit much. Now he had to hope they didn't die on the spot. That would suck.

To cover, he turned to Tanya without giving Daniela time to answer.

"Wouldn't that be cool if Daniela really was? Working for Estevan, then the Expediter, then the Captain? Sorry, being silly, I know. But Escobar was before my time," he turned back to Daniela. "And we missed out on Gerald before the DEA took him down. I've always had a thing about shooting for the very best. The Marines always thought they were such hot shit before they discharged my ass. Those jarheads couldn't have touched Estevan's crew if not for that *la Princesa* bitch. Besides, it's not as if that Major wasn't already an ass before I rolled his Mercedes. I was just trying to show his wife a good time—apparently he was a 'minute man' in the worst way. Not like he was with us when I rolled it or anything. Dishonorable, my ass. Like to see him hit that damned stop sign at a hundred meters. Hell, a hundred *feet*. Dumb Marine bastard."

Daniela offered Chad a noncommittal nod and walked back to where the others were waiting by the plane. Though she made no signal to call off Silva and the other guard behind them.

"Marines?" Tanya whispered.

"Always glad to slag some other crew. Usually I make it the 75th Rangers—that was Duane's outfit—but I didn't want her thinking Special Ops."

UNLIKE MOST MEN, Chad had learned how to create a whisper that wouldn't carry five feet. He and Tanya were turned partly away from each other and she'd wager that it would look like he was sitting in perfect silence, just going over his rifle.

Tanya was trying to make sense of *la Capitana's* look before she'd walked away. Something had shifted during Chad's "frivolous chatter" moment, but Tanya couldn't pin down what it was. They weren't dead, so it wasn't that he'd raised doubts in *la Capitana's* mind. No, it was something inside Daniela herself.

"Never touched Analie Sala," Chad continued softly.

"Tell someone who cares." And yet Tanya felt relief about that. She hated herself for wanting to know. And couldn't stop the next question, "You didn't let her actually get away, did you?"

Chad scoffed, little more than a heavy breath under the circumstances, as if she'd wounded his manly pride. But then he sounded deeply chagrined. "I helped. But that was Richie's doing."

"Richie took down the Expediter?" If ever there was something to stretch the imagination past belief, that was it.

Richie, despite being Delta Force, was brilliantly naive. That he could outfox a seasoned pro like Analie Sala seemed almost ludicrous.

"And what were you doing while he was doing that?"

"Enjoying the ride, sweetheart. Just enjoying the ride."

"Screwing some woman and shooting the shit out of things."

"Absolutely! I—" And then he caught that she'd trapped him.

She turned to look at him in time to see him blush. Chad actually blushed. About screwing a woman other than her. That was a ridiculous explanation, but it was the only thing that fit.

"What are—"

A high whistle cut through the night air. It came from… above. The roof of the hangar. Now that she knew to look for it, she spotted a ladder over in a shadowed corner that lead up to a trapdoor in the ceiling. They'd been very lucky that the lookout had been facing the side of the field away from town as they approached.

The few lights in the hangar were doused. A single lamp was set up on a stand facing the line where the two main hangar doors met. Someone flicked it on. Actinic white light splashed against the inside of the door.

At a second whistle, the doors were slid open until the gap was two meters wide. Anyone looking in from the outside would be unable to see anything of the hangar's interior or the people there. They might not even be able to see the plane.

A mixed line of burros and llamas were led in by pairs. Each was unloaded of hundreds of pounds of product onto a pre-positioned pallet, then guided back out. In between each load, the doors were closed. The full pallet was removed with a small forklift and replaced with an empty one—empty except for a small pack that Tanya quickly figured out was money. When the door was reopened, another pair of beasts was led in, unburdened onto the pallet, then loaded with the small pack of money and led out.

It was an old, primitive form of delivery—a form that scented the soft evening breeze blowing into the hangar with the ripe scent of the animals and their guides. It was also a form of delivery that could cross the high border by lonely mountain tracks rather than braving the Ipiales-Tulcán border crossing. The blinding light kept delivery men, if captured, from revealing anything other than the location of their delivery.

While the animals were being unloaded, Tanya and Chad

were waved over to join the human chain that unloaded the pallets into the plane.

Each tightly wrapped bundle felt as if it held twelve blocks of one-kilo bags—twenty-six pounds of coke each. Fifteen to twenty bags per pallet...four to five hundred pounds. She lost track around seventeen pallets, but it turned out to be one of the last.

Three tons of cocaine. And this far up the supply chain, it would still be very pure to keep the bulk down. Each kilo would probably become two by the time it hit the States or Europe. Actually, with this coming out of Colombia onto the Pacific coast via Ecuador, it was headed to the US or Japan. Technically not her problem, but she couldn't imagine what they could do to stop it.

If she and Chad hadn't inadvertently inserted themselves into the heart of *la Capitana's* operation, the Delta team could do something.

But...now?

She knew they still could. There were six top shooters out there in the dark. It would take only a few signals to lower the boom on this crew.

And yet Chad wasn't calling for that.

Why?

Instead, he'd gone to great lengths to ingratiate himself with Daniela.

Again why?

And that's when Tanya decided her brain must still be sex-addled. Daniela was *la Capitana*. She was the kingpin to the largest remaining smuggling operation other than the *Golfo* —since *Golfo* had wiped out their Colombian rivals, *Los Rastrojos*. Taking Daniela down now would solve today's problem. But someone would show up to take the helm of the operation. If they could burn out a second level of leadership, the loss of knowledge would merely cripple a whole segment of the operation. If they could take out the midlevel operations people, then the entire framework might collapse.

Yes, it was worth hanging on to see if that was possible.

She eyed Chad. He'd started whistling to himself as he lifted and tossed bundles of cocaine as if they weighed less than feathered pillows.

Noticing her attention, he shot her a big smile of delight.

Just happy to have a job, others would think, watching him.

So ready to chow down on this canary, she could hear him thinking about Daniela, though perhaps in a Delta Force way rather than a man-and-woman way.

Worth hanging on to? That was the question she still couldn't answer for herself.

14

"*H*ow do you feel about walking?" Daniela asked as the plane rolled out of the hangar and headed to the runway. No sign of the llamas or burros.

"These boots were made for it," Chad pointed at his feet.

Daniela, Tanya, and Silva looked at him nonplussed.

"Nancy Sinatra. These boots were made for walkin'…" he tried to sing it in a sultry Nancy tone, doing the whole hip swing-fake stomp-sexy shoulder shimmy thing. Still he got no reaction and heaved a sigh. Maybe if he was wearing a micromini and had some cute backup dancers. Please let Daniela keep thinking that he was just a goof of a good ol' boy who could shoot better than other people out there.

He had no problem playing just a little bit dumb, but it was clear that didn't come at all naturally to Tanya. *Just don't blow our cover, girl.*

His whole excited babble thing had hopefully cued Tanya that she was to play the brains of their outfit. But there hadn't yet been a chance to see if she'd caught that and how she might play it out.

Now there were just the four of them standing in front of

the dark and empty hangar. All of Daniela's enforcers, other than Silva, had either left on the plane or melted back into the night. With the dull roar of its turboprop engines, the heavy plane headed aloft. It circled west to clear Tulcán, but he could see its blinking nav lights finally straighten out onto a southeasterly course that would place it either in Quito or at the coast beyond. If anyone thought that it was odd to have a late night departure from this daytime airport with no actual scheduled flights anymore—nobody came by to make a point of it.

"Tulcán," Silva pointed at the town west of the airport. "Ipiales, eight kilometers by road," he pointed northeast. "San Luis Airport, ten kilometers. No road." He was pointing due north.

"I need to be in San Luis an hour before dawn," Daniela concluded, offering them their choices. With her to the airport or go to hell—probably with a bullet in the back of the head.

Chad glanced at his watch. Midnight. Six hours to cross ten kilometers of hard terrain. By Delta standards it should be a cakewalk, but he made a show of considering his choices.

Tanya finally slapped him on the back of the head, just the way she was supposed to. Good. She had taken the leadership role. That would allow him to be less noticed when he had to set up something nasty.

"For that you take point," Tanya snapped at him.

"Guess we're walking," he rubbed the back of his head. She hadn't needed to hit him quite that hard.

As they walked the length of the airport, Chad could feel Duane tracking him. The whole team must be. By now they would have figured out that he had a new plan and not to screw it up. Too bad he didn't. Follow along. Get integrated in. Learn what he could.

Oh, and live to tell about it.

It wouldn't matter if the team called in an Ecuadorian military takedown of the loaded plane—or found some other way to take out the delivery. *La Capitana* would know to expect a certain percentage of loss in her shipments. A twenty-to-thirty percent failure rate was well within the scope of the normal. Too bad he hadn't had a tracker to slip into the shipment.

But how would the team react to his walking out with *la Capitana?* Sofia would have identified her by now, of course. Especially with Tanya's earlier tip-off.

"Sorry," he told her as they walked in the lead.

"For what this time? Treating me like your bitch?"

"No, for doubting you back at the ferry. When did I treat you like my bitch?"

Tanya didn't answer.

They paused for a moment to inspect the stop sign. The big hole punched by the .338 Lapua had struck the upper right edge of the R in *PARE.* Tanya's 7.62 NATO round had left a smaller hole to the lower left of the A. About equidistant from the center. So, nothing to favor one or the other of them.

"Just walk," Tanya snarled.

So he walked.

Out past the airport, the two-lane road turned east toward the Colombian border and Ipiales. They followed it in silence for just a few hundred yards until they were clear of the last sleepy houses of Tulcán. He glanced at Silva, who nodded and waved north.

Chad led them up the steep embankment of the road cut through a small copse of spindly trees—stunted poplar maybe. He wished he dared pull out Tanya's NVGs, but they were the very latest generation and that might be too big a giveaway. He had his hand on his flashlight when he realized that he could see enough to survey the landscape ahead.

This close to the equator, the Milky Way threw enough starlight for night-adapted eyes to see both the general lay of the land and enough nearby detail to walk without falling off an unspotted cliff. Farmland spread over the face of the steeply rolling hills. They were too high in the Andes for dense jungle, but the hard peaks lay mostly to the south. The area of the Ecuador-Colombia border was relatively tame.

So why had Daniela been worried about covering ten kilometers in under six hours—it should take less than two. Was it a test? Yes, but not in how fast could they move. She wanted no trace that she'd come this way, and that took more work and more time.

He found a recent set of tractor tracks headed in the right direction. The compacted soil wouldn't reveal their passage.

———

TANYA WISHED she could talk to Chad yet was thrilled that she couldn't. The only moments they were side by side was when he stopped to survey the next stretch. He was following some kind of a corkscrew path that had made little sense at first. Only as he made about the tenth illogical turn did she catch on. A quick recall of the path so far revealed that just as they were following no trail, they also wouldn't be leaving one.

The more they walked, the more she appreciated his fieldcraft. Occasional glances up revealed that he was navigating by the stars. The North Star was out of sight, very near the horizon from Colombia, but he obviously knew his sky as well as she did. He made it easy to fall into a simple rhythm behind, freeing her mind for other thoughts.

She did her best not to contemplate that two armed and dangerous cartel leaders were walking no more than ten steps behind her. On the road the two had held farther back. But to follow exactly in Chad's tracks, they'd come much closer. They didn't seem to be simply waiting for a remote enough area to kill them both.

What she couldn't change, she would ignore.

The list of things she couldn't change also clearly included Chad Hawkins. However, she also obviously didn't understand him, which made him very hard to ignore.

Perfect woman?

Such a lame line. But the look on his face as she'd made her shot at the stop sign had been clear and open. For him, shooting was nearly as good as sex and he had looked impossibly pleased with her in that moment.

She'd never cared what others thought of her except her instructors.

But that look of pure joy on Chad's features—on the face of a top Delta Force sniper—was both unexpected and overwhelming. She'd put everything she had into that shot—by far the hardest she'd ever tried. And without Chad's final tip— that the Coriolis Effect was so much stronger at the equator— she'd have missed completely. Chad had revealed no hint of smugness that he'd had to remind her of that. No *Good thing I told you so.* Just pure and simple joy.

She had been beyond noticing his expression when he had ravaged her. But he had held her as she curled up around him. As she tried to, piece by piece, tuck the experience safely away. It didn't want to fit into the place where she forgot things—like her father and the death of her sister. Neither would it slide into good, but dangerous, memories—like the last time Tanya had heard her older sister laugh, truly laugh at one of Tanya's antics.

She finally had to build a new place as he held her as if she was important and precious. A place for a memory too good to set aside. It sidled up close beside the memory of serving with the Delta team three years before. And then he had violated that memory. Unless he hadn't.

But what was the good of even deciding if it was a good memory or bad? Three days from now, or whenever this mission ended, Tanya would be on her own again. No Chad. No Delta Force team. And after the reminder of what it was like to fight beside the most lethal fighting force in any military, there would be no returning to any merely skilled UN team.

Scheisse! She had always done best on her own. What had she been thinking by choosing any other path? Not a mistake she'd ever make again.

Chad signaled for a halt by a rushing river.

She hadn't even noticed that they'd been descending sharply for the last few hundred meters.

Zweimal Scheisse! She was letting herself so rely on Chad's leadership that she'd dropped her situational awareness. Unacceptable!

"Lose the NVGs when we cross," he whispered quickly before Silva and Daniela caught up with them.

She nodded. Good idea. They were in the burlap bag she'd kept slung over her shoulder, along with their water bottles. She dug out the bottles and handed one over as they sat at the river bank. Then attempted to hold the bag as if it was empty.

Daniela and Silva came and sat beside them.

"Any idea where the best crossing is?" Chad asked easily. As if they were two couples out on a happy Sunday trek.

"No," Daniela's voice was as beautiful as she was, even raised over the sounds of the rushing river. "I have never walked across this border before."

And again Tanya felt the shiver of just how likely it was that her and Chad's corpses would be floating down this river in the next few minutes. She could hear it running fast over rocks. The other bank wasn't far, but the volume of water moving over the rapids told her this wasn't likely to be fun. She rocked forward enough to dip in her fingers—and pulled them back quickly. Glacier cold.

"Pathfinders," Chad chortled. "Cool!"

Again Chad in his happy-doofus personality.

"I'll scout upriver, you scout down, honey. A hundred paces, then come back to here."

"I'll go with Tanya," Daniela announced.

Silva rose and took a couple steps to show he'd head upriver with Chad.

Tanya tried to get a read on whether Chad planned to kill

him while their forces were divided, but unable to see more than the starlight glimmer off his golden blond hair, she couldn't. Surely, if he was planning to, he'd give her some sort of sign. Wouldn't he?

"Anyone need a burlap bag?" Tanya didn't wait for anyone to respond. She stooped and tossed a big rock into it, big enough that there wouldn't be any sign of the weight of the NVGs. Knotting the top, she tossed it out into the current where it disappeared with a loud *plonk!* She didn't want to be answering any impossible questions.

Silva might be a fighter, but there was no questioning who had the brains of the operation.

She and *la Capitana* headed downriver.

Tanya hoped that she'd get to see Chad again. No matter what confused whirl her thoughts were in, her emotions were definitely in favor of spending more time with him.

"BEEN WITH DANIELA FOR LONG?" Chad eased through the brush heading upriver. It was thick this close to the bank. He listened to the water, but he used the brush as an excuse to constantly turn to keep an eye on the trailing Silva. Hold a branch until Silva grabbed it. Point at a surprise rock or hole. Every five steps or so he could see that Silva's sidearm remained in its holster.

He hoped the fact that he'd taken Silva upriver would indicate to Tanya that Chad wasn't planning to kill him. Because, if he had to dispose of the body, the river would be an obvious choice. But by being upriver, the body would then float down past Tanya and Daniela, giving away what he'd done.

Or was that too convoluted a message even for him? Would Duane have followed that logic?

Probably not.

Would he himself?

Nope.

Shit! He was overthinking everything around Tanya. The woman was messing with his head. He'd never bedded a true sniper before. It had taken everything in him to not jump her there and then, lying in front of the airport hangar after that amazing shot she took. She was a supercharged version of anyone he'd ever been with. *Anyone!*

"*Amigo?*" Chad prompted. Silva still hadn't answered.

"What do you mean by *with?*"

"Come on, *hombre*. There is no way you aren't wanting a piece of something that looks that good." *Just two guys, strolling along, talking about women.* If they were going to embed with *la Capitana* long enough to learn anything, he'd better start making friends fast.

"She chooses her men very carefully."

"Since she can choose any damn one she wants, can't blame her."

"Even you?" Silva made the question casual, but Chad could hear the territorial edge behind it.

"Swore myself to Tanya and almost screwed that up, literally, once. Not gonna lose her again. No how. No way." And in that instant, Chad knew it was true. He'd walk right off the team if it came down that fork in the road. Instead of her flying solo, maybe they'd walk that path together and see just how much pain they could unleash on the heads of people like Silva and Daniela.

"Daniela has a hard past. It is difficult for her to trust."

"You're avoiding the question, dude." *Fifty.* Chad had been keeping a silent count in his head. He had another fifty paces to find out something, because once they started the return, they'd naturally be moving much faster and talk even less.

"She is…impressive." Silva finally admitted.

"And?" *Seventy-five.*

Chad kept his silence and slowed as they neared ninety. Guy

sure wasn't given to bragging, but Chad couldn't think of how else to nudge him along.

"She took me off the streets two years ago. I was a runner in Gerald's operation. Now I am in charge of this border crossing for her. I have a nice house and enough money to entertain a woman whenever I want."

Sounded like the guy was making up the story as he went along. Whatever the truth, two things were clear: he wasn't sleeping with Daniela, and he would do anything *la Capitana* asked of him.

That meant she wasn't using sex to run her team, but she was still building absolute loyalty. Easy to respect that.

One hundred! And not a decent crossing along the way. Two sets of hard rapids. And only minimal information. But, a mission's intel was rarely built in a day. He just hoped that he had more than a day to build it.

"How did you forgive him?"

"Who says I have?" Not the question Tanya had been expecting. They had shifted ten steps away from the bank where the going was easy enough for them to walk side by side. It also gave them a better view of the width of the starlit river without getting all scraped up by fighting their way through the brush at the bank.

"Your voice. Your attitude. Your little whispers together. I know they are not all about me. His body movements shift when he speaks to you about things that are important to him."

"I hadn't noticed." And she hadn't. Somehow too close to the situation to see it clearly? Didn't sound like her.

"He…softens. I can see the fighter in him. I can see the training in both of you. He reminds me of one of my martial arts instructor's sayings. *To get your black belt, you learn forms, patterns, timing. There are as many levels of black belt as there are to get from white to black. Those are so that you can unlearn forms, patterns, timing.* You and he have both unlearned your forms. However, he is a white belt around you—clumsy and awkward when he shouldn't be."

"What did you study?"

Daniela's silence said that was the wrong topic.

"I…" Tanya couldn't say the word Daniela would be expecting. She tried, but if she could hear the falsehood in her head, so would her companion. *I just love the man.* She couldn't sell it.

She didn't believe in love any more than she believed in just one man.

"I…" her second attempt wasn't faring any better than the first.

The truth.

What was the truth about Chad?

"I've…never met anyone like him. He is charming, infuriating, the best lover I ever found, handsome, a total philandering bastard, and when he shoots like that, I want to jump his bones so badly it hurts like an ache in my chest." Her words had accelerated until they spewed out almost as fast as the river ran, laden with a full flow of doubt and confusion. She bit down on the inside of her cheek.

Had she meant what she'd said?

Every word.

Never in her life had she wanted a man the way she wanted Chad. Regrettably, that wasn't a choice she could live with because he was exactly as she'd described him.

Daniela was silent for a long way. Just at the turn, Tanya spotted the only possible crossing and they moved forward to investigate. The stream slowed as the banks shifted apart. By the sound and the white foam catching the starlight, there was a hard rapids ahead, but if they swam across fast, they should make it before they were dragged down into the rocks.

"Is Silva a good swimmer?" Tanya asked, and knew she was

asking a different question. Did Daniela have a man who did for her what Chad did for Tanya?

"He can cross the river." Silva wasn't *la Capitana's* lover, just her henchman. But the sadness in Daniela's tone spoke of her never finding that for herself with any man.

She looked sharply down at Tanya's hand when it rested on her arm.

Tanya didn't even think about it before she placed it there.

Daniela's gaze drifted up to look directly at Tanya. "There was a man once. For a while. But no more." Then she turned around and walked out from beneath Tanya's light touch as if it wasn't even there.

Tanya hoped it wasn't the one that Chad had reported shooting when they stole the motorcycles.

Wait! When did she start caring about *la Capitana?* The woman was going to die in the next few days, or be incarcerated for life spilling out her guts about her operation. Yet Tanya could feel pity for her.

They didn't exchange a single word as they crossed back to their starting point to await the men's return.

15

*C*had almost balked when they arrived at San Luis Airport in Colombia. A small plane awaited them.

If he and Tanya boarded, it would be impossible for the team to follow them. He'd been careful to not give away that they were following, not by glance, not by a single turn to see if anyone was over his shoulder beyond what would be normal for a man leading a small team across the Ecuadorian farmlands in the middle of the night. But he had no doubt that even now his Delta companions were arrayed strategically around the airport, ready to act on a moment's notice.

The little twin-engine, low-winged Beech Baron seated six and could fly fifteen hundred miles. She could reach anywhere from the Yucatán or Miami to Bolivia in a single flight. *La Capitana's* test hadn't been for them to walk from Ecuador to Colombia. She probably had a hundred ways to make the crossing that would be far easier than the icy plunge into the river—paying the border guards fifty US apiece came easily to mind. The trek had merely been a way to meet the newest members of the team.

This was the test. Would they completely commit to her service, cutting all ties behind them?

San Luis was no more brightly lit than the airport in Tulcán. It was even smaller. A single hangar that might hold three personal planes and a terminal building for no more than thirty people. The two-story control tower perched among a pretty garden, and the reader board announced one flight per day. Which was one more scheduled flight per day than Tulcán currently boasted though it was twice the size.

"You can leave your weapons here if you like," Daniela said casually as if it was no more than a suggestion.

"Why would we do that?" Chad braced himself for a fight.

That's when he noticed that he'd lost track of Silva. Not good. Very not good.

Tanya was watching the far side of the hangar.

For what?

Chad tried to brace for the worst, but wasn't sure what it would be. A cartel's worth of shooters hiding around the back of the hangar awaiting Silva's leadership? A hidden explosive in the plane that Silva didn't want to be killed by when he triggered it to wipe out the three of them? Or—

A five-year old Toyota SUV with a battered front quarter panel pulled around the corner and rolled up close beside them with Silva at the wheel.

"Or you can tuck your rifles in the back of the truck. They'll be safe there. No one would touch my truck or my plane."

"Where are we going?" He knew it was bad form to ask that of a new leader, especially one who just might run a massive, illegal drug smuggling operation. But he didn't want to leave his rifle anywhere.

"To Las Lajas neighborhood down the road," Daniela tossed her M4 in the plane's cargo compartment, then closed the little door before crossing to the SUV and sliding into the passenger seat. "Time for breakfast soon. You can wait here if you want, but I don't run a take-away service."

Chad squinted up at the sky. The stars that had guided them through the night were slowly fading. Though there was no other sign yet, dawn would soon be approaching over the tops of the Andes.

"Breakfast sounds good," Tanya slipped her rifle behind the rear seat of the SUV and climbed in. Wondering if he'd just failed some test, Chad lay his rifle to nestle beside hers, then climbed in as well.

They wound through the small city of Ipiales but didn't slow. Only a few kilometers from the airport, but the drive was long enough for the sky to lighten. By the time they entered the town, lights were coming on in several of the houses. Ipiales sprawled over the hills, rarely reaching a third story. A few office buildings on the hill towered to an impressive six, but the twin steeples of a not very impressive church dominated the town easily though it lay in the lower swale of the valley that defined Ipiales.

There were a couple of food stalls already up and open for business and the smells had Chad's mouth watering.

He knew about these. They were for the early workers who would service the rest of the people when they got up. From Indonesia to Somalia to the back alleys of Detroit, it was always the same. The cheapest, and often the best, food was very simple. These early vendors' clients didn't have money for fancy spices or widely varied meals. A corn *arepo* smeared with thick white cheese. Another wrapped around a fistful of white rice with peppers and chorizo sausage. Eaten quietly. The only talk was of what prospects the next day held, passing in soft whispers between chewing and sips of dark Colombian coffee.

But Silva didn't stop. He didn't turn in at any of the likely looking *restaurantes* either. Instead, he drove through town until they ran out of town. Beyond Ipiales, they entered a small hamlet that still lay wholly asleep. They seemed about to pass this by as well, but instead turned onto a small lane that wound past a few houses and suddenly rolled into a land of darkness. Another few houses went by on the right.

To the left, the landscape was wholly transformed. The crossing from San Luis Airport to Ipiales had been through the same type of rugged farmland that they had walked over for much of the night. It had smelled of dark soil, fresh growth, a heavy rain only a few days gone by.

Here, the hamlet perched on a knife-edge cliff. A river gorge plunged through a deep cleft in the mountains, its bottom lost in darkness despite the pink and gold light already dusting the land. The road crawled along the cliff edge as if clinging for life —the chasm lay so deep in shadow that seemed to go down forever. The cliff edge wove in and out, which must mimic dark twists and turns of the river far below.

He was watching the road's edge, so close by the SUV's wheels, with no guard rail, when Tanya gasped. He spun to face her, his sidearm half-drawn, but she was looking out the windshield.

He looked.

Blinked hard.

Looked again.

Blinked again.

But it was still there.

"I'm not seeing what I'm seeing."

"Me either," Tanya whispered softly.

"*Santuario de Las Lajas,*" Daniela stated as if that explained everything. "The Las Lajas Sanctuary or literally, the Sanctuary of the Slabs. There has been a church here for almost three hundred years. Ever since the miracle of the deaf-mute child who spoke aloud in amazement when she saw a miraculous image of Mary and Jesus etched into the rock. The cathedral that replaced the old church is approaching its first century."

Sticking out from the cliff wall, like William Tell's arrow after it split the apple and slammed into the tree, was a Gothic cathedral. It didn't make any sense, but there it was. Its central spire towered fifteen stories above the bridge that supported it. Gray stone rose in pointed arches and flying buttresses, bracketing stained glass windows between. The windows glowed from candlelight that yet managed to overpower the coming dawn.

"It is an amazing place to watch the sunrise," Daniela said as Silva parked the car and they all climbed out.

They descended through a narrow paved lane of closed tourist shops and down a broad stone staircase. All along the right-hand cliff face were plaques. Chad pulled out a small flash to see them more clearly. Hundreds, maybe thousands, in all shapes and sizes had been cemented in place.

"They are placed by pilgrims giving thanks to the Virgin Mary. Some for deliverance from disease. Some for a joyous marriage. Some for a peaceful death."

"Do you have one here?" Tanya asked with a perception that Chad hadn't had.

They completed the descent of the broad stairway and Chad had repocketed his flashlight before Daniela spoke again.

"I did. I don't."

She'd been thankful for something, so thankful she had commissioned a plaque to the Holy Virgin. And lived long enough to learn the nasty truth and take it back down. If Chad had a plaque made, what would he put on it? What would survive long enough that he wouldn't want to take it down again? He was thankful for a lot of things, but it didn't take a genius to know that nothing lasted long enough to cement a plaque to a wall. What had *la Capitana* once been so naive to tack up there? He considered asking, but decided it was the woman's own business. Probably some hot lover who'd shafted her—and not in a good way.

"The sunrise is best from the bridge. The cathedral stays in shadow at first light and only emerges during the day."

The bridge spanning the deep gorge and the river below was nearly as broad as the church. It was paved with great square stones. Carved balustrades ran down either side of the area almost as big as a soccer field. Atop them, angels with trumpets, harps, and other musical instruments were perched at intervals —some watching the heavens, others watching over the people below.

The rapids were audible, echoing up the canyon walls with a dull roar. Chad moved to one side and, looking way down, he could see the white foam churning over the rocks. There was a clear span of dark water directly below, but it was a rough river.

"Forty meters?" He asked Tanya, mostly to check in with her.

"Closer to fifty."

Fifteen stories from river to canyon-spanning bridge. And the cathedral towered above them for another fifteen. It was one of the most peculiar and powerful sights he'd ever seen.

All his years of hanging out in the backs of Detroit churches for warmth had left him with little belief in anything. He'd seen the worst of men stroll in, ask forgiveness, and stride out as if a priest's blessing meant something. Even the priests didn't buy in on that.

But there was something majestic here. Someone had thought this one place important enough to erect a Gothic cathedral in the wilderness of the Colombian Andes.

The rising sun touched a high peak to the west first, catching it like a torch. Then the tops of the canyon walls. The first beam of sunlight splashed down upon them like God's hand striking down from the sky. The uppermost edge of the sun shone through the high notch of a twist in the canyon.

"Did Ra the Sun God hang out around here? Cause if so, he could make a believer out of me."

"No," Daniela said quietly. "But it might be the work of Inti, he was the Incan sun god who worked around here."

"Whoever thought this landscape up was an amazing dude."

"*She* was. Pachamama was the Incan Mother Earth," Daniela acknowledged. "Now…jump."

TANYA KNEW she was missing something.

"Jump?" Chad sounded as bewildered as she felt.

Then there was the ominous sound of the safety coming off on two separate weapons at the same time, and neither of them was hers.

She turned very slowly.

Daniela no longer stood beside them. Daniela was nowhere to be seen. She had morphed back into being *la Capitana*. She had also eased away until she stood halfway across the twenty-pace span of the bridge with her pistol leveled at Tanya's chest. At ten paces with her weapon already drawn, she was too far away to charge.

Silva stood well out of reach, an additional ten meters along the bridge toward the cathedral.

The three of them had shed their rifles to "go to town." ·

Silva had not.

He had an Uzi knockoff aimed at Chad's chest. But Tanya didn't doubt how fast he could sweep the Uzi across Chad and onto her.

" 'Jump' you say?" Chad's Mr. Casual tone was back, but Tanya knew it wouldn't do him any good.

"Ten seconds," *la Capitana's* voice was cold.

"You know…" Chad glanced at Tanya and tipped his head toward the balustrade.

And Tanya knew exactly what he was thinking. "No, Chad. Just… No!"

"But we…" Yes, they'd done it before, just two days ago out of a helicopter and over a waterfall.

"Just because we did, doesn't mean I want to do it again."

"Chicken. Buc-buc-buc-bu-caw!" Chad started dancing in little circles with his thumbs tucked in his armpits, flapping his elbows like a psychotic chicken.

"Five," *la Capitana* called out.

"You stay out of this!" Tanya pointed a finger at the woman aiming the gun at Tanya's heart. First she had to get Chad straightened around.

Except Chad was anything but stupid. But she didn't know what his play was.

However, *he* did. And would be pushing her internal buttons to get the reaction he wanted. Damn him! He should not know so much about her.

But not daring to do anything other than play out her role, she forged ahead.

"I'm not jumping to my death on some childish dare by you!" She stabbed her finger at Chad this time. "Her? Maybe. You? No way in hell!"

"Buc-buc-bu-caw!" Chad crowed as he circled again.

"It won't work, you know," *la Capitana* said almost conversationally. "I'll shoot him first, if you like—it might be a kindness. But I won't be distracted so easily."

"Aw, and I had such high hopes," Chad stopped like a deflated little boy.

Then he dove to the pavement and shot Silva.

At the same instant, Tanya dodged away from Chad, drawing *la Capitana's* attention toward her as Chad continued his roll to take the woman out at her knees.

Except she wasn't there.

She'd hopped over the rolling Chad and landed lightly on her feet despite his attempt to grapple her as he passed beneath her.

Tanya had her weapon out now, but *la Capitana*…didn't. Instead, she folded her arms lightly across her chest and looked at Tanya.

Tanya swung her weapon to point at the sky but didn't holster it.

"You haven't shot me," *la Capitana* said in a perfectly calm voice.

"Why not?" Chad looked up at Tanya.

"She doesn't want me to. That's not the point." Tanya knew that much at least. And Chad, of course, knew that, but was feeding her the next line.

Silva groaned. "I hate this part." He sat up slowly, rubbing at his left breast—directly over his heart. "Someday someone is going to fire armor-piercing bullets. Or shoot me in the face. Double vest and it still hurts like a bitch in heat."

Which explained why they'd been told to leave their rifles behind. Her MSG90 might not have made it through the armor, but it definitely would have broken some ribs even if it hadn't. Chad's powerful Lapua would barely hesitate before plowing through both Silva's armor and Silva.

"Very few succeed in hitting you at all," Daniela noted. Her persona had come back from the austerely beautiful cartel leader to the lovely-though-still-dangerous woman.

Tanya and Chad glanced at each other just as the sun finally cleared the canyon wall and shone full upon them.

"Why the risk?" Tanya asked because it was clear that Chad wanted her to continue as the "brains" of their team.

"Risk?" Daniela nodded toward the Gothic cathedral. High up the spires, the sun finally caught light—the sharp, hard light that might be reflected off a rifle's scope. Daniela had a sniper up there watching them. No more than fifty meters away—flight time roughly five hundredths of a second—Tanya would have been dead before she could fully lower her weapon to fire. She'd just come within an instant of death—wasn't the first time. She wasn't dead, so it wasn't that big a deal. She holstered her weapon.

Chad still lay on his side on the ground, like he was some lounging lady from a girlie magazine—elbow to the ground, head propped on his fist. Tanya stepped over him, sat on his hip, and stared at Daniela.

"How many are so fearful that they jump?"

Daniela shrugged, "Half."

"Of which almost none survive, but *la Capitana* no longer cares about them."

Daniela nodded an acknowledgement of Tanya knowing her identity.

"But you have no use for team members who aren't brave. How many beg?"

"Most of the other half."

"Do you toss their bodies down or do you chase them away? Never mind. Don't answer." Tanya knew the choice she would make if their roles were reversed—some secrets were best protected, including *la Capitana's* recruiting techniques. Tanya didn't much like the brutal choice or that she knew she'd do the same herself if their roles were reversed.

"And the ones who fight?"

"They are the ones I need," Daniela continued, standing at perfect ease. "I need the brave, the daring…and the smart." She made a hand gesture, and Tanya could see the distant sniper leave his position in the spire and head down.

Tanya could feel Chad's grunt of acknowledgement through his hip and her butt.

Had he guessed all that in the split second after they'd been told to jump and before he'd started his chicken dance? It would explain why he'd shot Silva in the heart rather than a spinal-cord cutter in through the nose. At this distance, he could have hit either easily, even while diving to the pavement.

"And how do you tell if we're traitors trying to infiltrate your operation?"

"By how you walk."

"By how we walk?"

"Yes," and again Daniela waited.

"Because…we don't walk like soldiers."

"Not anymore," Daniela nodded, then began strolling toward the cathedral. "I can see your training. I could see it from the first moment. For one of you to shoot the stop sign at that distance and in darkness might have placed you as a civilian, but both of you making a shot I wouldn't like to try myself—clearly military. But you no longer walk like military, which tells me you have both been out long enough that you could have served with Estevan. And only someone who knew Analie Sala personally could have those details about her."

Tanya hoped that Daniela didn't recall the conversation along the stream of how the levels past a first-degree black belt was about unlearning all of the patterns. It was the first "miss" Tanya spotted in *la Capitana's* amazing skill set—she didn't fully understand Special Operations. Operator training was like none other in the world, whether it was American Delta, British SAS, or Israeli Kidon. All the patterns of military weren't trained out —they were discarded, wholesale, and replaced with flow and presence.

She and Chad had passed the test because they were *too* good. How narrow a group was that? Tanya considered the range and span of the test and decided she and Chad were lucky to be alive.

AS THEY APPROACHED THE CATHEDRAL, a priest opened the front doors. Before they stepped in, a man with an M16A4 and a Leupold Mark 4 scope stepped out. He offered them a pleasant nod before continuing on his way—just a friendly neighborhood sniper. He carried the rifle with the ease of deep familiarity. Chad knew his guess had been right: come up with a solution fast—or die even faster. But he'd thought it was a final desperate play.

He'd shot Silva in the chest because his diving roll had already twisted him too far to get an angle on the man's head.

Tanya was the one who'd taken it to the next level by *not* shooting Daniela.

The cathedral's shadow was like a cool curtain across the already warm sun, inviting them to climb the broad stone steps.

Inside, the cathedral was a wonder.

Great white pillars rose to a midlevel golden collar. Soaring high above that, the great arches of the long nave crisscrossed like a golden web over the white stonework. Though the direct sun had yet to brush the outside, the windows shone with blue, gold, and clear glass, making the church seem too bright to be possible. The only remaining interior light was a small lamp behind the altar.

The entire altar wall of the cathedral, rather than continuing the form of the arches, was made up of the solid stone of the cliff's face itself. The lamp shown on an image of the Mother Mary and the infant Jesus wearing mighty crowns of gold as Saints Francis and Dominic worshipped at their feet. The fact that the two saints had lived twelve hundred years after the shiningly Hispanic Mother Mary was the sort of thing that the Catholic Church was so good at ignoring. He was down with that—the little details were often best ignored.

Now he sat at the back of the pews, Tanya beside him and Silva across the aisle, while *la Capitana* confessed her sins to the priest. Chad had only tried that once or twice, mostly to see just what it took to shock the clergy. Once he made up a bunch of crap and the priest had practically yawned in his face through the little screen. The second time, he'd given the litany of a life on the Street—poor old guy had looked visibly shaken for days afterward. Chad had always felt a little bad about that.

How did *la Capitana's* priest take her confessions? Amoral sins weren't erased by a couple of Hail Marys and a spell as a missionary to darkest Detroit.

"Anything you want to be confessing?" Chad whispered to Tanya.

At her unexpected silence, he turned to look at her. She startled him sometimes. When she was quiet like this, it seemed that he was with a different woman entirely. The sarcastic, funny, all-the-way-to-the-bone warrior was familiar. That's who was still front-and-center when they were snarled up in each other's arms. It had been easy to imagine her expression in the darkness under the topiary—fiercely still herself.

But the quiet blonde who sat beside him with her hand lightly wrapped around his biceps, he was far less sure of. It was as if she should be the one shining in one of the glass windows. No hint of the lethal operator he admired so much. No sign of the lover who leapt into sex with such complete abandon.

Instead she was the sort of woman who made a guy actually consider the question of what *did* he want after Delta Force. He wasn't like Kyle and Carla. They'd climb ranks, driving themselves upward. If they ever reproduced, he could easily see Carla leading one of the brutal qualification hikes with the kid riding on her back. The kid would be able to shoot before she figured out how to suck her thumb.

He wasn't that, but he wasn't sure what else he was. Being a Delta Force operator was the extreme sport of the military. Maybe in another decade, definitely by the time he hit forty, his body wouldn't be able to hold the standard.

Old Delta operators didn't die, they imploded. Old joke. Sad joke.

One day his time on a 20K, full rucksack march would be longer than the cutoff time, beyond his ability to recover it. His shooting score would fall from sniper to designated marksman to —god help him—standard operator. Who would he be then?

Shit! No wonder he didn't like thinking about the future. Made him as depressed as all hell. Next thing, he'd be blubbering like a Navy SEAL ringing himself out of testing for the total failure he was.

He almost told Tanya they should just get out now. *La Capitana* was still in her ornate little priestly confessional booth. Silva wouldn't stop them. Or live if he tried. This time he'd get a pair of rounds straight through the nostrils—never have breathing problems again.

"Confession?" Tanya whispered as if coming back from far away. "I miss the team."

And that simply, she reminded him of everything he loved about being a Delta operator. Never boring. If home was the place you belonged, their team was just that.

"Fighting beside them is the best thing I've ever done."

She was right, too. Serving with this team had been the best four years of his life. From the moment when they'd all qualified for the Operator Training Course, right through the addition of Melissa and Sofia—they were the best.

And if he left?

He'd probably lose touch with Duane, and that thought hurt and hurt bad. Even though Sofia was the newest member of the team, he'd already miss her brilliant insights and her bright laugh.

"Fighting beside *you* is the best thing I've ever done."

Surprise rippled through him. That was true as well. He and the team had shared flow and mutual awareness born of their intensive training. With Tanya, he'd had that from the first second—ever since the moment she'd come up to them in the Venezuelan bar. She'd sat down with five Delta operators on a mission as if joining them for a tea party. Woman had balls the size of the *Titanic* and they'd totally sunk him.

He kissed her temple. Sitting here beside her, joined at the hip in an undercover operation with Colombia's Number One drug runner, he couldn't think of anywhere he'd rather be. Or anyone he'd rather be doing it with.

"You're getting no complaints from me, lady."

No complaints from him?

How about from her?

Tanya listened inside. Being a lone operator, it was where she was used to spending a lot of time.

Chad the warrior was impossibly attractive. She'd never operated so smoothly with another person—not in her Mossad training or even the micro-teams that Kidon used in emulation of Delta Force tactics. But she could picture more, better, longer associations with Chad.

She was a survivor. Tanya knew that much about herself. The surprise was that she cared enough about anyone around her to feel one way or the other about *their* survival. Feeling awful about the injuries and death of her UN team was just part of what happened. But she didn't *miss* Carl. She could barely remember what he looked like. That he'd died while on her team was too bad and she'd have done anything she could have to prevent it, because that's what leading a team was about. But the loss of Carl himself? All she could do was shrug.

She would care more about the loss of Melissa or Sofia, who she'd barely met, than she felt about Carl after months of serving together. That she didn't understand it didn't make it any less true.

Sitting beside Chad made her feel safer and more capable than she ever seemed to on her own.

And if something happened to Chad the man? Well, she could only hope that she went down in the same mission so that she'd never know about it. Bit by bit, she held his arm tighter, as if that would keep him safe and by her side.

"You a wine or a beer person?" Chad asked quietly.

"Beer. Why?"

Chad shrugged. "Me too. Just thinkin'. Don't look so surprised. I do that sometimes, you know. Sofia is like a super-wine heiress. Someday she and Duane are gonna settle into that big winery of hers and squish grapes together. Wouldn't want to compete with them or anything, but I could see setting up a brewpub in the heart of the Oregon wine country just to keep Duane and Sofia on their toes."

"What do you know about brewing beer?"

"Squat. But I like the idea of us doing something like that together someday. Sounds like fun."

And Tanya's ears started buzzing until they drowned him out, though she could still see his lips moving.

Chad was talking about...*after.*

No one ever talked about *after.* Not at their level. Especially not Chad. And absolutely not her. Even if she was the one who'd started the whole conversation back in Ecuador.

"What is going on in that tiny brain of yours?" She cut him off in the middle of some weird-ass fantasy about stone walls and aged wood beams, with a fireplace and who knew what the hell all.

Chad opened his mouth, then closed it. For a moment his eyes crossed as he considered her question.

"Damned if I know," he finally answered.

"You picturing me with a couple kids in that backwash you keep inside your skull?"

"Huh!" Chad gasped as if she'd just sucker punched him. Then he unleashed that killer smile of his. "It's weird. But I think I've gotta answer that one with a big 'Roger that!' A little-girl version of you is a damned awesome image, Tanya. Bet you were tough as hell—ready to take on the world—and damned cute."

Tanya tried to think back to her younger self. It was hard. In some ways, the Tanya Zimmer she was today had been born the day her sister went into the ground and her father "stumbled" into traffic—a speeding garbage truck had appeared at the perfect moment. (It was so perfect that it still counted as Tanya's sole evidence of the existence of the Bible's Old Testament vengeful God.) Who had she been prior to that? Had she had friends? Jumped rope or played kickball on the streets of Tel Aviv? Or had she gotten into schoolyard fistfights? She honestly couldn't recall. But she knew how she would raise a daughter herself. Tanya would show her the real, often cruel world, but make sure she knew that there was one place where she would always be safe and respected—that she'd always have a home.

She could feel the ache. Home. Only the vaguest images

clung around that word. Nothing concrete. Nothing definite. But so real that she could feel the sweet pain of it in her chest where such thoughts didn't belong.

Tanya spotted Daniela stepping out of the confessional and coming their way.

It helped Tanya get her thoughts back where they belonged. Surviving the mission. Taking down *la Capitana* and her cartel.

Picturing Chad with a kid tucked under each of his massive arms like sacks of grain as he was surrounded by their giggles had absolutely no place in any reality. Not even in her imagination.

Time to go?

Good!

She rose to follow Daniela and Silva outside, leaving Chad to trail behind.

But she couldn't seem to leave behind the image of Chad playing with children. With *her* children.

16

*D*aniela dropped them at a small hotel after breakfast at one of the tourist shops. Daniela's money for the meal was refused.

"It is run by a friend," she'd explained.

The same was true at the hotel—a friend who had eyed them as if they were DEA agents and he might sneak up and kill them in their sleep. It wasn't their rifles; it was them. Without Daniela vouching for their safety, Tanya might have tried fighting her way out here and now.

Tanya tried a smile, but it didn't make any difference. She supposed that was fair, she didn't feel it much inside either. Exhaustion rippled through her system in indeterminate waves that threatened to take out her knees as they ascended the narrow stone stairs to the second floor. There was no third floor.

Multiple near-death experiences on too little sleep had taken it out of her.

"Alone at last," Chad said the instant the door closed.

She tapped her ear to indicate that anyone could be listening.

He offered her a "Duh!" eyeroll. "Conversation isn't exactly at the top of my list right now, lady."

She turned to see if the attached bathroom included a shower, but Chad snagged a hand around her waist and hauled her back against his chest.

"No." There was no way they were going to have sex while images of children were dancing through her head. Children had been everywhere since the moment they'd left the church. Families arriving for the morning service had included children of all ages rubbing sleepy eyes. The young boy who had served their coffee at breakfast. The small group playing soccer in the road as they walked toward a tiny schoolhouse. Normally she never much noticed children and now she couldn't seem to see anything else. Tanya wanted nothing to do with that either.

Much to her surprise, Chad let her go right away when she protested. His release caused her to stumble forward into the room. It wasn't much. On the double bed, a woven wool bedspread in brown and white appeared to illustrate serpents and flowers. She looked for an apple, but it was no Garden of Eden. Three walls white, one dark blue. Floor of half-meter squares of white ceramic tile. A dresser that wouldn't hold more than a few clothes, but it didn't matter—they only had what they were wearing.

The view out the one window made up for everything else. The hotel perched at the edge of the cliff. To the right stood the Gothic spires of Las Lajas Sanctuary. Opposite was a high, thin waterfall spilling down into the deep canyon. And when she moved close to the window, she could look down at the river they'd been told to jump into. It was now light enough to see the hard rapids that ran toward the church's arching bridge. There might be smooth water directly below the bridge, but it still didn't look very survivable.

She leaned her forehead against the glass and only slowly became aware of Chad leaning his shoulder there as he looked at her.

"Why no wrestling match?" She'd have expected him to let her go when she asked, eventually. They'd been through enough together that it would be a playful moment rather than a threatening one. But still, the instant release had surprised her.

"Not sure. You're definitely worth wrestling with." In her peripheral vision she could see his friendly leer. "But it doesn't seem to be what I'm after."

"What are you after?"

He shrugged those nice big shoulders of his uncertainly. "You talking about the future, and what comes after all this, and kids…That's not shit I'm used to thinking about. Probably not any more than you are. Makes my head hurt."

Hers too. She went back to staring at the scenery to avoid leaning into Chad's personal magnetic field. The July sunshine struck down from the north. Their view faced south, so she could watch the shifting shadows on the scenery without the sun beating in the window. It left their room cool and shadowed.

Chad harrumphed to himself. "Tricky bit of it is, I gotta admit that I like the way some of that stuff we were talking about sounds. Wasn't kidding about it either. I figured joking about the future—settling down and all that other crap—was unkind. Used to do it as a kid, but Wollson taught me that there was such a thing as a code of honor. Must say, you're confusing the crap outta me."

Tanya had liked the way it sounded too, which bothered her at least as much as it was bothering him.

"I'd much rather that we just screwed each other's brains out and moved on. Simpler. At least I'd understand that."

"And now?" Maybe the exhaustion rippling through her wasn't exhaustion. Maybe it was crashing waves of uncertainty that made her feel flipped upside down. *Warning! Bad rapids ahead.*

"Don't know what it all means, but I'm still in a mood to lie down with you, woman. I've got a real bad desire to do that."

It was good advice. Live in the present. It's what they both did the best.

He slid a hand around her waist. Not aggressive. Not suggestive. As if it was just where his hand happened to belong. She allowed herself to be pulled slowly against his chest.

She knew that he could make her forget. Forget herself. Forget the mission. Forget the hundred close brushes with death. The round that had found Carl could just as easily have found her. The fall from the helo should have killed them both. And the waterfall. Chad shooting her. The motorcycle crash. Had she actually aimed her gun at *la Capitana,* the sniper would have taken her down.

Was she willing to let go for long enough to forget?

He'd done it to her once.

Did she want that again?

She leaned her head against his chest and felt his arms come around her.

Yes.

IT SEEMED that Tanya was melting against him one little piece at a time. A hand touch. A shoulder lean. Resting her cheek against his chest.

And with each tiny bit of giving in, he held her more and more gently. His past experiences with Tanya had been wild romps. Up against the front door. On the kitchen floor, their entire bodies well lubricated with cooking oil. The bed used only as a place to collapse when they were finally spent.

This odd gentleness was new, but he didn't want to break it either. Ever so slowly he undressed her and then carried her the three steps to the bed. He looked down at her as he undressed himself.

Yes, she was a warrior in her prime.

Yes, she was exceptionally beautiful.

Yes, they had roughly the same number and severity of scars.

No, he couldn't quite believe that she lay waiting for him. Watching him with those shining blue eyes.

When he lay down beside her and pulled her against him, she didn't attack. No grabbing, teasing, tickling—none of that. Instead she curled back against him and snuggled into his shoulder.

"You're snuggling."

"No, I'm not." She found some way to move even closer.

"You do any more of not doing it like that and we'll be sharing the same body."

"Do you always talk at moments like this? I do not remember you doing such things."

"Maybe because I don't." Sure, while still in the bar or spinning a line. Once he'd helped a woman get him exactly where she wanted him wasn't a moment he'd ever felt called for a whole lot of words.

"Then why are you doing it now?"

"You don't seem to be escalating the situation much yourself."

"No. I'm not." From what he could tell, her voice sounded puzzled from where she murmured against his collarbone. "Why do you think that is?"

He had no better answer for why she was acting non-Tanya-like than why he was acting un-Chad-ly. While he was thinking, he traced his fingers over the round scar at her hip of a bullet she'd once told him came from a Hamas shooter when she was still serving in Israel. Then up the long slice over her ribcage from a Mexican machete—a Sinaloa enforcer who hadn't lived out the next ten seconds. Finally the lightest brush over the slight puckering where he'd shot her.

"I'd take that one back if I could."

She nodded her belief of that.

Down over her back, to the lovely curve at the base of her

spine and a line—not on the skin, but beneath. He could feel the deeper scar tissue there.

"What's—" But she placed a fingertip over his lips, leaving it there until she was assured he wouldn't ask.

He traced the same route again, but she shuddered slightly when he traced that hidden line once more. After that, he kept his hand clear of it.

Slowly, ever so slowly, she relaxed and finally fell asleep in his arms.

He watched the long waterfall out the window as the sun moved across it. The steady flow was interrupted by gusts of wind up the canyon, or maybe whimsy of the water. With each tiny shift, it caught and reflected the sunlight in unexpected ways.

Was that what was happening? Had Tanya somehow shifted in the light?

Three years ago she had embodied the unexpected—the wildly sexy, outrageous warrior. Now she was something else.

And he wanted her more.

Ever so slowly, Chad retraced the line at her waist. Then as he let his hand drift up her back, he felt more lines. Deep, subtle, not on the skin but under it. They lay like a hidden map that he slowly followed while the sun splashed and the water shone.

The lines almost followed the twisting lines of the falling water.

But not quite.

Then he knew, and he couldn't suppress the cold chill of rage that ran through him.

He remembered Joncey. A jockey at Hazel Park race course, he'd won a horse race he was supposed to lose. He'd been whipped nearly to death, then dumped in the street near his and Wollson's squat. Joncey managed to live until the medics arrived —they were never in a real hurry to enter that neighborhood. He was DOA before they closed the ambulance's back doors. His back had been crosshatched with bloody gashes until there wasn't a patch of skin bigger than a man's palm that wasn't sliced. Whipped worse than any horse.

Tanya's back wasn't *that* cut up, but it was bad. And it was deep. Not with the cruelty of the cuts, but with age. How old had she been when she'd been given those scars? They were healed now and covered by clean skin. Only slow and tender inspection revealed the deeper scar tissue.

Revealed a past she had shrugged away like no more than an unpleasant memory.

Crap! And he thought that he'd had it hard growing up.

TANYA WOKE in a place she didn't recognize, couldn't recognize no matter how many times she blinked at it.

The hotel room lay in evening shadow, the sky just shifting to a darker blue. *La Capitana* had sent them here.

All that she understood.

Chad's arms still wrapped around her even as he slept…that she didn't understand at all. They'd slept together without sex. Without so much as heavy petting or even a kiss.

He was up to something.

But…what?

She couldn't imagine.

If taking such complete control of her body beneath the topiary had seemed utterly manipulative, then what was this?

If that *hadn't* been manipulation, but rather just sexual play, where was the overeager *quid pro quo?*

Or had it been a kindness—a gift—offering her a release unlike any before that moment? If it was the latter, then her current situation was even more confusing. Instead of being a friendly fuck between sex partners, it was the act of a companion. Of a lover. She had no history to equate that to. No frame of reference to even consider such a thing.

To fight beside Chad was a joy (other than being shot). To

screw both their brains out, that was great fun. But to have real meaning suddenly in bed with the both of them simply wouldn't do. *Very* dangerous rapids ahead.

Well, she knew how to cure that.

Chad had given her a great ride; it was time to move this whole thing back into that arena.

"Hang on, boy. One great ride coming up." Her whisper seemed to echo about the small room. She found the string of condoms that Sofia had insisted on tucking into the tiny med kit before Tanya had stuffed it in her pants pocket.

She took her time about it, teasing him awake. Half a dozen times she stopped just the moment before consciousness slipped in, letting him ease back into slumber. When he groaned in his dreams, when a smile touched his lips, that's when she sheathed his slow arousal and, lying full upon him, kissed him almost violently hard.

She'd come awake in his arms. Let him come awake in hers and see how he felt about it.

Between one heartbeat and the next, his deep blue eyes flashed open. Unlike her own hesitancy, he seemed to know exactly where he was and what he wanted.

Her attacking kiss was returned in kind—deep, penetrating, and undeniable.

One of his palms rode up over her behind and pulled her against him. It was easy to forget Chad's thoughtless strength until he used it. His big hand cradled her easily and held the sweet pressure solidly.

It was his other hand that distracted her. With the lightest of pressure, he traced his fingertips over her back. At first it was the contrast between the strength of one hand and the gentleness of the other that began firing her body up. The power and the thoughtfulness combined into a heady mix.

Slowly, so slowly, he traced a pattern across her back. A pattern that she'd forgotten until last night when he'd traced the buried scar tissue at the base of her spine.

Then it had been a mere twinge of recognition.

Now it was a hammer blow that had her jerking back. Driving her palms against his shoulders to get distance.

But she couldn't, because his big hand still clamped their hips together.

"I'm not asking," Chad's voice was husky and still rough from sleep.

"And I'm sure as hell not telling." No one knew except her mother and sister, and the surgeon she'd eventually paid to fix those scars. She didn't mind the battle wounds—they were badges of honor hard won. But a little girl whipped with her father's belt, that wasn't honor. She had tried to tackle her father as he abused Tanya's sister in other ways. He had thrown Tanya down and whipped her while he was still driven deep into Jimena. It had been a mark she'd been unwilling to wear.

Tanya had bled on the sheets all that night because her mother had not wanted the awkward questions that a hospital would ask. Hadn't wanted to lose her husband.

To hell with that, Mom.

Tanya's back had bled for the last time from the force of helping her father stumble in front of a garbage truck seven days later. Gone before he could desecrate Jimena's funeral with some stupid lies.

And now—

Her struggles to get away were futile against a man of Chad's strength.

"Let me go!" It came out as a snarl he didn't deserve but she couldn't alter.

He narrowed his eyes at her for a long moment before replying.

"No, I don't think so. Not this time. I'm not the one who marked you. And I'm not asking who was. But I think if I let you go, you won't be coming back and I'm finding that I don't like that thought much."

All she could do was snarl again.

"You see…" And there was the Chad tone again, "I don't give much of a shit about the Tanya of the past. No more than I care about the loser kid Wollson beat out of me until I left the little shit behind on the Detroit streets. Damn but that man was fast with a backhand when I screwed up, which I did plenty early on."

Tanya stopped fighting, but kept her arms straight and stiff against his shoulders as he continued to trace his free hand over her.

"Now *this* Tanya. This one I've had to do a lot more thinking about. You tell me I could find a better woman anywhere and I'm thinking I'm gonna have to laugh in your face. Besides, it would sound a mite bit disrespectful, seeing our current positions." He shifted his hips slightly side to side to remind her of where they were still pressed together.

All she had wanted was some good, distancing sex. Use each other and call it done. Because that she understood.

"Now, you wanna make love with me? I've got no complaints. I've been wanting that ever since you sailed away three years ago out on Lake Maracaibo. You want to lie back down and talk about something, guess I'm okay with that too. But you running away from me again—not so much down with that. Didn't even like it when you closed that bedroom door in my face a couple days back in Medellín."

Tanya glared at him…and believed him.

She'd gone out of her way to get Chad all fired up. And in the midst of that heat, which she could still feel where his big hand kept their hips pressed together, he was being kind and calm and rational.

"You promise you'll never ask?"

In reply, he kept his lips firmly sealed and didn't look away. But neither did he release her to cross his heart, which she'd been half-hoping for. Now, he held her in place because he wanted just one thing.

Sex. He wanted sex? Fine.

She shifted her position enough to line everything up and took him in.

It was difficult to hide her gasp of surprise. She'd forgotten how it felt to have Chad inside her. He filled her like no other man ever had. It wasn't mere physical scale, though Chad certainly didn't lack in that department at all. It was *the way* they fit together. As if their bodies had been specifically honed for one another—he wasn't a good fit, he was a *perfect* fit. The spread of his hips pressing against her inner thighs as she knelt over him. Their torsos that she knew could let her lie on his chest with her head tucked up against his chin or, like now, placed his lips upon her breast as she arched back and he rose to greet her.

A moment ago, she had wanted to flail against him and be done. Now, she wanted to mold her body to his and never let go. She scooped an arm about his neck to keep him in place and could feel the tug of his lips and tongue all the way down to her bones.

Burying her own face into his so-soft hair, she breathed him in. Breathed in the scent of the outdoors. No, of the wilderness that always seemed to cling to him.

When he began to move beneath her, she pushed him back to the bed and studied *his* chest with *her* lips.

It *was* a beautiful chest. Powerful, scarred but healed, definitely a chest only a top soldier could possess.

But it was more than that.

She lay her cheek upon his breastbone and could feel that chest. Could feel his arms about her—one still clamping their hips together, emphasizing every motion with the pressure. But the other wrapped around her back as if no marks of her failure lay beneath the skin. As if he'd never let go.

No wild rhythm took them over. Instead, the slow build lifted them millimeter by millimeter upward.

The long climb left Tanya time to think.

And time to feel.

Normally, sex for her was only about time to feel the ascent, the break, and the descent of a good release.

This time she felt what it would be like to lie with Chad one night after another. One year after another. What it would be like to be held by a man who understood that some wounds were too deep to talk about, especially in a world where most wounds were a badge of honor, not despair.

Tanya dug her fingers into his pecs and hung on as the slow build finally forced them apart—forced her back until a thin slice of air lay between their chests. A place where they didn't touch, but instead came together.

Chad's heat radiated off him as his chest heaved with a shortening breath. In contrast, hers ran slow and deep as if she was breathing all the way down to the soles of her feet, up her legs, through their joining deep inside her, and only then passing upward through her body.

This! This is what it felt like to have a man inside her—a Man with the capital M.

His release slammed her over the top. Because it would be impossible to contain the surge of energy he delivered. The wild energy streamed through her body, slamming her in its stormy passage until she could do no more than hang on and shudder.

This, some part of her mind echoed as life rolled through her.

Yes, *this* was something special. So outside her past experience that she didn't know how to think about it except for how good it was to be held and made love to by a man.

Did he love her?

That hadn't been just sex—he'd certainly made love *to* her. Was that the same thing? She didn't know. Tanya only knew that there had never been anything else like it in her life.

CHAD DIDN'T CARE about women.

He knew that for a fact.

He *enjoyed* women, but he didn't *care* about them.

Not while they lay together in the gathering twilight.

Nor a little later while taking her up against the cool tile wall in the tiny shower, which was far closer to what he'd expected than what they'd done in the bed.

Even over late-night dinner in a tiny *taberna* where they ate goat empanadas dipped in cheesy chile con queso with Silva and Daniela.

Chad Hawkins did *NOT!* care about women.

It was the code of his life.

So why was his leg pressed against Tanya's as they returned to the airport in the back of the Toyota SUV? Why the *hell* was he holding her hand rather than his rifle? Why was he trying to figure out how to join Kidon—it shouldn't be *that* hard to transfer from Delta Force. Should it?

And why did her quiet smile as they both boarded the Beech Bonanza airplane make him think about joining the mile-high club? Oh, he'd done it with a couple of stewardesses on a big jet, but he knew that with Tanya it would have a whole different meaning.

Meaning.

Sex wasn't supposed to have meaning. It was supposed to have…sex.

"What the hell have you done to me?" He whispered to her.

"You tell me, then I'll tell you and we'll both know." Tanya's dazed look was mitigated by the squeeze of her hand in his.

"You're making my head hurt, woman."

"You're making my *heart* hurt, man."

And…

Nope! He didn't have a good answer to that either.

The one thing he knew: he wasn't letting go this time no matter what.

Actually, two things. He would die to save her. Not the way he would for any of his teammates—because merely giving your all wasn't enough to qualify you for a Delta team. Delta was what it was because its operators treated every moment as a chance to go above and beyond.

But for Tanya Zimmer?

He'd take a bullet if it would just take a single one of those hidden scars off her soul.

And that didn't seem normal.

The Chad Hawkins he knew didn't care about women that way...except now it seems he did. And what the hell was up with that?

17

_T_hey flew north with the first hint of the sunrise, Silva at the controls and Daniela riding shotgun. However literal that was, she mainly faced forward and kept her thoughts to herself. Tanya sat with Chad in the second row of the three pairs of seats, narrow enough that her and Chad's shoulders brushed with each little bit of turbulence. It was very distracting, so she did her best to focus out the window.

Oddly the farther they flew from the heart of the Andes, the rougher the terrain became. Personally, Tanya had spent far more time in Venezuela over these last years, so the typical low-lying jungle there was more familiar, with its peaks that rarely crossed five hundred meters.

In Tulcán and Las Lajas, the landscape was alpine meadow and plateau—most of it near three thousand meters. The occasional river sliced down into it and the tops of the peaks struggled aloft, but they didn't climb far past the plateaus.

As they passed over Cali and then Medellín, the land dropped away but the peaks did not. They weren't as high, but they had resisted, held out against their inevitable demise.

She was going to avoid any personal metaphors here—the

terrain was just terrain, not some analogy for the razor-thin edge she walked as a Kidon operator. Nor for how even a few nights with Chad was carving changes in her body, in her life. Sure, her physical body reveled in his—the man was like a pure cocaine high. And the crash was far less harsh; she just hoped that it stayed that way.

He was also carving changes inside her, as if ferreting out the rage that she kept so close to drive her ahead. That she was less sure about. Rage was a very useful motivator. If she let that go, where would she be then?

The rivers were bigger here, carving wide valleys over time. (Chad had better not be doing that to her or they were going to have some harsh words. She didn't like people, lovers or otherwise, knowing too much about her.) Here, the cities no longer perched along farmland and flooded valleys. They hovered at river junctions where valleys met and spread up the hills until people etched the shape of the valley, rather than the jungle.

"What's that?" Chad was staring sharply downward out the window on his side.

First checking her side—but all she could see was jungle— she leaned across to look down on Chad's side. It meant pressing her body against him, which she thoroughly enjoyed. It should be a flirtatious tease—it always would have been before. Now it was backfiring badly. She wasn't enjoying the tease—she was simply enjoying it. Far too much!

At least until her eyes focused on the valley below.

They were over a slender river. Instead of showing as a meandering line, poking its way through the jungle, it was an unholy gash of gravel-gray mounds and vast pools of sludgy water.

"That," Daniela's voice was chill, "is the true scourge of Colombia."

"Illegal gold mining," Silva tipped the plane so that it would was easier for them to see.

Gravity made Tanya's body press harder against Chad.

"We have a long tradition of artisanal miners. All of their digging and extraction left few marks on the landscape. But now the militias and cartels take over the operations, enslave the miners, and use devastating extraction methods of dredges, mercury, and arsenic."

"We're a cartel now, aren't we?" Chad asked it in his ever-so-innocent voice.

Tanya approved of the "we," but it seemed more heavy-handed than his usual ploy. That wasn't like him.

"We are. But slavery and destruction are not on *my* cartel's agenda."

Tanya could feel the wince from Chad where their bodies pressed together.

"Besides," Daniela twisted to face them. "This operation belongs to *el Clan del Golfo.*"

"The ones you have a bounty on," Tanya remembered Fred Smith showing it to them.

Daniela raised one of those perfect eyebrows in question.

"I saw the flyer with the three stars. I thought the money looked good, but," Tanya poked Chad in the ribs, "he doesn't like splitting up the profits. I say we need to round up some of the old crew before we go after them."

"Old crew?" Daniela's voice almost went *la Capitana* chill as Silva began descending toward some yet distant airport.

"You know. Folks we've met on one job or another. Taking out the grand *jefe* of *del Golfo* isn't going to be easy or it would already be done. He's dug in deep and heavily protected. Someone already took down the other two. I want this."

"I'm telling you, woman, nothing protects them when I can touch them from a mile out," Chad hooked a thumb at his rifle that lay on the seat behind them.

Daniela considered him for a long time before responding.

"You may get your chance."

CHAD SPOTTED Sofia as they flew into the little airport, not that she made it hard.

He'd anticipated that the team would have put a tracker on the plane in the night. Or maybe Fred Smith had done his CIA thing to get a drone launched up high to keep an eye on them, or even a satellite feed. The team must have been airborne and done the old trick of following from in front. Silva hadn't made any dodging turns—had no reason to suspect. They'd climbed out of Ipiales and flown straight here…wherever here was.

It was bigger than a drug runner's jungle strip, but not by much. The nearby town wasn't more than a hundred houses and half again as many hovels.

Sofia, who couldn't have arrived more than a few minutes ahead of them, was slouched as if fast asleep in a faded red leather bucket car seat that was missing its car. It was propped against the front wall of a small cafe that boasted a strange variety of similar battered accommodations. The cafe smelled pretty damn good the moment Silva taxied the plane to a stop and opened the door. Sofia had her boots crossed on the dirt, an M4 rifle in her lap, and her long dark hair spilling forward over her nodding head. She also wore a battered straw cowboy hat with a brilliant, Macaw parrot-colored scarf for a hatband. It looked pretty cute on her. Of course just about anything would look cute on her—it was just the way she was.

Taking the bull by the horns, he shouted at her as soon as he was out of the plane.

"Sofia! Haven't seen you since the whole General Aguado mess." The greeting would tell her several things: they were using their real names and to play it as if they hadn't seen each other in a year. The team had met Sofia when she'd called them in to take down Aguado's sex trafficking operation. The only sex Aguado was getting now was up the backside from whatever hard cores the CIA had locked him up with. Couldn't happen to a more deserving guy.

Aguado's name also might be another clue for Daniela of the kind of experience they had as "criminals."

"Where's your worse half? And what the hell are you doing here? This is Nowheresville." She better have a good cover story, because Daniela was smart and suspicious. And Chad couldn't think of a thing.

"Don't tell him!" Duane stepped out of the cafe bearing a big plate of empanadas, an AK-47 slung over his shoulder. "You do and he'll just horn in on the job. Asshole still owes me three hundred from that last poker game."

"Just payback for the five you owed me."

"That was five, not five hundred. Asshole."

Then they embraced as if they hadn't seen each other in a year. It *was* damn good to see him, even if it had been only a day and two nights since they'd parachuted over Tulcán together. Chad would like to ask him about how he'd come to terms with partnering up with Sofia. But now wasn't the moment.

Whoa! *Never* was more likely the moment. He and Tanya were not partnering up in anything close to that kind of meaning. Sure, walk Kidon together. Do a little shooting and a little screwing together; they'd make a good pair-up. That's all he was looking for.

The other three had come up, and Chad didn't miss Silva's hand on his Uzi or Daniela's on her low-slung M16. Tanya was carrying both of their rifles, one over either shoulder and gripping the straps, making a show of having her hands full so that she wasn't a threat.

"Hey, Tanya," Duane waved at her. "Can't believe you're still hanging with this asshole. Who are these other people?" Duane growled. "They gonna try and horn in, too?"

"Depends what you're onto, buddy. Something six can do better than two?" Chad could feel Duane stretching it out just to mess with him. He tried to figure out how to warn Duane that Daniela wasn't exactly a patient woman.

"Shit! I knew it. You always were grubbing for a dollar. You remember Richie? No?" Duane didn't give him time to answer. "Bet you remember his copilot, Melissa—hot blonde chick? Gave us a lift. They had a couple hundred kilos of packages due out at Buenaventura on the coast, but he promised he'd be back tomorrow."

That was good. It meant Chad didn't have to explain the whole team at once but they'd be available fast if needed.

Chad glanced at Daniela, but she shook her head infinitesimally.

Yes! She was trusting him enough to tell him that the shipment wasn't one of hers. Of course, the fact that the "couple hundred kilos" of packages would be the Delta Force team and their gear, not cocaine, meant that it *absolutely* wasn't hers. But she wouldn't know that.

Sofia spoke up for the first time. "There's a gold shipment comes here out of the jungle somewhere every Thursday and into this airport. We didn't see any reason to not take delivery of it ourselves," Sofia finally took him off the hook and dropped the plan. She or the CIA must have done some fast work to figure that one out in time for her to deliver the line.

A good cover, and not a bad play. He could see Silva and Daniela relax another notch.

"Is this Thursday?" Chad had no track at all. Missions always did that to him. Time flowed by the mission, not the calendar.

Duane snorted in disgust. "What are *you* doing here? You got something better up your sleeve?"

"Gotta ask the lady," Chad nodded toward Daniela. "She's the main honcho on this one."

Daniela inspected him carefully. Then, with barely a glance at Duane and Sofia, she turned to face Tanya.

Tanya, being the warrior she was, took it right in stride that she would be Daniela's source of choice.

"Sofia, she's one very smart *chica*. I don't know how she does it, but she finds things out. The muscle? He was a shooter and breacher for the US Rangers until he blew up his commanding officer."

"I didn't blow him up," Duane growled.

"No," Tanya ignored him and kept talking to Daniela. "He blew up the man's Humvee—with him in it."

"Guy was an asshole," Duane muttered. "Was doing the Army a favor, but instead of a medal or even a bit of fucking praise, they came hunting my ass. Been chilling down here ever since."

"And that's where I found him," Sofia made it sound as if she was the one who'd found a way to make Duane useful for anything. Women in charge—Daniela should like that.

Besides, Sofia *had* found Duane. Then she'd fallen in love with him and married him.

Was that what Tanya was doing to him? Instead of just playing the smart one, was she doing some kind of unholy end run on him? He was gonna have to watch the woman like a freakin' hawk. He wasn't saying happily ever after...ever! Not even for a woman like Tanya.

"What about..." Daniela asked Sofia in her soft voice—the same one she'd used to tell him and Tanya to jump off the Las Lajas bridge to their death. "How do you feel about taking down the *source* of the gold instead of the shipment?"

Duane and Sofia exchanged a long look, then Duane laughed.

"Shit, Chad. I guess I do miss hanging out with you."

Chad offered his best smarmy smile and stole an empanada off Duane's plate.

"Still owe me three hundred," Duane growled as he handed one of the pastries to each of the others before heading back into the cafe to get more for himself.

18

"What do you think she's thinking?" Chad's whisper was soft enough that it barely earned them a glance from an anteater rooting through an old log with his strong claws and sticky tongue.

Tanya wished she knew.

The jungle at midday was quiet, for a jungle. Some monkeys were chattering as they moved through the canopy far above— probably tamarins by the high pitch. She knew not to look up too often because, in a towering jungle, it was a sure-fired path to a vertigo-induced headache. The trees climbed forever. The vines wound around them. The animal and bird life flew in and out of the massive biomass. It was always a little startling. A small flock of parakeets settled on a branch for mere seconds to observe them before flitting aloft. And to the west, a soft ripple of the river.

There was an underlying note. Still a mile off, it was no more than a basso rumble. But it was steady, a low waterfall roar that came from no river. It was the low note of the miners' machines.

She and Chad had been sent to circle south so that they'd

approach from upriver when they turned back to the north. Sofia and Duane had been sent in the opposite direction. And *la Capitana* had gathered a force of ten fighters of her own to come at them from the side. They looked to be a ragtag crew, but hung on Daniela's every word and handled their weapons with the ease of experience.

Her rules had been simple: "Capture at least one leader alive—damaged is acceptable. Kill the fighters. And if you kill a single unarmed miner, you will join them in the grave."

Not the ruthless cartel leader, but perhaps a vengeful one.

"Daniela definitely has it in for *del Golfo*," Tanya summarized. "The bounty poster. Attacking this gold mining operation. It would be an easy bet that this operation is one of their largest as well. What does she have so against them? Something doesn't fit."

"I know. That itch is there, but I can't seem to pin it down."

Tanya had a couple of itches. She didn't believe in "women's intuition" for one second—she'd spent far too long honing her fighter's instincts to waste time thinking that some sixth sense held any useful answers. But even her highly-trained operator was definitely looking for a place to scratch.

Daniela and *la Capitana* were such a contrast—at one turn, a pleasant, thoughtful beauty and at the next, the cold-blooded leader of one of the biggest cartels functioning in South America. If she was all the latter, it would be easy to justify taking her down along with her operation. But most of the time she was the former. It was puzzling.

Which was better than her other itch. Her feelings about Chad had shifted into downright confusing.

The sex? Incredible.

The missions? Challenging.

The man? Thoughtful, handsome, kind.

The man's reactions to her? At one moment she felt like the most admired woman in the world who was being offered the Princess' Dream Package of happy ever after with a great man

—as if she'd ever want such a thing. The next moment Chad acted and spoke as if he was down in the blocks practicing the start for his sprint away from her.

She supposed that last part was fair. Right now she was leaning strongly toward the sprint-away option as well.

"What's she thinking? I just can't pin it down." For Daniela or herself. "When Gerald the Boatman ran his operation, he made a point of cooperating with everyone: suppliers, downstream delivery, and middlemen. I can't tell if *la Capitana* is in competition with *del Golfo,* has some grudge against them, or wants them completely erased from the face of the Earth and sent to hell in a suitcase."

"Handbasket. Any of the three is fine with me. Got no prob taking them out." He wove through a line of saplings that were battling for ownership of a small sunlit patch where a giant of the jungle had punched a hole when it had crashed down.

"Well, it makes a difference." At the first glimmer of the river through the trees, they turned to follow the bank north, staying well inside the jungle's edge.

"Why?" Chad spoke a little louder to overcome the steadily increasing roar of the mining equipment. As they moved closer, the wildlife dissipated like smoke on the wind.

"What *did* they teach you in Delta school?"

Chad held up his rifle. "Bang! Bang! You're dead."

"It's not *del Golfo* we're in bed with."

"Wouldn't mind being back in bed with you. Real soon. Without a whole lot of interruptions. You want to put both of us in *la Capitana's* bed? I'm game."

Tanya sighed. She wouldn't mind curling up with Chad for an uninterrupted week or three—even if she couldn't remember the last time she'd taken any holiday at all. But a *ménage* with Daniela? What kind of an asshole suggested such things? There didn't seem to be any way for getting Chad out of doofus mode.

He stopped so suddenly that she ran into his back, nose first.

She raised her rifle and began scanning for what he'd seen that she'd missed, but he turned to look at her.

"Tanya. What the hell happened to your sense of humor, woman? The only lady I want is the one about two inches away from me."

He didn't even pause long enough for her to gasp in surprise.

"Daniela wants *el Clan del Golfo* gone? Good riddance. As to her motivation? Option One: taking them down because they're competitors? Doesn't feel right. Option Two: she has a grudge against them? Makes me think a little better of her. Option Three: wants the entire Clan removed from the face of the map? That gets interesting. I'd love to hear why. Option Four: What if she's taking them out to help or hurt someone else? That's more complex and the answer could teach us a lot. Option Five: None of the above. And that's the one that's fascinating me. We've taken down a lot of drug lords since I joined the team. Took down a lot in Detroit too—Wollson felt it was our duty to the city. Always quiet, always on the sly. He was fighting for some higher cause that took me a hell of a long time to understand. What if something like that's her motivation, huh? Could be really good or really bad."

Then he turned and began patrolling forward once more. They didn't have long to get into position—again no radios, they were doing this strictly by the clock.

Her training made it automatic for her to fall into step behind him: check right, check left, a glance over the shoulder for anyone approaching, glance down to check that they were leaving no footprints, check right, check... Training was the only reason she didn't stand there numb until Chad had passed out of sight around the bole of a mahogany or behind a clump of banana or mango.

And in that moment Chad had demonstrated that Delta Force operators were far above average intelligence as well as top fighters. He made it easy to forget that about him, but it wasn't any less true.

He was absolutely right. If Daniela wasn't following any of the predictable paths for cartel leaders, then they had to find out what she *was* thinking. And—Tanya hated to admit it—but her *woman's intuition* told her that Daniela was anything but predictable.

Then she stared at Chad's back.

Speaking of unpredictable!

The only woman I want is the one two inches from me?

He'd said it as if it was simple truth.

When had that happened?

So MUCH OF Delta training was about timing. The enemy's timing. The attack's timing. Timing of actions between team members.

And suddenly his timing sucked.

They were about to go down on *el Clan del Golfo*, one of the best organized, most dangerous cartels running. Those guys used military discipline and ranking. They paid, even rewarded their people fairly. Infighting was rooted out with brutal harshness. They were a well-tuned machine—that had somehow drawn the ire of *la Capitana*.

And what had he just done?

Practically told Tanya that he loved her. He'd *never* wanted just one woman. Not that he'd had two all that often—though the Nakamura twins had left behind some particularly good memories. But that didn't mean he wasn't typically thinking about who the next woman might be before he'd left the present one behind.

With Tanya, he wanted *her*.

Not someone else. Not even the Nakamura twins, with their gymnastic flexibility, lovely lithe bodies, and thick cascades of midnight hair down to their tight butts. He wanted the blonde Kidon assassin in the khakis and body armor.

And he didn't want her for just this mission. Or just this week. Or—

Duane was gonna laugh his ass off.

19

*T*he river was a disaster area.

Chad knew that the big operations used mercury and cyanide to separate the gold out of the ore. That poisoned the water. Any fish that survived would be lethal to the fisherman.

But he'd never seen a big operation up close.

Normally the jungle overhung the banks of these small rivers. Here it had been knocked back forty meters to either side —half a football field—in places, even more. The narrow river was now caught in massive pools turgid with sludge, separated by vast dikes of chewed up dirt and gravel. It flowed, but in no relation to its original course. Silt-gray backwaters, massive eddies where the bank had been dug away—it was a meandering disaster.

Hundreds of workers were spread over the area doing incomprehensible tasks. Some wielded hammers, others hoses. But most of them appeared to be inspecting the contents of sluices—sloped troughs made of battered metal or even worse-battered wood. People fought heavy wheelbarrows into the head of the sluices. At the same time, a pair of massive excavators dumped bucketloads into industrial scale sluices. Daniela had confirmed there were no roads into the area and the river wasn't navigable—even before they tore it up. How in the world they managed to get the massive machines in here was a mystery.

The excavators had long flat-plate treads, bright yellow cabs, and long black bucket arms that might have once said John Deere. They were the sort of machines used to take down old shopping malls or dig basements for new skyscrapers.

Closest to his and Tanya's position was a floating dredge. It was like a large, two-story cabin on a pair of long pontoons. The pontoons were far enough apart that two powerful conveyor belts ran through the gap between them. One dipped down from the rear end into the river. It was a chain of large buckets scooping up stones and muck from the river bottom. Silt-gray water spilled everywhere as the buckets lofted up high enough to be dumped down onto the second conveyor. It, in turn, extended far out the other end of the central cabin, reaching past the bows of the pontoons to deliver a massive pile of wet rock onto the shore. There it was scooped up by the wheelbarrow workers and excavators and fed into crushers before it flowed down the sluices for inspection and hand sorting.

Diesel fumes made a dark, choking cloud in the midst of the pristine jungle. The normally blue sky was gray-brown. The workers were as gray as the slurry they worked with.

"Check out the clean ones," Tanya whispered from close beside him.

Sure enough, there was a contingent of people who, while not exactly clean, weren't gray with river waste. *El Clan del Golfo's* enforcers. The "clean ones" were also the ones with weapons. Those covered in gray were armed only with the tools of their trade.

"Seven minutes," Tanya reminded him.

La Capitana's plan had been simple. Overwhelm the militia with surprise and superior force in order to capture them. The superior force wasn't gonna happen, the enforcers outnumbered *la Capitana's* crew by three-to-one—or would if four of them weren't Delta.

"Doesn't seem very fair," Chad commented.

"Because they've made themselves such easy targets?"

"No," Chad smiled to himself. Even Kidon assassins didn't understand some things about Delta. At least not yet.

Chad sighted through his rifle's scope on where he would expect Duane and Sofia to arrive from their downriver approach. Sure enough, there they were, a half mile away.

"It isn't fair to just take them down. It takes the fun out of it, don't you think?"

"What are you talking about?"

This could be a fairly simple operation—using the team's sniper skills to pick them all off one by one. But Delta was about applying *overwhelming* force, not merely sufficient force.

Even as he watched, Duane and Sofia slipped from hiding and headed for the nearest excavator.

"Let's play with them a little," he whispered to Tanya, but didn't bother waiting for her reply. No way was Duane going to one-up him on this.

The dredge was out in the open, the center of its own circle of devastation. There would be no stealthy approach. Instead, Chad slung his rifle as if at absolute ease with his uncontested authority. The gravel had been bludgeoned into rough paths, making it easy to stride along. He could hear the crunch of Tanya falling in behind him.

As he walked, he ignored the workers completely; they didn't even look at him askance. He waved to one of the guards, who waved back uncertainly. There were enough of them around that they wouldn't necessarily all know each other. Almost all were Colombian-native dark, but there a few outlier mercenaries. None as light blond as him and certainly no one to match Tanya, but they only needed a few moments of doubt to make this work.

He ignored everyone else and focused on the dredge itself. It had several big hoses. Two led down the dredging arm, probably blasting away at the riverbed to loosen the gravel and rocks for the bucket dredge to lift. But the two hoses that interested him were up in a turret on the roof of the cabin. They were right where the bucket dredge dropped its rocks onto the shoreward conveyor. These hoses would be used for cleaning the equipment (a purpose for which they were clearly never used), and blasting out mud jams caught in the machinery.

"Well, lady. Last time you drove, you ran me over and we ended up falling out of a helicopter and over a waterfall. You want to redeem your reputation?"

"You're joking," Tanya spoke softly from behind him—her voice perfectly gauged to carry over the roar of the dredge's motor and grinding rocks, and no more.

But he could hear the smile in her voice. Damn but he wished he could turn to see it on her face. She didn't use it much, but her smile could melt steel. It hadn't taken much for her to get with the program. Not much at all, because Delta-level crazy was completely in her nature.

Chad's internal clock estimated that they were down to thirty seconds on *la Capitana's* mission clock as they jumped aboard the floating craft where one pontoon floated close by the shore.

An enforcer—identified by the pistol at his belt—stuck his head out one of the doors.

"*Hola, amigo.*" Chad had to shout over the grinding of the machinery as he clapped an arm around the guy's shoulders, pinning his arms to his sides, and stepped him back inside. Lunch was set out on a small table, four other enforcers around the table. Rifles hung over the backs of chairs…and the men were all relatively clean. He didn't have a lot of time, so he shot the four at the table with a silenced Glock. The guy he'd kept immobilized with a crushing sidearm embrace, he kneed in the crotch to take him out of action—then tied and gagged him. *La Capitana* said she wanted one alive.

A woman came out of a small door that must lead to a galley. Her hands were full with a big platter heaped high with *patacones, empanadas,* and other delicacies. He stepped over, took a *patacone*—he had a real weakness for fried plantain—and took a big bite, searing the roof of his mouth.

"Damn good," he told her. "Better than they ever deserved."

She looked at the four dead men still sprawled in their chairs and the bound one groaning at Chad's feet. She then offered him a radiant smile that lit up her plain, dark face—wide and flat, marking her as truly indigenous.

When he held a finger up to his lips, she smiled again.

"When it starts," she'd know what he meant when it happened, "just walk away from the boat as if you were doing a normal errand. *Sí?*"

"*Sí!*" She agreed and gestured for him to take another *patacone.* Then she dumped the rest of the contents on the table and smashed the stoneware platter against the head of the one on the floor. He stopped groaning—probably for good. *La Capitana* would have to get her survivor somewhere else.

The woman nodded that she was ready.

Chad stepped back out onto the pontoon supporting this side of the central structure just in time to see Tanya step into the small control cabin on the second level. A body tumbled out the door and dropped into the water. It didn't move when it resurfaced.

Moments later, the dredge began turning in place, and Chad knew she had control. The conveyor, which had been dumping a steady stream of gravel- to head-sized rocks onto the ground, slewed sideways. In moments, it had buried a pair of ATVs and the men who'd been sitting in them cleaning their rifles.

When he heard a soft, "Hey!" shouted even louder than the grinding dredge, he knew it was time to hurry.

He climbed the two-story steel ladder to the operations level atop the cabin's roof. The hoses here were three-inch monsters —more appropriate for a team of firefighters, but there was only one of him. He braced himself against a stanchion of the dredge's structure and unleashed the nozzle.

It bucked so hard that it required everything he had to not lose control of the hose and be tossed overboard. The water pressure made it want to flail and fishtail. But once he had control of it, he was able to look around.

They must have been gathering for lunch. A dozen guys with rifles still slung over their shoulders stood looking up at him in surprise. He raked the hose across them, sending them flying head over heels to the rocks. Only one tried to get up, but Chad hit him square in the chest and slammed him back to the ground.

The cook from the boat jumped ashore and shouted for other miners to help her make sure the enforcers stayed down.

Tanya continued turning the ungainly dredge.

Chad spotted a man leaping onto the pontoon and scrambling up the vertical ladder to Tanya's position. Chad leaned out enough to clear the edge of the roof and blasted the man. He flew off the ladder and plummeted into the murky river. Each time he refloated, Chad drove him back under with the blast of hose spray until he returned to the surface back-first and remained in that position.

He heard the roar of the engines as the dredge lumbered forward. It had a clear run of only a few hundred feet, but it began gaining momentum.

Able to slash at either bank equally, Chad used his hose to blast any soldiers. The miners figured out what was happening fast enough. Each enforcer that Chad slammed to the ground, the miners were all over in moments.

Chad saw Tanya's wave, leaning out the control room door.

He didn't have time to even acknowledge her. *Del Golfo's* enforcers had finally shaken off their lethargy and were starting to fire at them.

He slashed to the left and took out a trio of armed men.

To the right, he blasted a woman square in the face as she sighted her rifle in Tanya's direction. The blast drove her through a full, backward flip—until she landed facedown. A miner's shovel finished the work.

He glanced up seeking more targets.

Duane and Sofia were driving the big excavator forward—Sofia at the helm and Duane shooting anyone dumb enough to aim at Duane's wife. The man was so protective of her. It wasn't as if Sofia needed protecting—but something in Duane did that anyway.

Protecting Tanya?

She'd kick his ass if he even tried. *Damn it!* Yet another thing to like about the woman—feisty as hell.

Tanya glared at the cabin roof.

She was going to kill Chad.

Not shoot him through the thin plywood. No! She was going to stand face to face and dismember him one piece at a time.

Half the windows of the dredge's control room had been shot out. The glass was no more than a series of crazed cracks radiating out from holes that pure luck had kept from aligning with her head. She could only see what was happening by popping her head up above the control console long enough to peep out one of the tiny round holes. Mostly 5.56 mm caliber—though there was an ominous .50 cal hole that had punched sideways through one window and out the other, the round passing so close to her nose that it still felt sunburned by the heat of the bullet's close passage.

Up!

Peek!

Down!

Analyze what she'd seen.

Sofia's excavator had walked right over two of the biggest sluices, crushing them beneath the massive treads. With the bucket arm, she'd broken up a couple of the temporary dikes formed by the piles of gravel—the river leapt across and washed out a whole enforcer group.

The operator of a smaller backhoe-loader hadn't been paying attention and barely managed to bail out before Sofia ran the bucket's big teeth straight down into the cab, shattering the machine. As she raked it down, a fuel tank was breached, and in a moment, the backhoe was engulfed in flames.

Up!

Peek!

Down!

Three more rounds came in from the left, where Tanya didn't even have a flimsy plywood door for protection. She looked out in time to see Chad blast the two shooters with his big fire hose. They went down hard—hard enough that they were never getting back up.

The glance ahead had also showed that she was slightly off course.

She reached up a hand to goose the right engine throttle. But there was no longer a control there—just a shredded stub of the shot-off wooden handle. Good news that she hadn't been holding it at the time. Instead, she had to accept slowing down the left engine slightly—the only two controls she was sure of.

Up!

Peek right!

Down!

La Capitana's forces were moving in from the jungle's sharp-hacked edge. All attention was focused on the dredge and excavators, making their job easier.

Sofia was taking on the other big excavator, bucket to bucket. They were slashing at each other with steel arms that could reach out over two car lengths, wielding massive toothed buckets weighing tons.

Up!

Down!

A line of bullets raked across the windshield and finally knocked it out—covering her in a shower of glass while she huddled.

Another spate of fire.

Then she jumped up and dropped three enforcers with her sniper rifle—so close, she barely had to aim.

That earned her a moment of peace to survey the situation.

She'd gotten into the main flow of the river and the dredge accelerated. Right on target. Time to bail out.

Tanya leaned out into the open and yelled at Chad again to get his attention.

She did, but only for a moment as he whipped his hose around.

The man looked like a goddamn Greek god! His feet were braced wide on the cabin roof. The hose, as big around as her own arm, bucked against his every move. His arms bulged with muscle to wield it, but he did—like Thor wielding his hammer that no other person could lift. His t-shirt soaked by back spray left him looking naked. And he had a feral grin as he slammed down one target after another. His occasional barks of laughter were even louder than the still grinding dredge or the roar of the fire hose.

A rattle of gunfire turned her attention back to her own survival.

Two shooters had dug in behind boulders with their backs to the dredge and were targeting Duane and Sofia. *That* was unacceptable.

Tanya veered the dredge. The long front conveyor dumped half a ton of rocks on their heads. One pontoon crunched against the shore before she could veer it back into the stream. Though she was slammed forward against the console by the impact, the dredge was heavy enough that it pushed through and once more flowed with the river's main current. It wallowed like a hippopotamus stuck in its mud wallow, but it dragged itself free.

She ducked her head out and shouted at Chad once more. "We need to abandon ship! Now!"

He nodded in her direction, but she could tell that he hadn't heard her words.

Sofia managed to spin her excavator's cabin and arm through a full circle, crashing it into the other cab at speed. The second excavator died along with its operator. In an apparent rage, Sofia began using her bucket to disassemble the other excavator—tearing off sheet metal, shearing hydraulic hoses, and finally tearing up the motor itself.

La Capitana's people were busy clearing out the last of the enforcers.

And the dredge's time was running very short.

Again she tried to signal Chad.

Again he ignored her!

She really was going to have to kill him.

Tanya checked the dredge's heading one last time, then scrambled out the door.

A jump to safety—a bulge in the gravel bank—lay just ten meters ahead.

A glance aloft. The god of water was still chewing up the last of the troops.

Mierda!

She raced up the ladder—and almost caught a blast of the hose in her face. Managing to duck clear at the last moment, she rose to stand beside Chad.

"We have to get off!"

"One more! Just one more!" And he pummeled another shooter to the ground. The enforcers were few and far between now, but their attention was aimed at Sofia's excavator and *la Capitana's* troops coming out of the trees.

No one was looking at the dredge sliding down the river behind them. It was a perfect vantage.

Except for one detail…

Chad flattened a machine-gun nest. Then another dug-in shooter. Smashing them in the back with his brutal lance of water.

For half a moment, Tanya hung on to his arm and felt his power. Felt his skill. He was masterful. Never had she met anyone with skills to match or even exceed her own. Not even the fearsome Carla. But Chad she could spend a lifetime living up to his standards.

A lifetime?

A crazy thought for the moment…especially as the answer was yes.

And then she knew…that half moment's hesitation had been too long.

"Hang on!" She shouted at Chad and she wrapped both arms around his and held on for all she was worth.

The nose of the dredge dipped down.

It wasn't much of a waterfall, no more than three stories, but as the nose went down, the dredge's stern went up until they were five or six stories above the pool far below.

"You gotta be kidding! Not again!" Chad shouted as he cast aside the hose and wrapped both of his arms about her.

She buried her face in his chest and took a deep breath.

The fall seemed to last forever.

Soon, the dredge was falling vertically, nose down.

The long boom of the unloading conveyor entered the water first. When it hit bottom, it rammed the back of the conveyor straight at them like a massive spear.

Chad tugged her aside with millimeters to spare.

Then the dredge began to flip. Having buried its nose at the base of the waterfall, it was going to land upside down in the pool.

Standing on the rear of the cabin roof, it flung them out into the air.

Straight at the rocky shore five stories below.

Barely, just barely, they landed in the rushing river instead. Deep under water, surfacing just as the current dragged them downstream.

Tanya managed to turn in time to see the dredge crash upside-down behind them. The long rear-digger boom collapsed into the water not three paces behind them.

As they swam, then waded ashore, Chad muttered at her.

"Woman driver."

But the way he had held her as they fell, and the way he kissed her now in the shallows of the river, she knew that she had completely fallen for him.

One Kidon assassin going down.

And going down happy.

20

"They throw a hell of an impromptu party, bro."

"Damn straight, dude," Duane agreed with him.

The four of them lounged on a broad boulder along the flowing river. It was pleasantly sun-warmed, now that the sun had slid behind the jungle canopy. Evening would be falling soon.

Duane had laid some breaching charges on the second excavator—after Sofia had finished tearing up the other equipment with it. And now, in the light of the late afternoon, its fire was finally dying down as well.

He'd expected the miners to be pissed at all of the destruction, but it had turned out not. Most were little better than slaves, dragged in from farming, forestry, or simply having lives. The few who were miners by choice had always run small operations that didn't run by large machinery or use poisonous chemicals.

The people had celebrated. Food, even alcohol, had appeared from hidden caches until there was plenty for everyone. *La Capitana* was being celebrated as were her team of shooters. It had taken them a long time for their own Delta team to slip into the background so that they could sit alone and talk.

"What about the future though? What's to stop *del Golfo* from rolling right back in here tomorrow?"

Chad was sorry he'd asked. The other Delta looked saddened by the thought. They might have set back this one operation, but there were dozens of others and the setback wouldn't last long. Soon, new equipment and new enforcers would arrive in this corner of wilderness.

"We will give them something else to think about," Daniela stepped up and joined their circle.

"Like the sound of that." And Chad did. It was a good tactic —once you get an enemy on the run, keep them running. "You got a plan for that, do you?"

Daniela nodded. It was hard to think of her as *la Capitana*, even with the shattered and burning mining operation spread behind her. There was something noble about her that he couldn't pin down. Maybe Tanya knew. He'd have to remember to ask her later.

"Gonna tell us?" Tanya did an imitation of his voice that had Duane and Sofia laughing. A smile briefly touched Daniela's lips, but only for a moment.

"You are exceptional fighters."

"Best training in the world, the American military," Chad agreed.

"Yeah, until they boot your ass," Duane hadn't forgotten his role. "What did you go down for again, mate?"

"Rolling a Marine Corps major's wife," Tanya answered for him with just the right amount of irritation.

"Think he was more upset about his Mercedes. He was just a Marine after all. Couldn't really expect to keep a hot woman."

"Might you four be interested in another mission?" Daniela didn't join in any of the humor. In fact, if Chad was reading her right, she knew something that was making her ignore their stories. Again, couldn't put a finger on it.

"Still haven't been paid for the last one," Sofia nodded toward the devastation surrounding them.

Daniela reached into a small pack and tossed a small cloth bag to each of them.

Chad caught his. Weighed about the same as thirty rounds of 7.62 mm ammo, close to a kilogram. He peeked inside and the rich luster of pure gold winked back at him. A kilo of untraceable gold—a market value of over thirty thousand US.

"Hard to argue with that," Duane's comment was carefully neutral.

Chad glanced at him. Something was up, but he wasn't sure what. The gold felt heavy in his hand, heavier than it should have.

Sofia and Tanya shared a look, then turned to inspect the miners and freed workers who were still joking around and enjoying themselves. Today had been a good day for them. Tomorrow, they'd be back to work. Perhaps at the tasks of their choosing, but back to work.

Tanya was the first to toss her bag of gold back to Daniela. "Already paid me enough," she nodded toward the celebrants.

Sofia and Duane looked thoughtful, but Chad waited them out.

"Going to you?" Sofia asked.

"Going to the people," Daniela replied, still holding Tanya's bag in her palm.

Sofia handed hers over and a reluctant Duane followed suit. As serving members of the US military, they wouldn't be allowed to keep it anyway; but that wasn't the point.

Chad made a show of looking into the bag again. He pulled out a single nugget the size of the end of his thumb, then tossed the rest of it back.

"Just something to remember this by," he buttoned it in one of his pants' pockets. Her look completely softened. Just for an instant, Daniela was a beautiful young woman, alive with hope. He offered her a wink. Then *la Capitana* slammed back into place and the dangerous beauty was again watching him carefully.

Hope?

Why had his tucking away a bit of gold made her hopeful?

He'd thought to put it in the battered ammo box where he kept odd bits and pieces: the cartridge casing of the round that took down the last of Wollson's killers, the pin of the first grenade he ever tossed in combat, the medals he'd been awarded but had nowhere to wear, the stone from his shoe on the brutal final hike of Delta Force qualification, a small chunk of marble from one of the many holes he'd blown in the headquarters of Venezuela's SEBIN—their secret police. Oddly, now that he thought about it, there wasn't one bit of memorabilia about any woman in there. Well, soon there'd be a bit of gold. *La Capitana* was a woman worth remembering.

Tanya and Sofia were also looking at him oddly.

He glanced at Duane and tipped his head enough to ask, "Any idea what's up with them?"

Duane offered back a microscopic "You got me, man" shrug.

Well, he didn't know either. How was a guy supposed to read women anyway?

21

"*Y*ou are a very fine fighter yourself," Sofia addressed Daniela as they were walking back through the jungle by lantern light.

Tanya hadn't seen any of that. She'd been too busy during the battle except to notice that disciplined fire had flown from the tree line. Now she considered. Daniela had not lost a single shooter—not even a scratch. They had taken down an unexpectedly large force without injuring a single worker. And Daniela had captured *del Golfo's* camp leader—only slightly damaged. Her troops had then swept the wide area to make sure that every other enforcer was dead, someone even swimming into the pool at the base of the waterfall to check on the bodies Chad had told them about.

That was her man, taking down five attackers before the fight even began.

Her man?

For half a second, as he'd pocketed that bit of gold, she'd thought it might be for the ring he'd joked about replacing—the ring he'd only given her, then lost, as part of their cover story.

But he hadn't looked at her. Instead he'd winked at the beautiful Daniela. Was that why he'd done his Mister Studly Firehouse-Wielder act? To get *Daniela's* attention? If ever there was a master of mixed messages, Chad Hawkins was it.

Could she trust him? *Ever?*

Tanya's heart twisted with the answer. She couldn't see how it would be possible.

"I also was trained by the American military," Daniela spoke softly. Tanya actually stumbled into Sofia in surprise. Grabbing onto her shoulder was probably all that kept them both from falling.

Tanya looked around, but Chad and Duane were farther up the line with Silva and a couple of *la Capitana's* other fighters. The only people around them were the miners: some singing, some laughing, a few just glad to be slogging home without fear in their hearts.

"Do you know the history of Gerald the Boatman's demise?"

Tanya had heard it once, but couldn't recall the details.

"Washington Prado Álava was enticed out of Ecuador." Of course Sofia would know everything, including his real name. "Ecuador has a mostly nonfunctional extradition treaty with the US, but Colombia has a strong one. He was drawn to Cali, where he was captured and shipped out."

"And do you recall how he was enticed?" Daniela's voice had gone hard, though she continued to walk like the commander she was.

"You?" Sofia gasped out the question as something clicked in that neatly ordered brain of hers.

"What?" Tanya didn't know this story.

"You were the beautiful undercover agent of the Colombian military that he fell in love with?"

"*Dios mío!*" Tanya barely managed.

"I was sent to woo the man. To let him have *me* so that they could have *him*. He fell in love with me and I betrayed him." Her voice didn't show the least hint of emotion.

"That must have been hard."

"I wish I had killed the bastard myself," her voice came out as a hiss as she stumbled to a halt by a towering wax palm. They had broken into a clearing awash with moonlight and dotted with the odd trees. Twenty stories tall, with smooth trunks and a tuft of huge leaves at the very top. In the moonlight, they looked like dim guideposts for giants who got lost in the night.

Tanya didn't know what to say. By her silence, neither did Sofia.

"My grandparents were victims of the FARC militia seizing their farm. My parents were bystanders wiped out by *Los Urabeños*. I wanted every one of the bastards taken down. Slowly. Painfully. So I joined the Colombian War on Drugs."

"But—" Tanya wondered how she could stand to be a cartel leader then?

"But what did I get? I spread my legs for that bastard Gerald for the greater good. Then when I returned, they treated me as if *I* was the slut." She pounded a fist against her breastbone. "I was the one who took him down. But it was my commander who received the medal. It was that bastard Vicente who received the promotion to captain. And when I complained, he tried to rape me because I was an 'easy' woman. Now they will all pay."

And she stormed off along the trail, rapidly covering the ground to catch up with the other group.

"*La Capitana,*" Tanya whispered half to herself.

"She took the name of the rank that she had actually earned."

They followed in Daniela's wake. The set of the woman's shoulders said to leave her alone, so they did—offering companionship and silence.

Just before they passed out of the moonlight and once more entered the jungle, Tanya exchanged glances with Sofia.

It was clear that they both liked Daniela, despite their assignment to bring down her operation.

The pity was, there wasn't anything they could do about that.

22

"*W*omen are treating us strange, bro."

"Women are treating *you* strange, dude," Duane answered him back as he cleaned his gun.

Chad didn't like that answer much. Not much at all.

Well past midnight, they were the only two awake, sitting in the car seats in front of the jungle airstrip's cafe. He was on a green-and-gold front bench of a Galaxie 500—probably a '67 or '68. Duane was in a black bucket that came from a '72 Olds 442. Chad recognized them from his chop shop days. That had been honest work in comparison to drug money and had kept him and Wollson alive…until it hadn't.

"Started at the gold thing," Duane was mulling the thought over.

"I thought it was after the fire hose."

"Nah, that was cool. I notice you aren't cleaning your rifle."

"Didn't fire it." But he had taken it swimming with him. He swung it across his lap, fished out a cleaning kit, and began disassembling it more for something to do than any need. Then he remembered the four rounds out of his Glock handgun. He fished out four new rounds and popped the magazine to reload it. He must be losing it to not have done that right away. Even *thinking* about women was causing problems.

"It was the gold thing," Duane said after Chad had finished reloading the Glock, then decided he'd better clean that as well and began breaking it down across the car seat. They'd both been trained to do this in the dark, while talking about something else, while hanging upside down by their ankles. Not quite, but Delta training sometimes felt that way.

"What, because I kept a half ounce out of four kilos?"

"Your bag only weighed a kilo? I knew she liked me better; mine must have weighed two."

"Let Sofia hear you say shit like that and you're gonna be down a hole, bro."

"Don't say that kind of shit around Tanya either, dude."

Chad finished running a rag through the barrel of the Glock, then sighted through it at the moon. Then wished he hadn't—thing was damn bright. At least the barrel was clean as he blinked against the bright afterimage knocking the center vision out of his right eye.

Duane was still fussing with the bolt of his rifle.

"Why do I have to be careful around Tanya? We're cool."

Duane scoffed. "I never would have guessed it. You really *do* know less about women than I do. That's sad, dude."

"Now what shit are you slinging?"

"Genuine Grade-A USDA certified kind."

Chad offered a scoff, but didn't really feel it as he accidentally tried to pick up the bolt for his Remington that he'd disassembled first and latch it into the receiver of his Glock.

"You getting down with Tanya yet?"

"Why should I tell you, asshole?"

"Because now you've picked up your barrel and receiver without grabbing the slide first."

Chad looked down at his hands. Somehow they'd forgotten how to put a Glock back together. He could field strip, reassemble, and fire one in under fifteen seconds if he had to. Now, suddenly, he couldn't do it at all.

"So, you and Tanya?"

"Yes. But I'm not telling you a single goddamn detail."

"Spoilsport. Of course, as a man lucky enough to be married to Sofia, I don't have to seek any of my thrills vicariously. I've got the best that a man could ever want in my bed."

"Then why aren't you there with her?"

"Because you're out here being all weird in the moonlight, Chad. Why aren't you off with Tanya?"

"Because. Woman is treating me all strange. Told ya."

"When you did it, was it good?"

"Don't need a goddamn therapist." This time he was holding the Glock's magazine and the rifle's barrel. In complete disgust, he closed his eyes, cleared his head, and slapped the Glock together in under ten seconds. He chambered a round, popped the magazine, and replaced the extra round before slamming it into his holster. Now he could work on just the rifle.

"Was it that bad?"

"Fuck you, Duane. Tanya Zimmer is the best time I've ever had in my life. We didn't even do much and she blew the roof off the fuck-o-meter, okay? You happy?"

Duane nodded as he quietly slipped the pieces of his rifle back together. When he was done, he began refilling magazines. He kept at it through thirty rounds. That meant thirty *del Golfo* enforcers.

Even with his hose and the five in the cabin, Chad doubted if he'd gotten that many.

"Sofia does that to me. Not in a thousand years did I guess how much I was missing until she let me through the door. That explains why you've been so weird since Maracaibo."

"Since Maracaibo? That was three years ago."

"Uh-huh."

Chad checked the inside of his rifle barrel. Again forgetting to not aim it directly at the full moon. "You're saying that Tanya did something to me three years ago and it still shows?"

"Not just a little, bro. You've got it bad. But there's something I don't get." Duane kept fooling with his already perfect rifle.

"You're a jerk. Just in case you were wondering."

"Learned it from a master. Chad, Tanya is an amazing woman. You've been thinking about her for three years. Never known you to think about a woman three minutes after she's gone. Tanya's here. Now. So why are you fighting against it?"

"Because…" Because he didn't know why. Subject change needed—bad. "Why do you think she got all weird after the gold thing? All three of 'em did."

Duane clambered to his feet and slung his rifle. He stood for a long moment watching the moon.

Chad didn't want to kill his friend, but there was a certain temptation to shoot him in the back. Chad somehow felt as if he'd just been stabbed there—or at least rabbit-punched to the kidney.

"You could try asking her," Duane's words drifted back as he headed toward the shadow of the hut that the locals had offered to him and Sofia.

Ask Tanya why she was suddenly looking at him as if he was toxic goldmine slurry?

Duane usually offered better ideas than that—it was one of the worst Chad had ever heard.

CHAD SAT ALL ALONE in the moonlight. His rifle lay across his lap with those big hands of his wrapped around it as if he was holding a woman.

Unable to sleep and sick of waiting, Tanya had finally gone looking for him. And he hadn't moved from where she'd last seen him. Sitting in the moonlight, his fair hair aglow. His blue eyes catching hints of the moon. The watchful sentinel guarding over everyone else's sleep.

Was he demon or lover? Or both? She no longer knew. No longer knew how to tell. All of her past rules didn't seem to apply to Chad Hawkins.

Did he really want Daniela?

She knew her own attractions, but Daniela was *Playboy* centerfold beautiful.

Chad had said the only woman he wanted was Tanya.

Did he really want any woman for more than a couple nights? It was hard to imagine.

Was it hard to imagine because of the way he was? Or perhaps because of the way she was?

A long-term male fit nowhere in her life. Not tactically, not strategically, and definitely not emotionally. Her entire career had been based on being a solo operator—able to change tactics, personas, even looks at a moment's need. Her longevity expectations had never been set high. One mistake, one well-aimed round, and she'd be dead. Falling just five paces either way from the flipping dredger and she'd have been dead—splattered on the rocks. That fast.

And yet her feet were walking out of the shadow of the trees and over to where Chad sat, glowing in the light.

He looked…magnificent.

When she stopped toe to toe with him, he slowly raised his eyes to look at her, but otherwise sat unmoving.

She bent down to lift his rifle from his lap and set it aside. Then she knelt over him and settled into his lap.

All at once, as if a spring inside him had suddenly released, he buried his face between her breasts and wrapped his arms around her so hard that it almost hurt. Placing her arms about his neck, she buried her face in his soft hair and breathed him in.

The way he'd just looked at her, the way he held her, it washed away all of her doubts from a moment before. Swept them away like the rushing river until she couldn't remember what they'd even been.

Chad wanted *her*.

Some part of her wanted to tip her head back and howl at the moon. Another part wanted to hold this quiet, peaceful instant of time in a glass jar so that she could pull it out on some future day when she needed it.

She'd thought there'd be a moment like that earlier—they all had. When Chad held back that bit of gold, she'd thought he'd say something corny about making her a proper wedding ring from it.

She'd seen Daniela take hope at that moment, too. Only now did she realize that Daniela hadn't been hoping for herself. In fact, her face had gone blank the *instant* Chad had winked at her. Daniela had been hoping that Chad would use that gold to replace Tanya's supposedly sold-off wedding band.

And she too had felt that brief surge of hope.

Despite her training.

Despite who she knew she was.

Despite knowing that such a thing was impossible in her life even if she was foolish enough to desire it.

For that brief instant, she had so wanted to wear Chad's wedding ring. She could picture it on her hand. Something corny inscribed inside that would be totally and completely Chad: *Jump off a waterfall with you any time* or *Let's take the plunge*.

Then he had tucked it away and winked at Daniela.

So he wasn't a romantic. She wouldn't know what to do with him if he was. Didn't know what to do with him anyway.

And if he held her much tighter, she wouldn't even be conscious, just from lack of oxygen.

As if of its own volition, one of Chad's hands slid down her back, inside her slacks, and enveloped her behind. The other hooked around her.

He tipped his head back to look at her.

His eyes were awash with emotion in the moonlight. Doubt,

fear, need. She understood them all, felt them all squeezing against the inside of her chest as if they'd crush all life from her heart if they could.

But there was something more there, in his eyes, that she couldn't deny. She didn't want to label it. She shut out the part that knew what the label was. If she let it in, all it would do was scare her. Probably terrify him. But there it was on his face, in her heart, even without the word to label it.

She closed her eyes as she leaned down to kiss him.

It didn't hide the look. It didn't hide the feeling.

Slowly, ever so slowly, they undressed each other in the moonlight. They took a long time touching each other's bodies. It was as if they were newborn and on mutual voyages of discovery. And when he finally lay her back on the long car seat, she felt only welcome for the beautiful man watching her in the moonlight.

He tried to speak, but she didn't let him.

Some moments were too perfect to be tarnished by words— even good words. This was a moment she would take deep inside and hold precious for a long, long time. Perhaps until her last breath was snuffed out in some future instant.

For now? There was only the now.

The man in the moonlight.

His eyes glazing over as he finally entered her.

His weight firmly adding to the pressure that built inside her. Built beyond any mere welcoming of flesh in flesh. He filled her with the moonlight as well. Each ripple of his hips pushing the light in further and further until it chased away the shadows of her past. Until it blinded the doubts of her future.

With Chad inside her, there was only the present.

This one.

Perfect.

Moment.

CHAD KNEW he didn't deserve this…and he didn't give a damn.

The way the moonlight spilled over her face and her breasts. The blemishes of war that enhanced the female warrior were washed away by the softer light and left behind only the woman.

She'd welcomed him as none other had.

All the women in his life had been willing. Wollson didn't have to teach him that lesson and the orphanage certainly hadn't. It was something he'd always known: treat her right and she'll treat you right.

But what Tanya offered had nothing to do with being willing.

She gave *everything* of who she was. He could take all he wanted and she would meet that need, willingly and with her whole being.

And if she could do that, he could do no less.

He breathed her in: moonlight, jungle, old car seat, and a shower in a late afternoon rainstorm that had finally broken up the camp by the river as it began to wash away the blood splattered on the rocks.

He tasted her lips, her neck, her breasts until no other flavor would ever satisfy him again. And he gave back everything he could to show her that.

Yes, women could fake it. Pretty damned impressively, he'd been told.

But there was a point beyond mere passion when it tipped over into ecstasy. No woman could fake that. And he'd never helped any woman wander so far down that path.

The warrior faded further. Still there, but slid into the background.

The woman who came forward made him want to never let her go. If only he could find some way to keep her present— with him, right here and now—he would do anything.

It wasn't how good it felt to be inside her—though that was amazing, every powerful muscle working on him until he wanted to cry out in joy. It wasn't how she felt in his arms—though he could recall no other who had fit so well.

Crazily, it was how *he* fit in *her* arms. As if he'd found where he belonged: being held by this woman, being enveloped by her.

When his desperate need for her slammed between them, it seemed to travel in both directions. Her release became his. His doing. Her doing. All wrapped together into a single dynamic event more powerful than any fire hose, more exhilarating than flying through the air into the rushing embrace of a warm river, more complete than...he didn't know what. Delta training. Than firing a perfect score on the range. Than his single takedown shot out past thirteen hundred meters.

Tanya held him as if she, too, never wanted to let go.

When the aftershocks had eased enough, he lowered his weight onto her because he couldn't stand to be as far away as propped elbows.

Her happy hum told him she felt the same.

Her kiss was as deep as the jungle darkness and as bright as the moonlight that sparkled in her hair.

When finally they rested cheek to cheek with no energy to do more, he whispered a single word into her ear. It was the only word in him. Everything had been washed away except for that one word.

23

"*M*edellín?"

Tanya tried to make sense of the word. It was a perfectly normal word, but she couldn't figure out what to do with it in the light of day.

They sat on the car seats in front of the cafe: her, three Delta operators, Daniela, and Silva.

But all she could feel was the green-and-gold car seat where she and Chad had made love, and they were sitting once again this morning. Last night had nothing to do with sex and a great deal to do with making love. For a change, that shift didn't bother her in the slightest.

And all she could hear was the one word that had made so much sense as Chad had whispered it in her ear like a holy blessing: "Tanya."

How was she supposed to make sense of a word like "Medellín" when his whisper still wrapped around her? He'd breathed her to life with her own name. As if she'd finally, after all these years, at long last, taken possession of who she was. She'd become herself in his arms when he'd whispered her name.

"Tanya?"

The heat rose in her once more, just at the memory. Foreplay hadn't been some romp as she was used to. It had been as if they'd met for the first time, but already known each other for a lifetime of years. Each moment filled with both discovery and familiarity—no surprise, only wonder. As if—

"I think Tanya's gone out to lunch."

No she hadn't. They'd only just had breakfast.

"What the hell did you do to the poor woman, dude?"

Tanya's eyes focused enough to see Sofia poke Duane, "You, shush! Let her be." Sofia's smile was huge.

The others were looking at her with a wide variety of expressions. Duane was always the quiet, calm one of the Duane-and-Chad show, only rarely showing his emotions—but he was smiling at her kindly. Daniela's eyes were soft and speculative. Whereas Silva's eyes were rolling, clearly running short of patience.

And when she looked at Chad, she couldn't help blushing. The heat roared into her cheeks no matter how she tried to hold it back.

"You're blushing," Chad grinned at her.

"That's not helpful. I'd appreciate it if you'd stop smiling like a loon."

"Got a lot to smile about this morning." Which was the absolute truth.

Without bothering to dress, they'd made it back to the small hut set aside for them shortly before dawn. And there she'd tossed down her clothes and jumped him. He'd caught her easily and taken her: back against the central post, legs around his waist, wondering if the roof would come down on their heads and not caring. All of last night's passion forgotten in one roaring go that had left them both sweating and gasping despite its brevity. Relative brevity—Chad's stamina was awe-inspiring —but that had been no languid lovemaking. It had been *all* about the sex. The glorious, soul-filling kind of sex that—

She looked around the circle and put her hands back on her hot cheeks.

Chad was still grinning.

Tanya back-fisted him in the solar plexus. He released a very satisfying whoosh.

"Aaaaand, she's back, sports fans," Sofia bubbled out a laugh.

Tanya stuck her tongue out at Sofia, sitting all calm and composed in her black bucket seat.

"Medellín," Tanya tried to anchor onto the only other word that had penetrated whatever sex-induced intoxication had taken her over. She'd been right that Chad was as addictive as cocaine and she could only hope that habit didn't destroy her. She definitely didn't look forward to the future withdrawal.

"Finally," Silva groaned.

Daniela still watched her with curiosity.

"I'm here," Tanya confirmed.

Daniela's shift to *la Capitana* wasn't so clear this morning. She seemed more kindly disposed toward them. Tanya had been afraid that after Daniela's outburst in the jungle, she and Sofia would be treated as pariahs—outcasts from the Garden of Eden. It was clear that Daniela told that bit of her history to no one. Making it all the more curious that she'd told them. Even if Tanya still didn't know what to do with it.

"We all know about these three men," Daniela pulled out the same flyer that CIA agent Fred Smith had showed them in the Medellín safe house. "Two are gone, but they will be replaced soon at a meeting of *el Clan del Golfo*. In two days' time they will all be in Medellín."

"If you can find out where, we'll take them down." Chad patted his rifle. "Get me within half a mile, even three quarters, I can get it done."

"No, we aren't taking down the leaders of *del Golfo*." It was her *la Capitana* voice.

Everyone exchanged looks but no one spoke.

"We're taking down the entire clan. All at once. I want them erased from the face of the map."

Duane whistled softly.

Tanya could hear Chad try to do the same, but he was still wheezing a bit from where she'd slammed him.

The "entire clan" numbered nearly three thousand people. Of course most of those were runners and enforcers. Taking out the top three would be a brutal blow. The whole operation would probably fall into chaos—very violent chaos. Take out the top ten and it might be past recovery but its collapse would still be ugly. Take out the top twenty or so and they'd probably be out of action. Twenty cartel leaders in a single day? That was a massive operation. At the top levels, one per year was a success story.

"Two days?" Tanya knew about Delta Force in action. Had seen them do what they did enough times now to understand what they were capable of. But without a plan…

"Two days?" But Sofia asked the question differently. Instead of concern, there was anticipation.

Right. Sofia had been recruited from the Intelligence Support Activity. Tanya was used to planning one-woman operations, even small team ops, on the fly. The idea of cleaning out *del Golfo* seemed unimaginable. To Sofia, it would be second nature. Tanya wouldn't mind learning to do that as well.

"The day after tomorrow," Daniela confirmed. "It's Saturday morning now. They have a lunch meeting in Medellín on Monday."

"We could use some help," Sofia made it a suggestion rather than a question.

Daniela smiled. "Who do you have in mind?"

CHAD MADE it through the suite's door about thirty seconds ahead of the others. Per Sofia's signal, the rest of the team were all waiting for him. He started speaking the moment he crossed the threshold.

"Okay. Premise: Tanya's the leader and Sofia's the brains of our operation."

"Got that right," Melissa muttered to Carla.

Chad ignored her.

Ignored them both when Carla gave her back a high-five.

"We've all fought together before on various sides. For Estevan, against Aguado, for the Expediter until she double-crossed us, and no, we don't know where she's gone—certainly don't know that she's dead just because we downed her plane. Fred," the CIA agent was here as well, "you're procurement for this team, not CIA. So don't promise shit that you can't deliver."

"What's the target?" Richie leaned forward.

"She'll explain. I had a falling out with Tanya, but we're married—"

There were gasps around the room and he shook his head to explain this was backstory, not reality. Though reality was getting slippery for him where Tanya was concerned.

Melissa and Carla looked at him strangely—just as strangely as the three women had at the gold camp. No time to think about two more incomprehensible women.

"She and I have been together ever since Estevan and Lake Maracaibo. We're better now. We're all freelancing mercenaries about to go to work for *la Capitana*. And, yes, we've absolutely confirmed that's who she is."

There were voices out in the hall.

Chad raised his voice, but kept it light. "I can't believe you shitheads got a deal like that and didn't cut me in on it."

"Why would we have called you?" Carla picked up the cue right away. "Tanya, sure. But you? Especially after what you did to her, you bastard."

Tanya came into the room at the lead of the others and slipped her arm around his waist, "He's only a bastard part of the time. Hi guys. Haven't seen any of you in a long time."

Chad started to turn to introduce the newcomers, but Tanya beat him to it.

"This is Daniela. And the guy with the nervous hand on his M16 is Silva. He's one of Daniela's best, but he doesn't like strangers."

Silva grimaced at the truth of that, but only eased his hand off the weapon after carefully surveying the room.

He wouldn't know that, throughout the room, handguns hid inches from fingertips. Kyle's arm draped lightly on the cushion behind Carla's shoulder was probably gripping his weapon. The sofa pillow that Richie rested his hand on would hide another. Melissa's ankle holster where her leg rested across her knee. And who knew with Carla—she never looked armed until suddenly she was pointing twin Glocks at your face while you tried to catch the grenade she'd just tossed at you.

The only one who wasn't armed and ready was—

"Who's he?" Daniela nodded toward Fred Smith, picking him out as the anomaly in the room.

Silva's M16 eased over to point at Fred's chest. He really didn't fit in.

"Procurement's my game. Fred Smith is my name. You tell me what you need and I'll get it for you. Anything!" Fred sounded even more voluble than usual. He was always that greatest of oddities—a cheerful, pleasant, talkative CIA agent—but this was something more than usual.

"How about a tank?"

"Russian or American? The Israeli Merkava is also a nice option, though they're harder to get. How soon do you need it?"

Daniela offered a brief smile. "I could get to like you, Mr. Fred Smith."

"I like being liked. I hope you'll find I'm likeable." He actually clamped his mouth shut and blushed slightly as everyone turned to stare at him. Because of his red hair and fair complexion, the blush showed brightly.

Daniela moved easily into the room and sat in one of the

armchairs. Tanya sat on the arm of one of the sofas close beside Carla. Chad followed Duane's example and grabbed a chair from the dining table, swung it into the gap beside Tanya. Duane sat backward on his as Sofia dropped onto the couch beside Melissa. Silva remained standing with his back to the door, but his weapon aimed at the deep pile rug.

Unable to help himself, he slid a hand across Tanya's behind and tucked his fingers into her back pocket. He could feel Tanya's posture soften slightly at his touch. No woman had ever responded to him so completel—

"Tell me."

Chad opened his mouth.

"Not you." Daniela's gaze tracked across the group once more. "You," she pointed to Carla.

Chad relaxed. She couldn't have made a better choice. Nobody spun tales better than Carla.

"No, you tell me."

Chad sighed.

Tanya couldn't wait to see who won the staring contest.

Daniela sat as calm as a queen on her throne. Carla slouched on the sofa, her feet crossed on the low marble coffee table, her fingers laced together over her belly, and her head resting back against Kyle's arm. Two elemental forces.

Tanya had always prided herself on being an elemental force. And curiously, she now sat in a room full of them. Sofia's brilliance, Carla the out-of-the-box fighter, and the guys had praised Melissa as much as any of the others. If ever there was a group of women worth hanging out with, this was it. Too bad all of them were supposed to kill Daniela, who was equally impressive. And then, with the mission over, the Delta team would disappear back into the mists as if they'd never existed and she'd be on her own again.

Daniela didn't break eye contact, but she did offer one of her infinitesimal smiles. A smile that made Carla burst out with one of her barks of laughter.

"Okay," Carla spoke first, but didn't shift her position at all.

She looked so casual, which Tanya knew was a total and complete sham. Though she did it well enough that Tanya could almost believe her.

"Sofia said you had a mission and needed some help. None of us will give you a hand with sex- or child-trafficking—unless you want us to break up an operation. We'll do that for free. Anything else, we're open to negotiation."

"I want to hurt someone."

"I'm listening," Carla declared herself the leader. Kyle was their actual team leader and everyone knew that, except for Carla when she found it too inconvenient.

"*El Clan del Golfo* is going down the day after tomorrow. Sofia said that you and your friends might be able to assist me in this matter."

Tanya watched that ripple around the room.

She and Chad had had several days to understand that Daniela was not who she appeared to be. Sofia and Duane had had one. To the rest of the group, this was a facet of *la Capitana* they'd never imagined.

"The poster," then Fred clamped his jaw shut once more. "I told you so." Then he clamped it harder.

"We were discussing your bounty, *la Capitana*," Carla revealed that they knew who Daniela really was. "Ten million a head speaks of great motivation. You must want control of their operation very badly."

"I said nothing about maintaining their operation."

Again the ripple ran through the team and this time Carla waited her out.

Daniela glanced briefly at Sofia, then Tanya. Her eyes showed the pain that she'd revealed in the privacy of the jungle.

Tanya nodded that, for now, her secret was safe.

"My reasons," Daniela finally turned back to Carla, her face once again composed. "Are my reasons. The reward stands."

"How far down do you want to take them?" Carla had done one of her mental leap things as if all doubts were now gone and they were suddenly all on the same side.

"I will be grinding as much of their operation into dust as possible." There was no doubting the sincerity of Daniela's words.

Carla made a show of looking around the room, not that anyone would dare correct her if they didn't like her answer. But they *would* like it. Tanya had observed that this team was so deeply integrated that the seven individuals (even the outsider Fred Smith—who couldn't seem to rip his eyes away from Daniela) functioned with a level of group-think consensus that almost made them a single unit.

That's where she'd failed. All of a sudden, that was wholly obvious. She'd personally led a number of teams. She had *led* them. *She'd* been the one in charge.

Despite Carla's role as apparent leader, she was really just the spokesperson for the integrated team. And even during Tanya's brief mission with them three years ago, they'd welcomed her (once they'd decided she hadn't betrayed them— odd, she hadn't thought about that repeat of patterns). The first time she'd had to prove herself to Carla. This time she'd almost been killed over the much harder task of proving herself to Chad. What would it be like to stay in one place long enough that she *didn't* have to prove herself over and over again?

Tanya couldn't even imagine what that would be like. She'd been doing it every single day since her father had flayed her back.

Carla faced Daniela once more.

She didn't negotiate.

She didn't pretend there was any question.

Carla simply asked, "Have you got a plan?"

"For the top thirty."

Thirty would be a triumph, if it was the right thirty.

Tanya tried to picture the vast network of informants and shooters that would require. Each additional informant increased the chance of someone tipping off the target. One call and the entire clan's leadership would scatter.

In twenty minutes, Daniela laid out her plan—well-placed shooters with up-to-date information.

In two hours, no one had improved on it and they'd gone down to Estela's restaurant for lunch. Estella never let on that they were Delta Force—just the new badasses in town. It was a good break, walking out the front door and looking across the curving road to the top of the escalator. Locals stepped off as if relieved to be coming ashore from a long boat journey—down into the foreign world of downtown Medellín. Tourists stumbled off as they tried to assess the dangers (which were very few now) and gawk at the stunning view, getting completely in the locals' way.

Around the corner, they returned to *Paisan Comida* and its wild mix of cultural art and local flowers. Tanya let her mind wander as she watched Estela bubble over the team—expanding her cheerful influence to rapidly include Daniela and Silva as well.

Chad, however, seemed to be the center of Estela's adoration.

"She and Ramiro got together 'cause of me," Chad explained when she remarked on it. "Well, me and Duane, but he doesn't really count."

Duane clearly overheard him, was meant to, and chose the best option of pretending not to.

"Local drug gang hotshot," Chad continued in a softer tone. "Earned himself a trip Stateside…in a cage. She no longer pays *la vacuna*—the vaccine, as they call protection money. But most of their friends still do. We've been working on that."

"*Vacuna…*" Tanya rolled the word around on her tongue.

How had she traced people in the past herself?

There were only two directions. Follow the coca: up from the source, through labs and tiers of distributors, and finally to the money. Or follow the money back down to the source.

The money!

"Estela," Tanya flagged down the owner as she hurried by with large bowls of *ajïaco* chicken soup. "How well connected are you to the other restaurant owners in Medellín?"

"I married one of them," she nodded toward Ramiro's next door. "Yes, we have lived and cooked here all our lives. We know many and they know many more."

"And they are sick of *la vacuna?*"

Estela pretended to spit on the floor.

"I thought so. Thank you."

She watched Estela hurry off. Restaurants. Everywhere in Medellín there were restaurants. And they were all sick of the drug cartels. Of the drug cartels' militias' demands for money.

The money trail. It led up from *la vacuna. It also led back down to—*

"Fred," Tanya interrupted an intense conversation he was having with Daniela about the logistical structure of *el Clan del Golfo.* He appeared as fascinated by Daniela's knowledge as the woman's beauty.

Fred actually glared at her for the interruption—as intense an emotion as she'd seen in her few hours of acquaintance with him. Daniela merely looked at her and waited.

"Can you get me a million dollars in American cash? Even half a mill will do. No, a million would be better."

That garnered her everyone's undivided attention.

"How fast?"

Tanya made a show of looking at her watch.

Fred harrumphed, but didn't hesitate for long before rising up to go back to his computer upstairs. Before he left, he briefly rested his hand on Daniela's shoulder.

"Excuse me, ma'am. Duty calls."

Tanya called out a few other requirements that had him groaning as he left.

Daniela watched after him until he was gone.

When she turned back, Tanya tried to ask the silent question of what she was thinking.

Daniela's steady gaze didn't offer even a hint.

The others didn't ask questions. They simply looked at her, waiting.

She couldn't help smiling—*this* was what it felt like to be part of a team.

Tanya could really, really get to like this.

24

*R*ichie flew the big seaplane with easy skill.

"I like flying too," Melissa explained to Tanya, half-turned from the copilot's seat. "But Richie is so good at it that I prefer watching him fly to doing it myself. Sooo sexy."

Richie turned enough that Chad could see him blinking in surprise.

The geek odd couple—Richie constantly surprised by Melissa. Melissa goofy-gone on Richie.

"I ever get like that about you," he whispered to Tanya. "Just shoot me."

Tanya held out a hand and they shook on it.

He wanted Tanya. Even more than this morning if that was possible. She'd cooked up a plan while everyone else had still been trying to find the starting line. That was *his* idea of seriously sexy.

Sofia had been impressed too—even as she was embellishing and expanding Tanya's initial idea—which was saying something. It was real hard to one-up that lady when it came to planning. Then Daniela had pitched in with the last bit of information that made the whole idea snap together. Tanya was already making her mark.

Wasn't any question anymore, he was headed to Kidon. He'd have to ask her about it when none of the rest of the team was around. Telling the team? That was gonna be damn hard and he didn't want to face that before he had to. He'd miss Duane, but Carla was going to pitch a major hissy and experience had shown that those were very dangerous.

The Army had replaced their team's Twin Otter airplane that had been destroyed while taking down the Expediter. Moore Aviation—named for its putative owner, Melissa Moore —only flew intermittently, but it was always a good scam when they needed it.

This time, Richie expertly skimmed the Otter's pontoons into the rolling waves close by an aircraft carrier a hundred miles north of Colombia—well out into the Caribbean Sea. Even with Fred's clearance, Melissa had to do some fancy tap dancing on the radio to get them permission to approach the carrier group without eating a SeaSparrow missile. But between them, Richie and Melissa did their magic and the Twin Otter was soon rolling easily in the light chop.

Their plane couldn't land on a carrier, not even one as big as the USS *Harry S. Truman.* It simply wasn't built for so short a runway. From the water, the carrier didn't appear to be small at all. It loomed ten stories above them, not counting the command tower, and seemed to stretch forever end to end.

"Just in case we needed a lesson in feeling small," Richie noted, leaning forward to gawk upward through the windshield. He never got tired of rubbernecking around the big boats. Actually around anything mechanical.

Chad was busy watching the carrier's armament—which wasn't much—and the frigate floating to their other side, which carried enough of ten different kinds of firepower to obliterate an entire fleet of Twin Otters in ten different ways. SeaSparrow missiles, 20 mm Vulcan cannons, .50 cal heavy machine guns, 5-

inch artillery, probably even cruise missiles tucked away somewhere deep in its guts.

He almost missed seeing the little Zodiac launch that was lowered to the water from one of the carrier's lower decks and was making quick work of slipping over to them.

Chad shifted to the rear and swung open the twin doors near the back of the cargo bay. The Twin Otter was essentially a high-winged, two-propeller bus. The two large pontoons lifted the cargo deck about two meters above the sloppy waves. Only the most forward seats had been left in, just enough for the team —two on one side and one on the other with a narrow aisle between. The Otter's cabin was under five feet high, which made him feel like troll crouching under a bridge as he peered out at the approaching Zodiac.

Except it wasn't a four-man rubber boat as he'd thought. Again the sheer size of the aircraft carrier had fooled him. The boat coming to meet them was a rigid-hull SURC—Small Unit Riverine Craft. It was forty feet of nasty with a pair of M240 7.62 mm machine guns mounted at the bow and an M2 Browning .50 cal heavy at the stern. It was loaded up with nine guys, all in full combat gear, heavily armed, and looking serious as hell.

"Could have used you guys yesterday. Where the hell were you?"

"*Who* the hell are you?" They used a loud hailer even though they'd come to rest just a boat-length out.

"Me?" Chad sat on the edge of the deck and dangled his feet out over the water. "I'm just your friendly neighborhood drug runner who wants his pay." That was the role that Tanya had picked out for them and he didn't see any reason to break cover for a bunch of Navy pukes. And he could see the cases strapped down in the middle of the SURC's deck as if they were massive pallets of gear and not just a sack and two ZERO Halliburton aluminum briefcases.

"Having a problem, honey?" Tanya slid her long legs out

and sat beside him on the cargo deck's edge with her PSG sniper rifle casually resting in her lap in addition to her handgun, spare mags, and sheathed knife all on clear display. They were all dressed for the undercover role—boots, jeans, and black t-shirts—Tanya's of course fitting like a layer of greasepaint to her fine figure. Then she leaned over to kiss him.

No complaints from him. He let it run long enough that it was sure to really piss off the Navy swabbies.

"So," he turned back to them. "You got my money?"

"Identify yourself or prepare to be boarded." A lieutenant junior grade in his armored vest, life preserver, and helmet, armed with a sidearm and a loudhailer, was starting to go red in the face.

Chad turned back to Tanya. "Aren't they just the cutest things?"

"They are," she agreed happily. Damn but she was an amazing woman. She'd picked up on his messing with other unit's heads and was playing right along. Of course, swabbies were such easy targets that he could feel himself losing interest.

"Look, jerkwad," he addressed Mr. Lieutenant JG they'd sent out to guard the precious cargo—they really shouldn't let junior grades out of the oven until they'd cooked a bit more. "I'm the guy with all of the clearances to be allowed to land in the center of a carrier group. I'm also the one who knows what's in those cases you're carrying and I'd wager a fifty that you don't. So, do I call the admiral and get your ass busted back to an E-2 seaman apprentice or do you give me what I came for? Daylight's wastin'."

"Sir," a chief petty officer stepped up to Mr. JG and spoke softly.

"Do it!" the guy snapped out, then started to raise a camera. Standard procedure.

"You take a picture of us and you're gonna take a ride to Leavenworth so fast that you'll think a carrier jet launch is a slow and lazy way to fly." It wasn't true, but Chad wasn't going to tell him that.

JG put the camera away and pretended to look busy while the crew sidled the boat in against the pontoon.

The chief offered him a friendly shrug of "these are the burdens we bear."

Chad shook his hand as he took the two aluminum briefcases. Navy chiefs were what kept the Navy tolerable— about the only thing that did. Besides, it was good manners to shake the hand of a man who gave you a million dollars.

"Heard you also wanted these."

Chad looked inside the sack. Tanya looked very pleased at the hundreds of markers pens, even leaned down to kiss the chief's cheek, which earned her a big smile.

"One last thing." And he handed over a thermo bag that Chad could feel was still warm. The moment he cracked it, he wanted to cry. A whole bag of American treats direct from a US Navy mess. Life just didn't get any better.

"Tell that JG he owes you fifty for stopping us from shooting his ass."

"Roger that." The chief signaled his crew and in moments they were racing back toward the carrier.

Richie started the engines and Chad closed the doors while Tanya went forward to distribute the hamburgers and fries. The latter were cooling and soggy…and tasted like heaven.

DANIELA HAD PROVIDED the radio frequency and password.

And Tanya could only hope that it didn't get them killed. Daniela had made no promises on that point.

"Urabá Trader. Inbound Twin Otter. Over." Daniela had said to keep the transmissions short. The Gulf of Urabá was at the very north end of Colombia, close by Panama. Populated mostly by fisherman and drug runners, it was where *el Clan del*

Golfo got their name. This was *their* center of operation and if they decided that the team was military, or working for *la Capitana*, end of story.

"How much?"

"One million US. Betoyes." Daniela claimed that their passwords were a rotating list of paramilitary massacres that had been perpetrated in Colombia. Not necessarily by *el Clan del Golfo*, but still, a horrific practice. The more she heard, the happier she was with the idea of taking them down.

There was a long silence while the clan considered and Richie kept flying straight into the throat of the monster. The Clan controlled hundreds of tons of cocaine a year and tens of billions of dollars. Not even Daniela could make such a claim to—

"Where Route 90 touches the bay north of Tie," crackled in over the radio, which then went dead. Clearly the end of the conversation.

If their password was correct, they'd have a deal. If not, that's where they were going to die.

Melissa was consulting a map, "That's forty miles into the Gulf of Urabá. They're going to be watching us all the way down the coast."

"Let them try," Richie took them down lower until the pontoons were mere feet over the wavetops.

For twenty minutes he kept them skimming along so close to the water that Tanya couldn't look out the windows. She soon noticed that no one else was either. Even a whole team with nerves of steel were having trouble with it. This version of Richie taking down the Expediter almost made sense.

Certainly no radar installation was going to see them. And probably no lookout either unless Richie accidentally rammed a boat. She spotted only a few fisherman in the calm waters—any one of which could have a radio, of course.

Richie finally landed and eased them toward the beach, but holding offshore. Here, Route 90—fancy name for a partially paved two-lane—angled in from the northeast and looked as if it bounced off the shore to turn back to the southeast. For this one stretch of fifty meters, the road emerged from the low trees. They were thick here and hid everything except the curve of the road mere feet above the narrow sandy beach.

Five minutes later, a trio of Toyota HiLux pickups rolled into view.

"Guns visible, but aimed at the sky," Tanya called out as she moved back to the cargo bay door just as Richie slid alongside the shore, grounding one pontoon with a soft shush into the sand.

Melissa swung open the door on the copilot's side, which faced the sea. She stood on the door's threshold, allowing her to shoot her M4 easily over the roof if necessary.

Tanya caught her breath at the stifling heat that washed into the cabin. It was easy to forget they were so near the equator up in the mountains of Medellín. And the carrier group out to sea had been tempered by a light breeze. Here the air reeked of roasted mangrove swamp. She had to fight off the cough of her body trying to expel it from her lungs by telling it sternly that it would only have to drag in more of the fetid air if it did.

Meanwhile, Chad had popped the hatch in the ceiling of the cargo bay and stood on a couple of seats so that his entire upper torso stuck out of the top of the plane. He must have been a sight, three feet of his Mk 21 sniper rifle emerging before his head even came into view.

Tanya settled for her Uzi, taking speed of fire over pinpoint accuracy as Chad already had that covered.

The HiLuxes eased to a halt, spread out enough that they'd make difficult targets. More men than she'd like spilled out of the first two trucks. A variety of M16s, M4s, and AK-47s—but they were also aimed at the sky or the ground. It was the third truck that worried her. That one had parked head-on to their plane. It had a camper canopy with a wide window at the front. It was hard to see in, but there was a thin slit below the window that ran the entire width of the canopy. Just the perfect placement for a hidden heavy machine gun to exercise a wide field of fire. It could shred them and their plane in seconds.

What she couldn't fix was best ignored.

"Who are you?" The leader came to stand on the beach, just beyond the wingtip.

"Wrong question," Tanya called back.

The man smirked, "Okay, *señorita*, let me see your money." His tone implied there were other things he wanted to see as well.

"*Señora,*" Chad snarled from above. Out of the corner of her eye, she could see the long barrel of his sniper rifle lower until it pointed at the man's chest.

Was that anger real? Or all part of the undercover act? She still couldn't tell with him.

"*Señora,*" the man said a little more respectfully.

Tanya picked up two packets of fifty-dollar bills from the briefcase behind her and waved the stack at him. "Now let me see your product."

The man casually raised a hand. Signal to kill them all and steal the money or…?

One of his men reached into the bed of the middle truck and held up a kilo brick.

She hopped down onto the pontoon, then stepped on the sand. Walking alone up to the main guard, Tanya was glad that Chad had found an excuse to lower and aim his rifle at the man's heart. At least if she went down, she wouldn't be going alone. She was careful to walk enough to the side to stay out of Chad's and Melissa's lines of fire.

She traded the ten-thousand-dollar bundle for the brick—close enough to the right exchange rate.

"Fifties?"

"My client prefers the lower likelihood of counterfeit than US hundreds have."

The man plucked a note out of the middle of each bundle

and held them out to the man who'd brought the brick down the beach. He trotted up the beach with the two bills.

Tanya opened the plastic of the cocaine brick. Gray-white, just the right tone off white. She rubbed a pinch between her thumb and index finger—oily with no grit at all. Touching her fingertip to her tongue, the numb sensation slammed in.

"Very pure, *señora.*" The other man returned down the beach and handed back the notes. "Like your money. One million is a hundred kilos."

Tanya laughed in his face and he shrugged, "That is today's price."

"That is today's price in Mexico; we're still in Colombia." She handed back the brick and took back the bundle of fifties before he could argue. "You can keep the two bills for your time."

"Aww, lovely lady—"

There was a sharp click of the safety coming off on Chad's weapon, the only sound in the quiet morning. No gulls or other shorebirds. No cars on the lonely stretch of road to nowhere except for the three Toyotas. There was just the quiet lapping of the water and the sound of a pissed-off Delta operator.

For a long tense moment, no one moved. She didn't grab her sidearm, but she did casually position her hand for fastest draw and fire.

"Vasco?" Richie called from behind her and the man flinched. His hand actually dropped to his sidearm, but he had the brick of cocaine in one hand and the two fifty-dollar bills in the other.

Half of the guards reacted by raising their weapons, but the man stopped himself.

"Vasco, it's Richie. Moore Aviation," Richie dropped out of the plane and walked up the beach.

"Richie? *Amigo?* I thought you died in the jungle."

"I thought the same of you." They did one of those

249

handshake-in-the-middle, one-armed-hug-and-thump that seemed to be the world's standard greeting for macho guys.

Except Richie had about the least amount of macho possible for a Delta operator.

"Yeah, that Expediter bitch, she left us all to die. You ever get that sexy blonde?"

"Married her!" Richie hooked a thumb over his shoulder to where Melissa was still standing with her rifle resting on the roof of the plane.

Another manly hug-and-thump.

Then Vasco waved. Melissa waved back, but didn't leave her perch or shift her weapon.

Was Tanya supposed to know about this? Or not? She tried to remember her role here, but couldn't. Normally she had no problem keeping her cover story straight. But with Chad, the lines were blurring. Married or not. Three years apart—never apart. Took down Estevan together—worked for Estevan until someone else took him down.

She closed her eyes for a moment.

For Daniela, Tanya had been there, working for the Expediter.

For Vasco, he would know that she hadn't been there. Now her cover stories were splitting and multiplying. She knew from experience that was a bad sign. When a cover began to fracture, it was a sure indication that the mission was going to hell.

For now? Survive. She opened her eyes after no more than a blink, ready to get back in the game or go down fighting, but Richie spoke first.

"So what's this price bullshit?" He was playing the chummy guy in a way she'd never imagined he could pull off.

"We don't know you. Then you get first-timer's price."

"But you do know us. You gotta remember Chad, too," Richie waved a hand negligently toward the plane.

Tanya glanced over to see that Chad's rifle was still unwaveringly aimed at Vasco's chest.

"Hi, Chad. Sorry I no recognize you, *amigo.*"

Chad grunted a greeting, but didn't shift his aim.

"Some things never change," Vasco whispered.

"Nope," Richie offered commiseration. He was displaying a whole range of unexpected emotions. Richie's two modes were typically geek-like enthusiasm and super-geek-like enthusiasm. It was almost as if…

Tanya had to cough to cover her laugh. It wasn't almost; it was *exactly* as if Richie had studied Chad and was doing his best to imitate what Chad would do. And he was making it work. To cover her next laugh, she had to look away but spotted Melissa's smile. She was watching Richie with her isn't-he-the-cutest-thing-ever expression. It wasn't a smile of benevolence or admiration of a team member. It was a look of love as clear on her features as if the word was painted there.

Tanya glanced up at Chad. Because of the pontoon's height and his position standing up through the top hatch, he was the highest point around, even higher than the roofs of the trucks. Chad looked like a blond Nordic god—again Thor came to mind. A very pissed off, very protective Thor.

Tanya didn't want a man who was lovingly amused by her. But she didn't mind having an angry god of thunder watching over her shoulder. Didn't mind that at all.

By the time she, Richie, and Vasco had haggled a price, they actually had a relatively good deal—a hundred and fifty kilos of uncut cocaine in exchange for a million dollars US.

The money would be flooding out as payments to other members of *el Clan del Golfo* right away. Hopefully, a number of the bills would be streaming into Medellín, the nearest large city in the Clan's operations. That's the real reason she'd chosen the fifties over the hundreds—they were far more likely to be spent than stashed.

A million dollars in secretly marked bills—all traceable to this one transaction.

"COULD HUMP you blind right now, woman. You're amazing."

Unable to help himself, Chad hauled her into his lap as soon as they were airborne.

"I can't believe that you had the balls to laugh in the guy's face. You are the best woman ever."

Tanya did one of her inscrutable looks, one that might have had another laugh hidden in it, then she kissed him. It wasn't a laughing kind of kiss. It was the hard release of post-mission adrenaline. He knew it well. Finding a willing woman right after a high-stress mission was just the best combination. But holding the woman who'd been at the center of the mission? That was blowing his circuit breakers.

She lay her head on his shoulder, content to stay in his lap for the entire forty-minute flight back to the carrier.

And all he could do was hold her.

No need to talk.

No sex in the open cabin plane with Richie and Melissa sitting right there in the pilot seats—especially not with Melissa turning around to grin at him every five minutes. He stuck his tongue out at her and it just earned him a silent laugh.

Yeah, Chad Hawkins the Sucker!

Maybe he finally understood the others: Kyle, Richie, Duane. He'd always thought of Kyle and Carla as inevitable. The two best operators of their entire class—of course they belonged together. Richie and Melissa—a geek's delight, in both directions. And maybe he was getting some insight into Duane and Sofia. She wasn't just some hot babe with a brain even more amazing than her body that Duane had somehow landed.

Did they feel like *this* when they were together? The way he felt holding Tanya? For Duane's sake, he sure as hell hoped so.

Did they *all* feel that way? The "one right woman" crap?

What if it was actually true?

He tightened his arms around her and she sighed happily. And he could feel his cheeks were hurting. Even after he leaned them against her sleek hair. She made him smile so damn much that it hurt despite his face finally being mostly healed. How nuts was that?

Upon their return to the aircraft carrier, the same damn lieutenant JG rode out to meet them.

Good. Chad needed something to distract him from other thoughts that he wasn't ready to be having.

"Appreciate the loan of the million bucks."

Chad could see the JG flinch as he learned that he'd handed a million dollars in the briefcases to what he thought was a drug runner.

"Got some good value for your money," Chad began tossing bricks of cocaine to the chief petty officer. "Hundred and fifty kilos, about five million on the Street in the US. Yessir, five times return in value in just a couple hours. US military oughta just get into the drug trade since the drug *war* is such a flop. Wipe out your national debt in no time."

The chief was smiling, but the JG blew his cork.

He stormed up to Chad, yanking out his sidearm. "I ought to waste your drug-running ass. Right here. Right now."

Chad might have just ignored it if the JG had only targeted him.

But when he swung his weapon to cover Tanya as well—

Chad slap-grabbed the weapon out of the JG's hands. He released the clip and the magazine dropped between Chad's knees where he sat on the edge of the cargo deck. It bounced off the plane's pontoon that the boat was sidled against and disappeared into the waves of the Caribbean Sea.

Then he popped and dropped the slide, "Oops!" That bounced and sank as well. Finally he heaved the receiver in a high arc over the boat. Like a dumb deer in the headlights, the JG instinctively turned to follow its path and plunge.

Once his back was fully turned, Chad grabbed him by the

nape of his bulletproof vest and lifted him up until he was dangling helplessly a couple feet in the air.

"Facing away from your known enemy? Didn't they teach you crap?"

The JG began struggling, and Chad lifted him higher. His men were watching, but the chief signaled them not to raise their weapons.

"Oh dear," Chad snarled in the JG's ear. "Lost your sidearm on a friendly mission? And now you have seventeen rounds unaccounted for. That's *real* bad. You *know* what command thinks about that. You'll be lucky if they don't bust you a grade or two—knock your ass right out of any future promotion track. Wanna keep playing, buddy? I know so many ways to make you hurt without ever touching you, it'd make your head spin." Chad gave him a good shake, then pulled him in close so that he could whisper.

"You never, ever aim a weapon at that woman. You hear me?" He gave the guy another shake, then tossed him back on the deck of his boat where he crumpled to his knees.

Either the guy was going to learn the lesson and shape up now to make an exemplary officer, or he was going to crawl back into whatever officious civilian hole he belonged in. Chad didn't much care either way. But goddamn it! If you signed up to be an officer in the US military, you should damned well behave like one. Half the time, that's what was wrong with the military corps.

"Chief," Chad called out to him. "You better give this asshole the credit for 'capturing' five million in cocaine. It's about the only thing that will save his sorry ass. Richie," he shouted into the plane, "Get us out of here before I actually get mad."

He and Tanya pulled in their legs and he slammed the cargo door as Richie got them moving.

"Shit," Chad lay down on the rear cargo deck rather than moving to a seat. In moments, Richie had them skimming over the wavetops, making Chad repeatedly bang the back of his head on the decking without having to put out the effort to do so himself. It had been such a good day and then a guy like that made you wonder if you were even fighting for the right side.

When he opened his eyes, he saw Tanya looking down at him with wide eyes and a thoughtful expression.

"What?" It came out hard, so he eased off and tried again. "What?" Better, but not much. He was still too pissed at a US officer threatening to shoot her.

She finally shook her head and lay down beside him on the hard steel deck. He hooked an arm around her and she rested her head on his shoulder.

Well, at least one thing had gone right.

---

25

*T*anya spent the next two days wandering around in a Chad-induced haze.

He hadn't said he'd loved her.

Chad Hawkins might never do that.

But he'd shown that it was true beyond a shadow of a doubt.

He'd lifted that JG as if he weighed less than a sack of potatoes, not straining for a single moment. An Army sergeant beating on a Navy lieutenant? Even from one branch to another of the service, it was a court martial offense—not that the guy would dare to report it. Maybe Chad would be safe because the only people who had his name for the exchange were the CIA and they wouldn't care what a Navy lieutenant had to say. But she doubted if that thought would have changed Chad's actions in the slightest.

He hadn't done more than tease the guy until the moment the JG had threatened her. She'd seen Chad defending his teammates in dangerous circumstances. He was always casual, glad to deliver a joke along with his lethal sniper skills.

This time he'd been anything but calm.

She'd been in far more dangerous situations than this—many times. People had defended her as she'd defended them: because they were on the same team.

Not once! In all of her memory, not once had anyone ever tried to defend her because they cared about her. She had no answer to that. No idea how to react.

For two days they had worked to exhaustion laying the groundwork for Daniela's *la Frio Purga*—The Cold Purge. Tanya felt as if she knew every block of every street of Medellín. That was impossible, of course. The city was the fastest growing in Colombia. Roughly one in ten Colombians lived here. Along the outer reaches of the hilly *barrios*, whole new streets had probably been created just in those two days, as more and more of the rural population left the countryside to accrete around the edges.

Traffic was a nightmare, but the public transit system whisked them around Medellín with splendid efficiency. The main-line train ran up the middle of the river valley that was the heart of the city. A branch line followed the most populated tributary a short way to the west. And as fast as they could, they were adding cable cars up into the hill neighborhoods. With the ease of new connections, money was flooding up the hill as workers flooded down the hill. Meter by meter it drove back the drug trade that had thrived for so long in the poorer areas.

The team's own safe house lay at the top of a thirty-story outdoor escalator that was rapidly changing *Comuna 13*—one of the two most dangerous places in the entire city. The other was on the far side of the city. La Sierra sat at the end of a long run of cable cars and was the gateway to the region's coca fields.

"I own that now," Daniela had told them in her chilly *la Capitana* mode. "No one from the Clan would ever think to go there if they want to live."

Tanya could see the solidification of the rest of the team's certainty that the day after *el Clan del Golfo* went down, *la*

Capitana would be going down hard. She had wanted to spend some more time with Daniela, but preparations simply hadn't allowed it.

But she did have an idea.

---

26

*C*had was still scratching his head over this one, but Tanya had made it clear that he had no choice.

La Frio Purga was going ahead full bore.

Everyone was mobilizing.

Not just the Delta team. Not just *la Capitana's* team either. Somehow Tanya had roused the restaurateurs as well, without telling them exactly what was coming. She'd started it with Estela and Ramiro, but it seemed to flow across *Comuna 13* like an underground wildfire. Chad was used to undercover infiltrations—small teams slipping undetected deep into unfriendly territory—but Tanya had mobilized an entire section of the city.

Last night, both of them too tired for sex, she had still curled up in his arms as if they'd always been that way.

"There is one man you must meet. We need to be able to contact him at a moment's notice and have him act."

"That sounds like your dance, sweetheart. You just wiggle a finger and any man in his right mind is gonna come running."

"Not this time. We need him to trust *you.*"

She'd refused to explain why. Just said that she couldn't do it for reasons she wasn't willing to explain. Arguing with the woman had gotten him nowhere. So here he sat at the crack of dawn, cooling his ass in the dude's outer office instead of getting some pre-battle wake-up sex. Wrong in about eight different ways.

Teniente Coronel Sánchez of the National Police of Colombia.

Chad really needed to shut his brain off. Tanya had been right about his drug-runner babe "Renata" actually being *la Capitana*. Hell, way back when, three years ago, she'd been right about Estevan and his narco-submarine empire too. Woman knew what she was doing. Who knew when she'd made this contact or what the hell they needed him for. But if Tanya said they needed him, Chad didn't need to know more.

But why couldn't Tanya do this errand?

Shit! Because she'd slept with the man! She'd sent him to call on one of her ex-lovers. Trying to figure out why just made his head hurt. Tanya had been very clear that he was to befriend the man, not kill him. He wished to hell she'd explained what game she was playing…but since when did women ever do that? Next time he saw her, he'd—

"Major Jenkins?"

"Uh… yo!" It took him a moment to respond to his fake ID's name. He'd chosen Duane's last name just to mess with him.

"I'm Lieutenant Colonel Sánchez. May I see your ID?"

Chad tossed it over. The guy's eyes didn't quite bug out, but he handed it back very respectfully. He was five-seven, compact and solid—though getting heavy at the belt line—and wore a sharply pressed uniform. Late thirties with medium skin and a dark mustache. He was clearly a man who spent some money on his appearance.

"Come into my office. What can I do for the United States 75th Rangers?" Duane's old unit. *Suck eggs, dude.* He'd thought about dragging Duane into this, but it was more fun besmirching his old unit's name first and telling him about it later. The office was big enough and clean enough to reveal that this guy had some serious pull. Definitely one of the Colombia anti-drug agency's rising stars.

"This is strictly between us, Colonel, if that's okay with you." Chad dropped the full name of the subordinate rank because lieutenant colonels always wanted to act like the real deal even though so few of them achieved the next rank up. Though this guy appeared politically savvy enough that he'd probably make the jump.

"Of course!" Foreign military always ate up the US secrecy thing, wanting to be the one in the know.

"My government has sent me down. We want to give Colombia a little more help in the drug war. We gave you fifty billion in aid and you guys only cleared fifty thousand hectares of coca fields last year. Only seventeen the year before that. I've been instructed to help you get back over the hundred thousand mark, preferably up to a quarter million."

"Well," the man rocked his chair onto its two back legs. "Perhaps you don't understand the difficulties and dangers we face down here."

Chad could just see the guy looking for the grease. How dirty was this guy? He'd apparently slept with Tanya, which was going to severely shorten his lifespan—might have already if Tanya hadn't insisted that they needed him. He obviously took his share of the aid money and probably a fair slice from the drug cartels to look the other way. A lieutenant colonel was no longer paid by individual runners—he'd have enough power to deal directly with the cartels.

"I'm laying the groundwork to jump in here with three companies. Maybe four."

The guy's chair legs clanked back down on the cement floor.

"Four?" He barely managed to gasp.

So sweet! A Ranger platoon of thirty guys could clean up most normal messes on their own. A company of a hundred guys would be nearly unstoppable, even if they were just

Rangers. Four companies? Four could own this country in a week's time. One of the secrets to a good lie was to make it so outrageous that your target would assume that you'd never be dumb enough to try and pass off such a fake—unless it was for real.

"Fully supported, of course. Command is talking about pulling an MEU into Urabá just for backup." An entire Marine Expeditionary Unit of two thousand jarheads launching off a helicopter carrier into the Gulf of Urabá didn't actually sound like such a bad idea.

This time the guy's jaw actually dropped. Right where Chad wanted him.

"Now I'm just the liaison, but our President doesn't want to tangle up a whole bunch of generals and politicians in this. We're talking about taking some serious action and explaining ourselves later. Friend gave me your name. Can you work with me on this? Gonna be a hell of a show and I need someone willing to climb right to the top with me."

And the arrogant little prick smiled hugely and held out his hand. "I'm exactly the man you're looking for. You can count on me."

Best bribe in the world—dude suddenly had his sights on a leap straight to Major General with three suns on his collar. He'd definitely do anything Chad said.

Chad really had to talk to Tanya about her taste in men. Though maybe—what with him being her current taste (thank you very much)—asking for that look in the mirror wasn't the best idea.

"How much are you setting me up?"

Tanya looked up into the mirror to see Daniela leaning against the door jamb. Someday Tanya was going to settle down. When she did, she would design her own bathroom—and give it a bank vault for a door. Not even Chad would get the combination. She spit out her toothpaste, then rinsed the brush and her mouth before answering.

At least Daniela had waited until after she was dressed.

"Honestly?"

Tanya thought it best to ignore the contact she'd sent Chad to make. Other than that…

"Less than you'd think."

"I think it's a lot."

"Try thinking it is just a little."

Daniela's dark eyes studied her closely, until Tanya had to struggle not to squirm.

"As long as you want to focus your ire on *del Golfo*, not a soul here will complain."

"And when I want to focus on something more?"

Tanya could only shrug. It wasn't a threat, not quite. It was more of a suggestion of what might be possible if Daniela decided they had betrayed her.

"For today, you have no concerns," Tanya offered. And that was true. This was the day of *La Frio Purga*. If everything went according to plan, a third of Colombia's cumulative drug cartels would be removed in a single day. The second third was held by a myriad of smaller and marginalized gangs—that could be hunted down and picked off one by one.

The final third was bothering Tanya—it was represented by the woman standing in in her bathroom. And according to Fred Smith, he saw no signs of an organization. Daniela had set herself up as the sole kingpin with *all* of the reins in her hands alone. Even Silva barely registered on Smith's data landscape. *La Capitana's* operation was all Daniela according to him—a fact that practically made Smith swoon each time he mentioned it.

"Knock her out of the picture and the whole structure might well fold up and disappear. It's a magnificent concentration of power and information. Just tell me who I have to kill to get all of that intel." So he wasn't just swooning after Daniela's exceptional body. She was an intelligence officer's wet dream: brilliant, focused, and powerful. What Fred Smith didn't know was the core of pure anger that drove Daniela.

It was a core that Tanya knew very well herself.

For now, if *la Capitana* had the information to take down the entire *Clan del Golfo*, she was going to get nothing but the best help the team could offer.

"Where is Chad?" Daniela showed no signs of moving from the door jamb, so Tanya began brushing her hair.

"Running a couple of final errands. Everything is as ready as we can make it."

Daniela appeared ready to say something, then changed her mind.

Tanya had long since learned that these were the moments to keep her mouth shut—living her life alone might have taught her that too well, but for now it might prove useful. She tossed aside the hairbrush and scooted up onto the counter to show that she was in no hurry, despite the hundred details she wanted to check.

It was exactly where Carla had sat to confront her so few days ago. Every time Tanya touched this team, time compressed in strange and impossible ways.

Ten days ago, she and Chad had fallen out of a helicopter together after not seeing each other for three years.

A week ago, Carla had intruded on her shower to sit in exactly this spot.

And now Tanya couldn't figure out what to say to Daniela or how she was going to live without Chad.

Ten days, and yet her life would never be the same. There had always been a pattern, a shape. Simply take down every single bastard who could have possibly created the drugs that her sister had used to kill herself. Shred them one by one if she had to, until—

"I recognize you." Daniela's face revealed nothing of her thoughts.

Tanya felt the hard chill and cursed herself for leaving her weapons on the bed after she'd dressed. Daniela wore a large fisherman's knife—perhaps Gerald the Boatman's—and her Cordova [.38 sidearm could punch a giant hole in Tanya's chest. Being recognized as the Kidon operative who had been wreaking havoc throughout the South American cartels for the last five years was as good as a death sentence. She prepped herself for one all-out attempt at survival, but Daniela didn't move.

"I know that anger. I see it in my mirror. I've learned to never look closely. How do you live with what you see?"

Tanya blinked in confusion. Unable to stop herself, she turned away from Daniela to glance in the mirror. When she noticed her glance skitter aside, she forced herself to look. Her face in the foreground, Daniela watching curiously over her shoulder. Tanya barely recognized herself.

The blonde fighter's hair was straight and her face was clean —typically the end of Tanya's interest in her own appearence.

The person seeking the death of others and not caring if that eventually included her own—crystal clear. Apparently that was the woman Daniela saw.

But there was a new overlay whom Tanya barely recognized. Hadn't been aware of until Daniela forced her to look. The beauty whom Chad was so captivated by was a woman she didn't know, as if she was peeking wide-eyed out at the world for the first time in her life. She shifted her focus to Daniela.

Long hair brushed, face clean.

And an anger and hurt so deep that Tanya could feel every bit of it etched on her own soul.

"I...don't know. I think I live with it by never looking." Tanya turned back to face Daniela and leaned against the mirror in the right spot to block Daniela's view of herself.

"Until it becomes all of who you are."

"Until it does that," Tanya echoed.

But she could feel that new woman, the one Chad saw, trying to look out of the mirror over her shoulder.

"Until it becomes something more."

"Death," Daniela declared.

"Hope." Tanya was as surprised by her own answer as Daniela looked.

27

C had arrived back at the safe house in *Comuna 13* with Sánchez's cell phone number and his promise to never be away from it for the next forty-eight hours.

He checked in with Fred for his final assignments.

Daniela's people would already be in place throughout the neighborhood—and another, thinner layer in the adjacent neighborhoods. Her enforcers were crossing the great divide of the Medellín River as it ran through the center of the city and the Aburrá Valley. *La Capitana* controlled the eastern flanks and *el Clan del Golfo* the west. An uneasy and—according to Daniela —unspoken truce had the troops rarely crossing the central dividing line. Today they had crossed it in force. Unfamiliar with the territory of the city's west flank, they were given very specific stations.

The only truly mobile element was going to be the Delta Force team. Their cover was simple: tourists—very heavily- and covertly-armed tourists.

When he turned, Daniela and Tanya came out of the bedroom into the living room looking as close as sisters.

Tanya raised an eyebrow in an infinitesimal question.

He offered an equally tiny nod of confirmation. Yes, he'd dealt with Sánchez.

Daniela looked at him as if he was a complete and utter mystery.

Great! What stories had Tanya been telling? What stories did he *wish* she'd been telling?

Now there was an old thought. He'd seen the dynamic before. Present girl telling friend how good a lover Chad was. So when Relationship One fell apart, the skids were already greased for slipping into Relationship Two. Would he be interested in Daniela if things fell apart with Tanya? No. He'd be chasing after Tanya trying to figure out how to get her back. That would be a first for Chad Hawkins for damn sure.

He made a point of walking up to Tanya and pulling her into his arms. "Hey, lover." Then he kissed her. He'd barely caught the words and shifted them. *Hey, my love* had almost slipped out instead. But if it did, it would be some casual line with as much meaning as *honey* or *sweetheart,* which was how he'd always used it in the past.

Calling Tanya "my love" would have all kinds of weird ramifications he wasn't ready to deal with.

So, instead, he briefly cupped her butt as he kissed her, then let her go.

Still Daniela was watching him like an alien, but Tanya's smile and the tingling memory of *her* hand on *his* butt left him feeling fine.

"Let's go."

And just that fast, the whole team was in motion.

Tanya sat in Estela's restaurant and pretended to linger over a breakfast that she couldn't taste.

Chad's unthinking greeting, as if she was the most important thing in the room, was still sending waves of smiles through her. Daniela's gaze had agreed with Tanya that maybe, just maybe, there actually *was* such a thing as hope.

Hope for a future. Hope for not just a better lover, but a better life.

And in that moment, seeing the flicker of possibility on Daniela's features, she was able to embrace her own feelings more completely.

She didn't just love Chad. She was Melissa-level completely gone on him. Her pulse rate had soared so high when he entered the room, she'd have been hard-pressed to make a sniper shot at a hundred meters, never mind a thousand.

Now she sat, eating by herself, pretending to read *One Hundred Years of Solitude* in Gabriel García Márquez's original Spanish. It was hard to resist the tale's opening of the gypsy who traveled the world without anchor and the peasant farmer who had a place in land and family but never seemed to see it. But she had to keep an eye on the patrons.

One after another, people came, ate, paid Estela, and left.

A lone diner, a nondescript man in his mid-thirties, stepped to the cash register to pay Estela.

Tanya's interest sharpened when Estela hesitated.

She, like most proprietors did in the region, often used counterfeit detection pens on any larger denomination American bills—the unofficial second currency of Colombia. They weren't flawless by a long stretch, but they exposed the lesser quality forgeries.

For today, almost every restaurant in western Medellín was using one of the test pens Chad and Tanya had picked up from the aircraft carrier—specially flown down from the mint in Washington, DC, by the supersonic F-35 Lightning jet that had delivered the two briefcases of money as well.

The team had told the restaurateurs to only use the special pen on American fifties. A single stroke across President Ulysses S. Grant's forehead.

Estela did just that.

Then she gave the signal by flipping the bill quickly facedown on her counter.

A second man rose from where he'd been casually reading a newspaper close by the counter. Tanya watched Daniela's enforcer set aside his paper, then, stepping up to the man at the counter, quietly press a handgun hard against the customer's kidney.

Daniela's enforcer escorted the man past the end of the counter and back into Estela's kitchen.

Tanya followed quickly.

As she passed the counter, Estela handed her the fifty-dollar bill.

In the kitchen, the enforcer had the other man bent over a wooden prep table, his hands Zip Tied behind his back. In moments, he'd been patted down and several weapons and a small sheaf of fifty-dollar bills were sitting on the table. The weapons and money went into a bag. Gagged and ankles bound, the enforcer tossed the man into a corner of the walk-in refrigerator.

Tanya followed them in.

"Get comfortable," she told the man. "This is only the beginning of *La Frío Purga.*" She held up the fifty in front of the man's face for him to read. Across Grant's forehead, the pen had reacted with the hidden ink and the words were now clear: "I am a criminal for *el Clan del Golfo.*"

She handed the bill to the enforcer.

As he'd been trained, he fished out the man's ID card and held it up along with the bill close by the man's face. He snapped a picture with his phone and forwarded it to the inbox Fred had made. Then the enforcer stuffed the bill and the man's ID back into his pocket.

The automatic system Smith had set up pinged back an immediate "received" message. Daniela's enforcer returned to reading his newspaper in the corner of Estela's restaurant. A backup sat in the other corner in case more than one clan member carrying the marked fifties came in at a time.

Moments later, Tanya's phone vibrated with a message. "Nineteen in the first twenty minutes," was Smith's message.

Twenty minutes? That's all she'd been waiting? It had felt like an eternity, wondering where the flaws were in her plan.

Estela stood close by the refrigerator door when Tanya emerged.

"I have known him for twenty years. He always tells me he worked construction."

"He is also a soldier for the Clan," Tanya told her.

Estela slammed the refrigerator's big door on him. "How long do I have to keep that trash in my refrigerator?"

"Most of the day, I'm afraid. If we let a single one get out or turn them over to the police, they might get word out of what we're doing. Better if they just disappear for the day."

"The Cold Purge," Estela patted a hand on the closed refrigerator door. "I like it very much. Maybe I will offer to make him a *raspado* when I let him out."

Tanya laughed. After a day of sitting in a refrigerator, being offered a cone of shaved ice with fruit syrup would be the final insult.

She headed out the door as Smith reported that the count across western Medellín was up to thirty of the Clan's men. None of the top three had been caught, of course. But Daniela had identified twenty "key personnel" that they wanted to be sure to take down. Three of those had already been caught in the restaurant sweep—a very good start indeed.

Tanya sent a message to the full team: *Phase III running.* Phase III encompassed the Tier III people—mostly runners and thugs, the "enlisted" men of *el Clan del Golfo*.

For the rest of the day, it would continue on auto-pilot. Unless something went very wrong, there would be no need for the team to be called and they could now focus on Phase II—

the twenty people who were the leaders' closest cronies, the "officers." The Tier I "generals" would be the final nut to crack.

Typically this kind of operation was run the other way, take out the top first. The problem was, then all of the little people would scatter.

She and Sofia had cooked up this idea.

They'd both liked it because they could think of a hundred different things that could go wrong.

CHAD HATED WATCHING the takedown of three of the Clan's people at a faux-American burger joint in Pajarito.

Pork burger with crispy pork rinds—okay, he'd have to be coming back to try that. But horse burgers and yucca fritters, how was that authentic US of A? His downfall was that they had pizza on the menu, and he hadn't had breakfast yet though it was already midmorning. Tanya had sent him off to deal with Sánchez at daybreak, which had taken longer than planned.

The two slices told him just how faux this place was. He should have known better than getting pizza at a burger joint in Colombia. Even lamer than horse burgers. All it did was make him homesick for a Detroit-style deep-dish pizza from Cloverleaf with the works. Best he'd ever had anywhere—and he'd tried pizza in over thirty countries. Medellín didn't even make top half.

The Pajarito neighborhood sat high in the hills three miles north of the safe house in *Comuna 13*. It was their operation's furthest outlier and Chad wanted in on the action.

But Tanya had been very clear about that: *Let Daniela's enforcers do their job. Don't interfere unless there's trouble.*

And there hadn't been any at all. Her enforcers had it down. Not as smooth as a Delta, of course, but these guys weren't slouches. They grabbed the Clan's people and put them on ice without a single customer in the restaurant doing more than glancing over, puzzled to see others moving into the back kitchen. It was happening so smoothly that the chances of any ripples running out into greater Medellín were pretty much zero.

Where was the fun in that?

Phase III running, pinged in on his phone.

"No shit, Sherlock."

Outside the restaurant, he stepped into the taxi that was waiting for him—a taxi driven by yet another of Daniela's people. She apparently owned the allegiance of most of the city's taxi and bus fleet. Lady was real smart—they were the connective glue of gossip in any city.

"Your honey has it down," Duane climbed in from the other side, coming from his own observation station for Phase III.

"She's not my honey." That's a phrase they'd both used too many times for the sweet things they found in bars and on beaches.

Duane looked at him, "Haven't had much chance to talk. Is it getting serious?"

The taxi driver pulled out, watching him in the rearview as much as he was watching the madness that Colombians called "driving" out the windshield.

"C'mon, dude, what're you feeling?"

"Feeling? You're asking about *feelings?* What the hell has Sofia done to you, bro? Besides, I…" Chad knew exactly what he was feeling. Didn't have any damn words for it, but he knew what it was. Kind of. A life of Detroit street girls and Spec Ops bar babes did nothing to prepare a guy for whatever the hell Tanya was doing to him.

Now both guys were watching him.

The taxi driver rolled right through a stop sign, not that such an action was unusual in Medellín. But he did it in front of a bus, which *was* unusual. Colombia's traffic psychosis had a very well-defined pecking order: trucks never stopped for anyone, buses came next, and SUVs outranked mere cars like the battered Chevy Spark subcompact they were presently squeezed into. Below cars came motos, then bicycles. Pedestrians were somewhere down with stray cats and dogs. Walking in Medellín, especially after dark when streets became raceways, was taking your life in your hands. Gridlock was your best bet for a safe crossing any time of day or night.

Subject change time. "The *Phase II* guys are going to be much more challenging, which means we should get to have *some* fun." Daniela had identified the twenty dudes who actually ran the day-to-day operations for most of *el Clan del Golfo*. He was careful not to mention the plan or any names to the taxi driver, just in case. Word wouldn't be out on the street yet about what was going down and they wanted to keep it that way for as long as possible.

Chad scanned down his list.

"Shit!"

"What?" the taxi driver actually twisted around to look back at him despite pushing hard through a stale red light.

"They already took out the first two on my list." Each pair on the team was supposed to have five targets on the Top Twenty list of key players. Suddenly he was down to three.

"But that's good," Mr. Taxi still wasn't doing such a hot job of looking where he was going.

"No! It means that my girl—"

He ignored Duane's raised eyebrows. So he'd never heard Chad call any woman that. Big deal.

"—is probably going to finish the day with a higher body count than I am."

The driver laughed. "You're right. That's not good. We'll work double time. What's the first address?"

Chad gave it to him.

"That's under the cable car. It will take some time to get there."

Chad leaned low enough to look up at the cable car through the windshield. Medellín had started putting these in around the city. The trains couldn't climb the hills. And there was only the one set of escalators—the steep section up to *Comuna 13*. But cable cars didn't care about heights and could span distances for the farther back communities like Pajarito.

Each gondola could handle eight passengers. Once traveling on the cable, it moved along at five meters per second—about ten miles an hour.

"Is the address *exactly* under the cable car?"

"*Sí.*" The driver missed several pedestrians by millimeters as he took their lives into his hands and dodged around a truck.

"Cable moves slower than a parachute landing," Duane seemed to have the same thought.

"Yeah," Chad waved at a racing bus in time for the taxi driver to avoid imminent death. "Drop us at La Aurora station. Wait for us two blocks downhill from the address."

Inside the cable car station, it took only a little bit of acting the noisy, drunk-in-the-morning Americans to convince the line of people waiting to board that they should take the next gondola.

As soon as the door closed, Duane reached into his pack and pulled out a minimal profile descending harness. Chad fished out the same and a length of 8 mm ultra-light climbing line.

Twenty seconds later, Chad had overridden the gondola's safety mechanisms and popped open the doors, which improved the view nicely. It was a lovely morning and the ocean-fresh air tasted good. Even a few hundred feet up and the smells of the city faded away. They rigged the midpoint of the line around a seat post and latched their descenders onto either side.

From their packs, they also pulled Glock sidearms, which they clipped to the harnesses, and a pair of FN P90s—both rigged with subsonic rounds. They spun on five-inch-long sound suppressors to avoid announcing their presence any more than could be helped. The P90 was ideal for this situation. Its compact bullpup design meant that they could carry an exceptional close-quarters-combat rifle in a twenty-inch pack.

Ready, they had a chance to look around.

"Great view," Duane noted.

"Sweet!" Chad wasn't about to be outdone for cool and casual. And it was beautiful. They were descending from one of the highest points in the entire city and the view swept from the far north where the Bello neighborhood marked the eastward turn of the Aburrá Valley. Directly below was the land of red brick. Ahead and farther below, the glass of downtown shone in the morning sun. South and west, the steep rise of other districts seemed to each glow with their own colors. One hillside was dominated by bright blues and golds, another by gentle tropical pastels. The parks stood out as dark green patches and the tops of the Andean peaks at this northernmost end of the range slipped quietly behind the city as the gondola descended quickly.

"Ten seconds?" Duane asked casually.

Chad picked out the right building, which matched the aerial image on his phone. It wasn't hard. In an area of tightly packed buildings and crowded, climbing streets, their target covered the area of a dozen buildings. Behind high walls, a small tropical paradise surrounded a huge swimming pool. The only one in this whole area.

"Sounds about right," Chad acknowledged, by which time they were down to five seconds remaining.

They almost out-casualed each other enough to miss the jump as they finally rose from their seats and stood with their backs just out the door and their toes on the threshold. Chad glanced over his shoulder, estimated speed of the gondola, their height, and how fast the descender would let them down.

No need to even glance at Duane, they made the same estimates from the same training.

They kicked back hard in perfect unison and let the rope fly.

Three seconds of near free fall, Chad kept his eye on the swimming pool.

Half pressure on the descender's brake lever to slow his fall.

Partial release.

Hard brake.

Let it go at the last second.

He landed in the pool, feet first in the shallow end.

Releasing the descender completely, he let the end of the rope slip away even as he swung his rifle into position.

Duane went into the deep end and completely disappeared from view.

Couldn't happen to a better man.

But Duane hung on to the rope, anchoring it in place. Because Chad had released his end, it slithered up and around the seat post in the departing gondola car. Moments later it splashed down in the pool with a snake-like hiss. When the car reached the next station, it would be empty and the door would be open. Unless the people in the next gondola were dumb enough to talk about the two guys who had jumped out carrying rifles, no one would ever know what had happened.

Without being conscious of it, Chad had assessed the state of the patio area as he'd descended.

Before the splash had even settled, he'd fired silenced rounds into the three guards standing discretely around the area. They barely had time to look surprised before he dropped an additional round into each and they collapsed to the stone flagging.

The man eating breakfast at a glass table froze with his fork in midair.

Weighted down by his gear, Duane resurfaced by plodding up the slope from the deep end, coiling the line as he went.

"Could cover me, bro."

Duane looked up in surprise. "Why? You got it handled. Besides, I'd hate to leave behind a good chunk of line."

Chad shook his head to clear the water out of his ears as he climbed the steps and scanned the rest of the pool area.

A very hot babe came out the door dressed in nothing more

than the towel she was carrying in her hand and bikini bottoms that were so brief they barely deserved the name.

Spotting Chad, she opened her mouth to scream.

"I wouldn't be doing that," he called out as he aimed at her voice box, ready to cut it and her spinal cord with his next shot.

She was smart enough to choke off her cry and close her mouth. Then she very slowly moved up to the target still frozen in midbreakfast while facing Chad. She bent down as if to kiss him on top of the head.

Then stood back upright with a handgun that must have been in the target's back waistband.

Chad sighed and shot her in the face just as Duane fired a pair of rounds into her cold heart right through one of those lovely breasts.

The target was smart enough to place his fork on his plate and his hands flat on the table as the woman slowly collapsed to the deck beside him. The subsonic 5.7 mm rounds of the P90s didn't have the knockdown power of a full load behind a 9 mm or a .357, but she wasn't any less dead before she hit the ground.

It took less than a minute to hide the bodies in the small pool house and lock the door. Another to check the house. No one else there, but a surveillance system showed that there were several more guards outside.

Down in the garage, they found a nice selection of options.

"Too bad the Lamborghini doesn't have three seats."

"It is," Duane agreed sadly.

Duane took the wheel of the up-armored Range Rover with tinted rear windows. Popping the garage remote, he rolled out onto the street, raised a hand as if to wave to the outdoor bodyguards—also blocking their view of his face—and turned down the hill. He punched the remote to close the garage door again. No one would think to check inside for a while— hopefully the rest of the day.

Two blocks later they pulled up alongside the taxi and dumped the bound-and-gagged target into the taxi's trunk.

The driver headed off to a hangar that Daniela had rented at the south end of Olaya Herrera Airport in the heart of Medellín. The airport lay in almost the exact center of the city, making it very convenient.

"Well, we had a nice swim. What's next?" Duane commented as soon as Chad had climbed into the front seat.

"How do you feel about horses?"

"Why?"

"No reason. That's the next target's nickname." Chad tapped the next address into the dashboard's flat screen system.

"Think it's that he's hung like a horse?" Duane headed south across Iguana Ravine to climb up into the El Moro neighborhood.

"We can find out if you're feeling voyeuristic."

"Rather be voyeuristic about what the hell is going on with you and Tanya."

Shit! Chad had thought he'd successfully left that subject behind.

TANYA HAD FINALLY FALLEN BACK to the safe house suite to sit with Fred Smith.

She and Silva had swept in to take down Number Fourteen on the twenty-person Phase II list, and found him in a meeting with Sixteen, Seventeen, and Nineteen. Small teams of Daniela's people had been sent to take out the few key players who weren't in Medellín today, but they'd been told not to act until the three leaders had been taken down. A special team had been sent out to the Gulf of Urabá to clean out the sales team that one of Smith's drones had traced back to their lair while the Twin Otter had flown away from them.

"We're running out of targets fast," Fred noted as he worked the lists.

Four of them had gone down fighting—Tanya had taken out one of those, Carla two, and Kyle another.

"What's the count on the Phase III guys?"

Fred chortled happily. "*La Frio Purga* has a hundred and eighty-seven of the 'enlisted ranks' so far. Your ploy with the fifties worked brilliantly. We're gutting their operation today. If we continue this for the rest of the day, we could easily get two-fifty."

"That's great." But Tanya had trouble putting much enthusiasm into it.

Phase III was running fine. The last few of the Phase II top twenty should be taken care of within the hour. That left only the three *generales* of Phase I.

If Daniela's intel was trustworthy—and no reason to think it wouldn't be—that should work as well. Which meant that by the end of the afternoon, this mission would be complete.

Then—Tanya had to get up and pace away from Smith to hide her feelings—Daniela would get taken down.

And the team would move on to another assignment and this safe house would probably be abandoned, leaving her rootless once again.

The temptation to bury her face in her hands in misery almost overwhelmed her training to present a neutral expression to everyone around her.

She liked and respected Daniela. She *loved* Chad. And she didn't know what to do with either of those emotions.

"Daniela is really something, isn't she?" Smith effused happily.

For the operation, he'd set up a trio of screens. One was his master lists. Another a map of Medellín so that he could assist any team who called in. The last, at least at the moment, had a full-screen shot of Daniela. Her image had the slight blur at the edges common with most security cameras—so Smith had tapped into someone's system. She had her handgun out, double-fisted, and aimed at someone just out of view. She looked like the apocalyptic horsewoman Death. Her face was beautiful, even in an angry snarl. Her figure was on clear display as she braced for a possible shot. She looked powerful. Indomitable.

And Delta's job was to take her down.

To take her down would shatter *la Capitana's* cartel. Take Silva as well and it might never be a factor again. But to do that now, after all she'd done to wipe out *el Clan del Golfo* wasn't right. But neither could they release her to go back to running her drugs.

Tanya had tried to arrange something for her, but that would only heal the moment. Then she would be shipped off to an American prison. It would be kinder to shoot her where she stood.

Smith continued looking at the screen in the same dreamy way she'd noticed earlier. She wondered if Daniela had noticed Smith and what her opinion might be.

"You're sweet on her." The words sounded ridiculous as she spoke them, but it didn't make them any less true.

"The way you are on Chad," he said absently, not looking over to her as another report flashed up on his screen. He tapped out a quick acknowledgement.

Tanya tried to respond. He couldn't be as gone on Daniela as she was on Chad. They'd barely met, whereas she and Chad were...what? Lovers? Yes. Warriors together as compatible as any Delta team? Sure. Committed? Not in any world that either of them lived in, because their worlds were so far apart. And about to become even farther.

"Pretty obvious on the two of you. Thought I was hiding it better," Smith seemed to be speaking to himself.

A CIA agent's sensitivity wasn't exactly going to be the most highly calibrated tool on the planet, but she'd thought she was hiding it better than "pretty obvious." If he saw that much, what did Daniela see? Or Carla? Or...herself?

No way was she going anywhere near a mirror or that "I'm

so in love with Chad" woman might pop back into view and Tanya couldn't deal with that.

"There must be something we can—"

The door to the suite opened and Daniela strode in with Silva, "That's Mr. Thirteen."

"And Eighteen," Chad came in close behind. The kiss he greeted her with was an absolute toe-curler. Even if she couldn't keep him, she was glad to have him for now.

Smith looked at her in question, but she shook her head slightly to call him off continuing the conversation.

Within minutes the rest of the team was back.

"All twenty," Smith practically crowed in delight as the team reported their final takedowns in person. He jumped to his feet and went through the team collecting high-fives.

Chad gave him the high-five, but Tanya could see his puzzled expression as he followed Smith's progression through the group. So even by the agent's inherently jovial character, this was pretty exceptional.

It was all explained when he reached Daniela last of all, even though he'd had to reach past her to high-five Silva before acknowledging her. Instead of holding up a hand for a high-five, he clasped Daniela's hand in both of his.

"I know we're not done yet. But I wanted to thank you. You're magnificent." Then he even managed a quick hug. He thought he was being subtle, which was kind of cute actually. Not a woman in the room missed it, including Daniela—who appeared pleasantly bemused.

Tanya checked to see if Chad had noticed, but he was chatting with Duane as he turned to the armory table and began reloading the magazine for his P90. Richie had moved to the computer to double-check Smith's lists while Melissa rolled her eyes at her husband's back. Kyle knew he'd missed something and was looking around for it. Silva hadn't missed a thing and he looked thoroughly pissed.

Silva was a deeply unexplained factor. He didn't appear to

be her lover, but he was as protective of Daniela as any Delta operator was of their spouse. He troubled her, simply because Tanya couldn't explain him. Having a wildcard factor in the final phase of this operation would not be good. Maybe by involving the whole group she could force an answer. Tanya raised her voice to get everyone's attention.

"We need to know——"

"They're in," Richie called.

Everyone's attention except Richie's.

It was the moment they'd been waiting for. The fact that it was happening exactly on Daniela's announced schedule merely confirmed the impressiveness of *la Capitana's* operation and exactly why it had to be taken out.

Tanya gave up. Too much was in motion—today the cards would have to fall where they would. *El Clan del Golfo*, Daniela, her and Chad: all of it.

Nearby, just halfway down the steep hillside of *Comuna 13*, the three leaders of the entire clan were gathered for a meeting. Nicolás had been captured months before and El Indio had been recently killed. Two new leaders were being gathered by Otoniel, the alias for the head of The Clan, for the continuance of the operation.

It was going to be their first and hopefully last meeting as leaders of the cartel.

Richie's comment meant that all three of their Tier I targets were at the same site.

They'd done it. It had been the critical challenge, to take *el Clan del Golfo's* operation out from under them without the three leaders realizing it. If they'd known, they'd scatter to the winds.

Everyone gathered around as Richie began bringing up various views. He didn't even appear to notice as he wiped Daniela's picture from Smith's third screen.

Daniela looked at Smith for a long moment—he'd managed to remain close beside her as everyone gathered close. Then she looked at Tanya and tipped her head toward Smith asking a question that was easy to interpret.

Tanya did the "considered moment" to show that she'd caught the question, then gave the small shrug and nod of "I don't know, but he seems okay to me." She wished she could ask Chad or Carla. To Tanya, Fred had been a voice on the phone three years ago and then the last few days. She liked him. She liked his innate cheerfulness and unthinking kindness. She couldn't help but be impressed by the resources he could tap. And, perhaps to his highest credit, his absolute passion for this team.

This team.

They had honored her by judging her worthy for both this mission and the one long ago.

They'd kept Fred Smith for three years, and she didn't doubt for a second that they'd have shuffled him off if he hadn't been a hundred percent on board.

She offered Daniela a more emphatic nod, a solid "Yes." Trying not to think of what that meant for her.

Daniela did her own thoughtful look as she considered the answer. Then her smile went bright, with a hint of a hidden laugh, just moments before Tanya felt Chad's hand slide around her waist.

He nuzzled her ear and mumbled, "Hey, beautiful."

"Hey."

"Took down three with Duane."

"Six." She didn't tell him that four of them had been together.

It earned her a curse, then an easy shrug of acceptance. "Still three to go, right?" Or not acceptance. Man was as competitive as she was. She was going to miss him so much.

And she was damn well going to take down at least one of them herself to make sure he didn't get ahead of her.

CHAD LOOKED at the screen and whistled. The leaders of the Clan, not knowing their entire operation was already toast, were in a building that had more in common with bin Laden's fortress than one of Pablo Escobar's lush estates. High walls bordered all sides.

The cameras they'd hung in the area over the last two days revealed an impressive layer of guards and armor. Not just up-armored vehicles, but a couple of the police's Hunter TR-12s were parked nearby—armored personnel carriers where they had no call to be at the moment.

"Those are gonna be fun," Duane sounded pleased. He was their explosives genius and would definitely enjoy taking those out of action.

"I'm on the ground with him," Sofia announced. "I'll be able to get a better view of what's happening if we walk in as a couple."

"Once it hits the fan, we'll need shooters covering these exit streets." Tanya pointed.

Kyle and Carla nodded their assent.

"I'm going to park a CREW Duke right here, then we'll join you," Richie indicated his and Melissa's planned position.

"CREW Duke?" Daniela asked.

"Remote-controlled IED suppressor. It also cuts off all cell phone communication. I'll leave open a single frequency for our radios, but the rest, we'll just shut down. They won't be able to talk without a landline."

"And that," Smith stepped forward, "won't be an issue. I'll drop phone and power just after Duane blows the vehicles. Helos?"

"No," Tanya had already decided against those. "Not in broad daylight. This can't look like a US military operation. We're going in flying Daniela's colors, so to speak. This is strictly an internecine conflict to anyone on the outside."

Chad looked at her quizzically. He was obviously thinking of his meeting with Colonel Sánchez.

She shook her head to remind him to keep that secret as he'd promised.

He shrugged an okay, with an afterthought of "Yeah, whatever." Hopefully he wouldn't shrug *her* off so easily.

"Daniela and Silva, you two know the area best. I want you to ride down the escalators, timing it so that you're alongside the building at the Go moment. We're looking to you to block any escape routes to the south and those huge staircases and sliding escalators are going to be your best bet. Daniela, have your people block the escalators at the right moment to keep the public off them."

Daniela spoke up. "I will also have taxis and buses sitting two blocks back in all directions creating a traffic gridlock. Nothing in or out."

"Only one thing missing," Tanya looked at Chad and smiled.

"You and me, my girl." For reasons that weren't clear he stuck his tongue out at Duane. "We need shooters with an angle inside those walls. Any brilliant ideas?"

"Yes."

And he laughed with delight rather than asking when she didn't elaborate. Exactly her kind of guy.

28

*C*had stood still and wondered just how crazy Tanya might be. If he'd ever thought there was anyone like her, she'd just erased that.

They stood side by side atop the highest end of the big outdoor escalator that connected *Comuna 13* to the city below. It wasn't actually a single escalator, but rather six segments, each one five-stories high and interconnected by colorful little plazas.

But they weren't *on* the escalator, but rather on the roof over it. There were no sides, just a roof for the days it rained—open-air travel. Each segment was covered by its own simple roof. Steel box girders half-a-meter square were painted a dark red—and punched with a thousand little holes to make them both decorative and lighter weight—creating the edges of the roof. Down the middle was a wide expanse of glass to let the sunlight in. It ran flat for the first few meters, then angled downward very steeply. At the lower end, five stories below, was another short flat segment for the runout of the escalator.

From here, the financial district far below was a shining beacon of glass towers. In contrast, above them vultures were circling, watching for dead things. It was an amazing view, enhanced by their precarious position. No safe balcony around them, no neat little handrails to keep pedestrians safe. They stood on glass, up above the city.

He glanced back over his shoulder to where four of Daniela's people waited on the roof of the safe house ten meters behind and well above them.

"You sure you aren't crazy?"

"Certifiable," Tanya admitted. "Crazy for you."

He faced her.

Her smile was tentative.

And he didn't like that on her face. Because it wasn't how he felt about it. Not at all. He might not have the words for Duane, but he didn't have that problem around Tanya.

"Plumb dead nuts I'm so crazy for you, lady."

And her smile lit up like a magnesium flashbang.

"Best feeling in the world being smiled at by you."

"Know what you mean. You ready, Chad?"

"Born that way, Tanya."

Then she raised her arm and slashed it down.

At her signal, they both broke into a sprint across the upper flat section of the glass roof. Just as they hit the change in the roof's angle from flat to a forty-five-degree downslope, the harnesses they were wearing snapped taut.

Hopefully, at that very instant, the guys up on the roof would let go of the massive canopies they held aloft. The next ten steps were either going to work—or the eleventh was going to hurt like hell.

He sprinted down the glass slope, leaning hard enough into the harness' back-drag that he was running perpendicular to the surface. Every few meters, the roof's windows were supported by steel ribs. He used those like runner's blocks to sprint down even faster. Everything depended on speed.

Five steps.

Six.

Seven.

He kicked harder.

Eight.

Suddenly Tanya was no longer beside him, but he didn't dare look aside.

Nine.

Ten.

Elev—

The harness finally hauled up and back, harder than he could sprint down, and his feet left the escalator's roof. One last glimpse down through the glass, he saw Daniela's and Silva's faces upturned to watch them.

Looking up, he saw that the broad paraglider canopy had unfolded properly above him. Not a lot of grassy hillsides for launching paragliders in *Comuna 13*. He settled the harness so that he was in the proper sitting position with the controls neatly to hand.

Tanya, being lighter, had lifted off several steps before he did and now floated neatly above him. She waved.

He waved back—and the paraglider entered a lazy turn the instant he eased the control toggle. Because Tanya thought of everything, she'd already rigged handle extenders so that they could steer with their feet and leave their hands free. He slid his over his toes as well, then, for a brief moment of incredible privacy, they circled silently above the city. The midday heat, baking off the heart of the city, was creating a glorious updraft all across the face of the hill. It was easy to climb and the ride was smooth.

His alarm beeped—two minutes.

He unlimbered his Mk 21 rifle and oriented it to point downward. Perspectives were strange from up here, but he found the target quickly enough. The escalator was thirty stories high—a vertical football field. He and Tanya had circled up to twice that until they were higher than most of the hills. The air was smoother up here, but had a tendency to head out to the countryside. He shifted his feet to crab across the wind, sacrificing some altitude but getting good position over the target.

At two hundred meters up and sitting in the harness, he would be a moving target—most importantly a tiny target, about the size of a quarter held a full car-length away. A tough hit for someone with iron sights, which was all the guards down there probably had. Drug runners typically fought their battles at a couple paces or while doing a drive-by. Two hundred meters was way outside their typical skill range.

"Never mind us, dudes. Just a couple tourists lost on the wind." They'd gotten the chutes from the paraglider outfit that flew on the mountains southeast of town. So they were a common enough site around Medellín, if not directly over the city. The fabric was the striped colors of the Colombian flag: half yellow, a quarter each blue and red. Looking up, they were stunning against the blue sky.

He zeroed in on the compound they were supposed to be watching, just as his watch alarm pinged the Go signal.

TANYA COULDN'T BELIEVE it had worked.

She watched him circle and move below her. He was such a joy to watch. Somehow, in the process of her falling for Chad, he'd fallen for her. It didn't mean she had a solution, but now she definitely had hope.

Her lighter weight had let her climb faster and she'd used her altitude to fly farther east so they'd have two angles on the action below.

Just as her watch beeped, down below, the three Hunter TR-12s were briefly outlined in brilliant light—the brilliant light of Duane's explosives cutting their axles. None of them would be going anywhere. Through her scope, she could see that one had actually lifted off, landing back in the same position completely upside down.

The outside guards raced toward the three explosions, away from the compound.

"Shoot random guards," Chad shouted across to her. "Wound or kill, doesn't matter."

That wasn't part of the plan, but she didn't argue. From her height, she was in the low end of her sniper rifle's range. On top of that she was shooting nearly straight down, making the math too simple.

She missed the shot by a full meter.

Why was—she laughed. There were no gravity effects. If anything, gravity would accelerate her round as it fell; it certainly would make it drop away from her target. She spun the dial on her scope to recalibrate from five hundred meters to zero, because that's effectively what was happening ballistically.

She punched down a guard with his rifle at his shoulder exactly where she meant to hit him.

Shifting over fifteen meters, she dropped another, and then a third. Now that she had the range and angle zeroed in, she went for thigh and upper arm shots.

Chad was doing the same and soon there were ten down.

Five more each, they'd barely dented the crowd. They changed out magazines.

"That should do it," he called over.

Tanya extended her right foot to circle once more over the street, except now it had become a battle zone.

Right. Otoniel was inducting two new members to fill out his leadership circle. None of them would quite trust the others yet and all would have brought the enforcers most loyal to each of them. She and Chad had just stirred up a three-sided war as each set of guards assumed the other two were shooting at them, so were busy taking vengeance. That's why it had been okay to wound. A well-trained guard, if only wounded, would probably hang on to his weapon—he would then shoot widely and indiscriminately, deciding he was in the battle for his life.

As the mayhem grew, she refocused on the central compound.

There was action there, but not mayhem. These guys had good control. Cell phones were out—tested, slapped, and finally heaved aside as useless. Richie's CREW Duke blocker was definitely doing its job. Landlines were grabbed, but Smith had done his work and those were dead as well.

Chad dropped one of the interior guards with a chest shot.

As everyone spun to look at the falling guard, Tanya dropped one on the other side of the open courtyard.

Now everyone had their guns out.

"Now?" Chad called.

"Now."

In the next ten seconds, every guard was down —permanently.

There were only the three leaders left, huddled back to back and looking around them in terror.

Chad spilled air out of his paraglider and descended fast.

As she followed him down, Tanya could see that the war out on the street was still going on. The various outposts they'd set up were cutting down anyone who tried to run—cross fire along the streets by the Delta teams kept them hemmed in on three sides. On the fourth side, Daniela and Silva slowly walked up the down escalator to keep their sights even with the southern escape route. Certainly no one on the ground was paying attention to the two paragliders now falling out of the sky.

The big chutes landed so gently that she barely had to squat to absorb the impact. Instead, she landed with her rifle zeroed on the face of Otoniel immediately in front of her. Chad had the other two covered as his chute collapsed behind him.

"Is there a reason you're still holding your guns?" she asked, doing her best to imitate that wonderful laughing tone of Chad's that always pinpointed the absurd in the moment.

One of the new leaders raised his weapon—Chad shot him

in the biceps and his sidearm clattered to the ground as he yelped.

The other two set their weapons down very carefully. The gunfire outside the compound was tapering off rapidly.

"Now." Tanya looked at him.

"No. Gotta kiss you first."

He spun her around so that her back was to their three captives. Before she could protest, she could see that he was watching their captives past her cheek. Under her arm, he still had his Mk 21 zeroed on them. Not a one looked like they were even breathing.

So she let herself melt into his kiss for just a moment. It felt like none prior. It wasn't about sex—she knew that one. It wasn't about post-battle adrenal lust—knew that one too. She wanted to label it as love, but that didn't fit…quite.

No, it was…pride! He was proud of her. She was pretty pleased with herself, but Chad's adulation was unmistakable. He finally let her go and spun her around until once more she was facing their captives, but now she knew she wore a ridiculous grin.

"Now," he declared. "Though its one weird-ass way to go about it." But there'd never been a woman like Tanya and he'd do anything she said.

Richie had turned off his jammer, so Chad dialed his phone, though he kept his weapon on the Clan's leaders while Tanya systematically frisked and bound them.

Teniente Coronel Sánchez of the Colombian National Police picked up on the second ring.

"Major Jenkins!"

Jenkins? Oh, right, he'd used Duane's name.

"I hadn't expected to hear from you so soon." But Sánchez sounded delighted that he had.

"I need a favor."

"Anything, *mi amigo.*"

"I need clearance to transport some folks out of the country. I picked up some guys while I was looking into things and want to get them extradited before their friends find out."

"Extradited?" Sánchez's voice was suddenly strained. "That isn't the easiest thing to arrange."

Chad knew that, but Tanya had insisted that was exactly the card they had to play, so he played it. Chad answered his concerns with silence.

"How soon?"

"Can you do it in the next thirty minutes?"

"What?" Sánchez practically screamed into the phone.

"Well, if you can't help me, I can always ring Gonzalez—" Sánchez's direct boss and the man Sánchez would be hoping to replace with Chad's help.

"No! No. Your friend Sánchez will take care of it for you. Thirty minutes?" He started sounding worried again. Exactly as Tanya had predicted.

"I've got a runner outside the front gate of your building," Chad continued on the script Tanya had set forth. "Sitting in a taxi. He has a couple of bundles that might help any squeaky wheels."

"Okay. Okay. I know someone."

Meaning a crooked judge.

"For how many people?"

"Why don't you leave that blank and meet me at the southwest gate of the Olaya Herrera Airport, the one near the medical response group? Half an hour. Counting on you, buddy." And he hung up.

29

*C*had met Sánchez at the gate. It had taken him forty-five minutes, but the instant he spotted Chad, he held aloft an envelope proudly.

"Excellent! Come with me. I'll show you what's going down." Chad led him through the gate and the back door of the run-down hangar. Red brick placed around gray concrete beams. The high roof was a graceful semicircle of rust-pocked sheet metal, marred further by the missing windows here and there in the panels under the eave. The rear door might have once been blue-painted steel, but now it was rust red shreds of flake.

They stepped across the threshold and Sánchez stumbled to a halt.

"You said a couple."

"Nah, buddy. I said *some*, but let's not quibble."

Three hundred and seven guys were lined up in chains of fifty—literally. They were bound hand and foot and all still wore gags. The three leaders and their twenty main assistants were in a chain of their own. All of the rest had been Tier III people captured by *La Frio Purga* that had been run by the restaurants of Medellín. Those guys tended to be huddled together for warmth and the fight had definitely gone out of them. There was another chain of the ambulatory ones left over from the primary strike on the three leaders. The wounded had been shipped off to a local hospital.

Tanya had told the restaurant owners that they were done. If they kept checking fifties, they'd start running into second-hand money and might be arresting the wrong people. Not a single civilian injury, though there had been a few wrestling matches reported and Daniela's people had shot seven of the guys before they behaved. The Red Cross medics were checking them over now.

Chad pulled the envelope out of Sánchez's nerveless fingers and handed it over to the airport manager and the customs official they'd invited over to witness the event.

After careful inspection, they announced that everything was in order.

The manager picked up a radio and called his tower. "Authorized to land."

Moments later, the roar of a big jet coming in hard rattled the hangar. Then another—and a third.

Richie and Duane slid open the big front doors as a trio of US Air Force C-17 Globemaster transport jets rolled up and parked in front of the hangar. An Air Force Security Force team debarked with weapons drawn. The younger guys stumbled in surprise, but the senior master sergeant simply grinned.

"Now ain't this a purty picture. I'll be taking them off your hands right quick."

Smith handed him a dossier and a thumb drive including all of the photos of the criminals with their marked fifties. "Inside that case," he indicated a large trunk that two of the Security Force guys were struggling to load, "is enough evidence to lock most of them away for life: all the laptops and master files we could lay our hands on. Payouts, bribes, murders—I only did a first scan, but there's more real good stuff there. Choose the right state, at least three might face the chair."

"Outta my hands, but I'll sure make the suggestion," the sergeant turned. "Load 'em up!" That got his men moving.

Sánchez was still watching, goggle-eyed, trying to figure out how much trouble he was in.

"*Teniente Coronel* Vicente Sánchez." Daniela came to stand squarely in front of him. "What are you doing here?"

Sánchez swung his jaw, but no noise came out. Looked like the man had just stepped in some serious shit that wouldn't wipe off any time soon.

Daniela glanced at Chad with a look that could curdle steel.

"Not me," he held up his hands palms out. "Talk to her," he nodded to Tanya as she approached.

"I thought you two ought to meet," Tanya said as if she was introducing a couple on a blind date.

Sánchez looked back and forth between them, then found some backbone.

"I've been so worried about you, Daniela. How have you been? What have you been doing?"

Daniela now aimed her soul-killing gaze at Sánchez.

"Oh," Tanya spoke as if surprised. "I didn't realize that you knew *la Capitana.*"

Sánchez stared at her as frozen as if he'd spent the day in one of the refrigerators.

Then he snarled and yanked out his sidearm.

Chad broke his wrist, then handed Sánchez's weapon to Tanya.

He needed popcorn for this. Or to sell tickets. He could make some serious money—the rest of the Delta team had drifted over as the Air Force security guys took over the prisoners. Silva too came over to listen.

Then Chad noticed there was one more in the circle than he expected. It was…

"Holy shit!" He snapped to attention. You never saluted a

superior officer in the field because it drew the attention of snipers with mischief on their minds. But it was hard to resist the urge.

The others all looked at him in surprise, followed his gaze when he rolled his eyes to the right. Then each snapped to attention in turn as they noticed Colonel Michael Gibson had joined their circle.

Except for Tanya, who simply looked at Daniela and they both shrugged in confusion.

Chad thought about explaining just who had joined them, but decided it was safer to keep his mouth shut.

"At ease," Gibson growled.

Kyle, with the balls of steel that made him the leader, stepped forward and shook the Colonel's hand.

"Can't say as we were expecting you, sir."

"I'm here. Carry on as you were," Gibson nodded to Tanya.

Tanya shrugged as if she didn't know what was wrong with the rest of them. She spoke to Daniela as if the commander of all of Delta Force—and the most highly decorated soldier in the Unit's history—hadn't just appeared out of thin air.

"I wanted to give you a choice. You kill Sánchez here and now, no one on this team will blink."

"We won't?" Chad didn't like the guy, but that seemed harsh. He glanced at Gibson, but the dude was as unreadable as ever.

Silva spoke for the first time in a long time.

"My sister—"

"Oh," Tanya said softly. Chad had figured that out a couple days ago—it was the only reason a single, straight guy wouldn't melt into a puddle of guy protoplasm around Daniela. That or the single straight guy was in love with Tanya—which took him out of the running.

Maybe it had been circling in the sky with her, or landing in the middle of the battle, or falling out of the helicopter together forever ago. Didn't matter, still true. No one else in the world for him—that much he knew for certain.

"My sister," Silva started again, "gave her body to Gerald the Boatman in an undercover sting operation to bring down South America's largest drug trafficker. She was a second lieutenant at the time. Sánchez here took credit for it, took the promotion to captain that she deserved, then tried to rape her in the bargain. When she refused him, he announced she was a slut, an 'easy woman.' For that alone I could kill him."

"Or take off his goddamn balls!" Chad jerked out his knife and held it out to Daniela handle first. Now he understood why a woman would do that to a man. Someone tried to do any of that shit to Tanya, castration would be the least of his worries.

Daniela shook her head slightly.

Chad waited a moment in case she changed her mind before putting his blade away.

"However," Tanya spoke up. "There is another option. He just bribed a judge with a hundred thousand dollars of clearly marked drug money—all in fifty-dollar bills. The judge is aware of this and has reported it to the authorities. However, he stands behind his extradition order. He signed an additional order so that we can send Sánchez to the US along with the rest of these worms. Or we can leave him behind to be tried here in Colombia."

"Where will they treat him the worst?" Silva's voice was bitterly cold.

"La Modelo Prison, here in Colombia," Daniela said thoughtfully.

"Yes," Tanya agreed. "The judge actually suggested that as the most suitable place for him to contemplate his sins. Both the right- and left-wing factions of Colombia—who basically control the two sides of the prison—will want to shred him alive. One side for all the arrests he made, or at least took credit for. The others because they were jailed for corruption and want to take it out on someone other than themselves."

"No! Not there!" Sánchez squeaked in terror, his skin gone as white as Chad's.

Tanya stepped forward and plunged a shot into Sánchez's arm. In moments, Chad had to catch him as he sagged.

Tanya waved forward one of Daniela's taxi drivers who'd been waiting off to the side. In moments, Sánchez was loaded into the trunk with instructions to deliver him to a Judge Hermosa.

TANYA WAITED until the taxi had pulled away and all of the prisoners were loaded aboard the C-17s with a one-way ticket to the US.

"Well?" Daniela asked her, her arms folded over her chest.

Tanya didn't have a good answer, but she knew one thing. She turned to the compact man that had shocked everyone—surprised her too because she never saw him arrive. He seemed to keep fading slightly from her attention from one moment to the next.

"Your load is complete. Feel free to dump them in the ocean if they give you any trouble."

"Just might have to consider that," he said in a wry tone that had her liking him.

"Are they ever going to introduce you?"

The man shook his head in a tight negative.

"Not until I see how you solve the rest of this."

He waved a hand at the Air Force Security Forces. In moments, the C-17s were raising their rear ramps and ramping up the engines they'd never wholly shut down.

Soon the jets were on their way.

Only the action team and the unknown man remained in the vast space that smelled of old concrete and many men's weary curses.

That's when Tanya realized who the man was. She'd heard

whispers of him from her first days in Mossad—America's super soldier. As if Captain America existed outside the comic books and movies. No wonder he'd been able to sneak in with no one noticing, this was the fabled Colonel Gibson.

He didn't look like much. A few inches shorter than she was, not particularly broad-shouldered, blue-gray eyes, and graying at the temples. He looked like someone's aging dad. Then she started to notice his stance…that wasn't a stance. And his hand position that wasn't poised, but appeared perfectly positioned for any action. *Any action*—no matter what it might be. She remembered her martial arts instructor's metaphor. If ever there was a tenth degree black belt, his name must be Gibson.

Yet the moment she looked away from him, he seemed to disappear. When she glanced back to assure herself that he hadn't, he offered her the briefest smile, then slid back into his neutral space.

No one spoke until after they'd watched out the door and all three of the massive jets roared down the runway to head aloft. The echo inside the hangar had time to die completely away before Daniela was finally the one to break the silence.

"I've never seen a Delta Force team in action. You people are formidable."

Gibson eyed Daniela curiously, but didn't say a word.

"They are, aren't they? I *love* this team," Fred Smith hovered nearby. And Tanya now knew that he meant it. Chad told her that today had been a demonstration of how far above and beyond he often went to deliver whatever they needed to complete a mission—once they'd gotten him broken in, of course.

"When did you know?" Tanya asked her.

"I knew you were American military when you and Chad both shot the stop sign from twelve hundred meters at night—"

"Dude," Duane whispered softly.

Sofia slapped him on the back of the head.

"Ow! You too, Tanya." He rubbed a hand where he'd been hit.

Tanya and Daniela ignored him.

"I have no shooters that skilled. My suspicions grew the way you worked together when I tried to make you jump off the bridge."

"And you didn't kill us then either?"

"You weren't trying to kill me…ahh. Which of you was it on the motorcycle?" Daniela turned to Chad.

"That would be this amazing woman," Chad pulled her into a one-armed embrace and kissed her temple.

"I'd have caught you, too, if Chad hadn't shot me." She elbowed him in the gut, but not too hard. Her elbow just bounced off his rock-solid abs anyway.

Daniela briefly raised her eyebrows before continuing.

"How did I know? Remember, before *la Capitana*, before Gerald the Boatman, I was a trained narcotics officer for Colombia. We were trained by the very best, members of your Delta Force. I knew who you were for certain the way you fought at the gold field—all four of you. No one else fights like that."

"Actually," Tanya grimaced. "I'm not Delta. I'm with Israel's Mossad."

"Yeah, about that." Chad started to let her go.

This was it. This was the moment where it all came apart. She closed her eyes for the coming blow. Chad wasn't even going to wait until they were somewhere private. He was going to tell her goodbye right here and now in front of everyone. And they'd all get to see her heart shatter.

She steeled herself for it. Knew she had no way to hold it together, but by God she was going to try.

"I, uh…" Chad let her go completely and the chill shook her.

Maybe she'd been the one locked in a refrigerator all day. It certainly felt that way.

"I, uh... Look, I'm really sorry, guys, but—" he turned to face Colonel Gibson, actually saluting sharply. "Sorry sir, but I quit."

There was stone silence.

Tanya opened one eye.

Everyone was looking at Chad in shock. Except Gibson, who was still doing his I'm-so-neutral-you-forgot-I-was-here-again-didn't-you thing. She had.

She opened the other eye.

Chad however looked completely serious.

"You...what?" Carla asked perfectly calmly. It was her most dangerous mode and even Chad recognized that enough to take a step back. Then he shook his head like a cornered bull and stepped forward once more.

"I quit."

"Dude!" Duane sounded hugely disappointed.

"I'm going to apply for Kidon."

This time Tanya felt the shock as it rippled through her and the circle.

Chad turned to her. "Only way I can figure to wind up next to you, Tanya. Which is the only damn place I want to be. Figure if I go Kidon, maybe we can make up a team."

"Like a husband-and-wife team?" She didn't know why that was the first thing she'd said. Getting married had always been something right down there with the crime that had placed her father into her family.

Chad's big hands flapped uncertainly for a moment. Then, with a muttered, "Shit!" he actually went down on one knee.

"Wouldn't want anyone else, lady. Hadn't thought about the marrying part, but you want that, I'll sign up."

Did she want that? Ever after? Consecrated as her husband according to the laws of Moses and Israel, or whatever they said in the US?

With Chad? The answer was easy.

"Yes."

"Cool." He took her hand, and for one shining moment, Tanya's world almost made sense.

"Bullshit!" Carla snapped out.

And the image crumbled.

"No goddamn way are we letting you leave this team."

Chad rose until he towered over Carla, who was most of a foot shorter. "You got no say in this, pint-size."

Tanya wanted to cover her eyes. Carla was the team's elemental force. This was going to end so badly—along with a dream she'd never dared have.

"I got plenty of say, you idiot. Why the hell would you leave our team, when it's exactly where Tanya belongs? Huh? Answer me that one, Mr. Hawkins."

Chad squinted down at Carla, still trying to digest that one.

Tanya was feeling a little bewildered herself.

"You deserve to be with this team," Daniela spoke softly. "The way you fight together? There is no other option."

It wasn't an option…because never in a hundred years had she thought of herself as deserving to be on a team like this one. She was the whipped girl. The loner. The one fighting all out until fate decided it was tired of her and killed her off.

But with this team, she'd…belong?

"Duh!" Carla must have seen the doubt on her face.

Tanya looked at Chad. She wished she could take him aside and talk it out. He was still frowning down at the spot that Carla had stepped away from. Frowning so hard that something must be wrong.

"Damn!" But it was suddenly his cheerful voice. He grabbed Daniela by the shoulders and kissed her right on the mouth. Quickly, but it surprised Daniela no end.

Then he grabbed Tanya's shoulders until they were practically nose to nose.

"What do you say, lady? Want to come fight for the good guys?"

Tanya opened her mouth, hoping that she'd somehow find

the words to say how good that sounded before her heart simply busted from joy.

"Hey!" Chad cut her off and turned away before she could answer.

She practically stumbled forward into the sudden vacuum.

"That's it!" He practically shouted at Daniela. "How about you coming to fight for the good guys, too? You took down *el Clan del Golfo* so sweet. Asshole Sánchez as a bonus. Good thing I didn't know about that before or I'd have beat him to death with my bare hands. You could join us and help us take down your old operation. What do you think?"

"Duh!" Carla answered for her.

"Okay, so I'm a beat slow," Chad grumbled.

Now it was Tanya's turn to pull him in close enough to kiss his temple. It felt as if she was holding all the hope in the world.

"Daniela," Tanya was amazed she could speak. "You started out with the good guys. Just the wrong good guys. Come on back. Make Fred a happy man."

Smith blushed brighter red than his hair.

"He loves you for your brain, trust me," Chad laughed as Smith impossibly went even redder.

Tanya had been so sure that Chad hadn't noticed. So, he wasn't totally oblivious, just a guy.

"We'll find a girl for you too, Silva. What you looking for? Can't have perfection, I already got her." Chad pulled her in tightly once more.

Tanya managed not to giggle happily.

Silva turned to Daniela, "I quit."

"Wait…what?" Tanya had nearly died when Chad had said those words. And now Silva?

Daniela pulled him to her, held him tightly, and kissed his cheek. When she turned back, she was crying.

"My big brother is married. He's a dog trainer. He came to help me after Sánchez. After…" her voice choked off as she brushed her hand down his arm.

"I stuck with her so that she didn't kill herself while chasing revenge. I couldn't stop her, so I decided that keeping her alive was my job as a big brother. But oddly, now my job as a trainer will be much safer. I trained drug-sniffing dogs. *El Clan del Golfo* had a very high price on my head, but I think that doesn't matter as much anymore."

"Well?" Carla asked Daniela.

Tanya could see the answer so easily that she laughed aloud. She couldn't help herself.

She turned to Colonel Gibson for his approval of two new people joining his team.

Except he wasn't there anymore. Or anywhere in the hangar.

Chad noticed her looking around. "Yeah, he does that. Kinda freaky."

As Carla twisted around looking for Gibson, Tanya spotted a white envelope sticking out of her back pocket and pointed it out.

"Uh," Carla pulled it out. "That wasn't there before."

Kyle plucked it up and pulled out the two sheets inside. Then he began to laugh softly before he handed one to Daniela and the other to her.

Everyone crowded in close to read them.

They both held formal offers to join Delta Force—signed by Colonel Michael Gibson. Tanya's was already countersigned by her own Kidon commander.

"Okay," Chad whispered in her ear. "Maybe he's *more* than a little bit freaky."

EPILOGUE

"*L*ong way down, bro."

"Damn long, dude."

Chad stared over the edge of the Las Lajas bridge at the river rushing so far below.

"Woulda died for sure," Duane declared.

"I dunno. Maybe that spot there?" Chad pointed at the hole of an eddy current far below.

"Nah, fish bait. But might be some good fishing down there."

"We could try later."

Duane slapped him hard enough on the back that Chad would have found out just how deep that hole was if the balustrade had been a few inches lower.

"Chad, got news for you. Wedding is one thing. Wedding night sex is another."

"I already know what to expect there."

"You haven't a clue, dude. Tell me that again tomorrow."

Chad eyed the Las Lajas Sanctuary speculatively.

Somewhere inside there, two women were getting dressed up

in wedding white. The three other female team members and Silva's wife would be fussing over them.

Chad leaned back against the railing and stared across the width of the bridge at the white marble-winged angel playing the saxophone. There was a drummer, French horn player, dude with a fat-bellied lute, but he liked the expression of the sax-playing angel. Looking like she was getting down with it.

"What's next?"

Duane shrugged uncertainly. "*El Clan del Golfo* is gone. *La Capitana* shattered her own organization. Wasn't hard, since she kept control of all the reins for just that purpose. Mostly just paying folks off and telling them to go home."

"Fit right in, didn't she?"

"Way Fred and Sofia go on about her, she's our next tactician. One thing we know. Whatever is next…"

"…is gonna be damn fun." Chad finished. "Glad to just be a shooter."

Duane fisted bumped him. "Shooter on a hell-a team, dude."

"Damn straight, bro."

Kyle came up to them with Richie. They had a dazed Fred Smith in tow. Three months to finish the cleanup of the worst of the cartels, and Daniela still had his head spinning.

Actually, Chad could feel that in himself, too—not that he'd ever admit it.

"Ready to do the married thing?" Kyle had his of-course-you-are tone in place. Which was how he led the team whenever Carla wasn't watching.

"Long as it's Tanya Zimmer waiting at the head of the aisle, I'm game."

Kyle gave him one of those looks.

"Easy, boss. I'll say 'I do' and mean it when the time comes." Kyle eased back.

"Great idea for the rings," Fred commented as he and Chad fished them out to turn them over to the best men.

Chad read the inscription to himself: *Shot straight to the heart.* He hoped she liked that. That and the shining blue sapphire that matched her eyes; the white gold already matched her hair.

"Wish I could claim it, but the idea was Duane's." He was the one who'd suggested they should make the rings from that lump of gold Chad had taken as a souvenir from the river camp as a keepsake.

"Actually," Duane looked uncomfortable. "Might have been something Sofia mentioned. She said something like, 'it might be a good idea.' But she had this odd tone, the one like it isn't a choice?"

Chad was getting to know that tone. Why would Sofia have thought of that? He'd already forgotten about the thing, tossed in the bottom of his rifle case from the cartel takedown mission and forgotten there.

"Won't they be surprised when we tell them." Fred was happily inspecting them one last time before handing his over to Richie.

Chad glanced at Duane. Yeah, fifty today gets you a hamburger next Tuesday that the women were all in cahoots on this already. Oh, they'd act surprised and never in a thousand years admit knowing, but...

"Inscrutable," he whispered to Duane.

"Till their dying day, dude. Till their dying day," his best man confirmed.

Chad decided it was better not to think about it and turned to Kyle.

"So, you heard from Gibson yet about what's next?" Chad could never slip a subject change past Carla or Tanya, but sometimes he could get it past Kyle.

Richie's smile lit up. "Did he ever! You wouldn't believe where we're headed. We're—"

Kyle clamped a hand over Richie's mouth and sighed. "After the honeymoon."

He remembered what Duane had said about married sex being even better than engaged sex.

"I'm good with that."

There was a friendly round of laughter and backslaps.

Chad locked arms with Fred and began heading for the church.

"Gonna be so good," Fred assured him cheerfully.

"In so many ways."

It was hard not to compare the fifteen stories of Gothic majesty of Las Lajas Sanctuary with the run-down neighborhood Catholic church back in Detroit that reeked of desperation—his own and that of the others who cowered in the back. He had come impossibly far...yet it felt like the journey was only beginning.

Chad took one last glance at the radiant blue sky of the Colombian Andes.

"Bring it on, bro," he whispered. Then he focused on going in and marrying the woman who brought it like no other.

WANT MORE? TRY FLYING WITH THE NIGHT STALKERS!

(EXCERPT)

TARGET OF THE HEART (EXCERPT)

*M*ajor Pete Napier hovered his MH-47G Chinook helicopter ten kilometers outside of Lhasa, Tibet and a mere two inches off the tundra. A mixed action team of Delta Force and The Activity—the slipperiest intel group on the planet—flung themselves aboard.

The additional load sent an infinitesimal shift in the cyclic control in his right hand. The hydraulics to close the rear loading ramp hummed through the entire frame of the massive helicopter. By the time his crew chief could reach forward to slap an "all secure" signal against his shoulder, they were already ten feet up and fifty out. That was enough altitude. He kept the nose down as he clawed for speed in the thin air at eleven thousand feet.

"Totally worth it," one of the D-boys announced as soon as he was on the Chinook's internal intercom.

He'd have to remember to tell that to the two Black Hawks flying guard for him…when they were in a friendly country and could risk a radio transmission. This deep inside China—or rather Chinese-held territory as the CIA's mission-briefing spook had insisted on calling it—radios attracted attention and were only used to avoid imminent death and destruction.

"Great, now I just need to get us out of this alive."

"Do that, Pete. We'd appreciate it."

He wished to hell he had a stealth bird like the one that had gone into bin Laden's compound. But the one that had crashed during that raid had been blown up. Where there was one, there were always two, but the second had gone back into hiding as thoroughly as if it had never existed. He hadn't heard a word about it since.

The Tibetan terrain was amazing, even if all he could see of it was the monochromatic green of night vision. And blackness. The largest city in Tibet lay a mere ten kilometers away and they were flying over barren wilderness. He could crash out here and no one would know for decades unless some yak herder stumbled upon them. Or were yaks in Mongolia? He was a corn-fed, white boy from Colorado, what did he know about Tibet? Most of the countries he'd flown into on black ops missions he'd only seen at night anyway.

While moving very, very fast.

Like now.

The inside of his visor was painted with overlapping readouts. A pre-defined terrain map, the best that modern satellite imaging could build made the first layer. This wasn't some crappy, on-line, look-at-a-picture-of-your-house display. Someone had a pile of dung outside their goat pen? He could see it, tell you how high it was, and probably say if they were pygmy goats or full-size LaManchas by the size of their shit-pellets if he zoomed in.

On top of that were projected the forward-looking infrared camera images. The FLIR imaging gave him a real-time overlay, in case someone had put an addition onto their goat shed since the last satellite pass, or parked their tractor across his intended flight path.

His nervous system was paying autonomic attention to that

combined landscape. He also compensated for the thin air at altitude as he instinctively chose when to start his climb over said goat shed or his swerve around it.

It was the third layer, the tactical display that had most of his attention. At least he and the two Black Hawks flying escort on him were finally on the move.

To insert this deep into Tibet, without passing over Bhutan or Nepal, they'd had to add wingtanks on the Black Hawks' hardpoints where he'd much rather have a couple banks of Hellfire missiles. Still, they had 20mm chain guns and the crew chiefs had miniguns which was some comfort.

While the action team was busy infiltrating the capital city and gathering intelligence on the particularly brutal Chinese assistant administrator, he and his crews had been squatting out in the wilderness under a camouflage net designed to make his helo look like just another god-forsaken Himalayan lump of granite.

Command had determined that it was better for the helos to wait on site through the day than risk flying out and back in. He and his crew had stood shifts on guard duty, but none of them had slept. They'd been flying together too long to have any new jokes, so they'd played a lot of cribbage. He'd long ago ruled no gambling on a mission, after a fistfight had broken out about a bluff hand that cost a Marine three hundred and forty-seven dollars. Marines hated losing to Army no matter how many times it happened. They'd had to sit on him for a long time before he calmed down.

Tonight's mission was part of an on-going campaign to discredit the Chinese "presence" in Tibet on the international stage—as if occupying the country the last sixty years didn't count toward ruling, whether invited or not. As usual, there was a crucial vote coming up at the U.N.—that, as usual, the Chinese could be guaranteed to ignore. However, the ever-hopeful CIA was in a hurry to make sure that any damaging information that they could validate was disseminated as thoroughly as possible prior to the vote.

Not his concern.

His concern was, were they going to pass over some Chinese sentry post at their top speed of a hundred and ninety-six miles an hour? The sentries would then call down a couple Shenyang J-16 jet fighters that could hustle along at Mach 2 to fry his sorry ass. He knew there was a pair of them parked at Lhasa along with some older gear that would be just as effective against his three helos.

"Don't suppose you could get a move on, Pete?"

"Eat shit, Nicolai!" He was a good man to have as a copilot. Pete knew he was holding on too tight, and Nicolai knew that a joke was the right way to ease the moment.

He, Nicolai, and the four pilots in the two Black Hawks had a long way to go tonight and he'd never make it if he stayed so tight on the controls that he could barely maneuver. Pete eased off and felt his fingers tingle with the rush of returning blood. They dove down into gorges and followed them as long as they dared. They hugged cliff walls at every opportunity to decrease their radar profile. And they climbed.

That was the true danger—they would be up near the helos' limits when they crossed over the backbone of the Himalayas in their rush for India. The air was so rarefied that they burned fuel at a prodigious rate. Their reserve didn't allow for any extended battles while crossing the border...not for any battle at all really.

It was pitch dark outside her helicopter when Captain Danielle Delacroix stamped on the left rudder pedal while giving the big Chinook right-directed control on the cyclic. It tipped her most of the way onto her side, but let her continue in a straight line. A Chinook's rotors were sixty feet across—front to back they overlapped to make the spread a hundred feet long. By cross-controlling her bird to tip it, she managed to execute a straight line between two mock pylons only thirty feet apart. They were made of thin cloth so they wouldn't down the helo if you sliced one—she was the only trainee to not have cut one yet.

At her current angle of attack, she took up less than a half-rotor of width, just twenty-four feet. That left her nearly three feet to either side, sufficient as she was moving at under a hundred knots.

The training instructor sitting beside her in the copilot's seat didn't react as she swooped through the training course at Fort Campbell, Kentucky. Only child of a single mother, she was used to providing her own feedback loops, so she didn't expect anything else. Those who expected outside validation rarely survived the SOAR induction testing, never mind the two years of training that followed.

As a loner kid, Danielle had learned that self-motivated congratulations and fun were much easier to come by than external ones. She'd spent innumerable hours deep in her mind as a pre-teen superheroine. At twenty-nine she was well on her way to becoming a real life one, though Helo-girl had never been a character she'd thought of in her youth.

available at fine retailers everywhere

ABOUT THE AUTHOR

M.L. Buchman started the first of, what is now over 50 novels and even more short stories, while flying from South Korea to ride his bicycle across the Australian Outback. All part of a solo around-the-world bicycle trip (a mid-life crisis on wheels) that ultimately launched his writing career.

Booklist has selected his military and firefighter series(es) as 3-time "Top 10 Romance of the Year." NPR and Barnes & Noble have named other titles "Best 5 Romance of the Year." In 2016 he was a finalist for RWA's prestigious RITA award.

He has flown and jumped out of airplanes, can single-hand a fifty-foot sailboat, and has designed and built two houses. In between writing, he also quilts. M. L. is constantly amazed at what you can do with a degree in Geophysics. He also writes: contemporary romance, thrillers, and fantasy.

More info and a free novel for subscribing to his newsletter at: www.mlbuchman.com

Join the conversation:
www.mlbuchman.com

Other works by M. L. Buchman:

The Night Stalkers
MAIN FLIGHT
The Night Is Mine
I Own the Dawn
Wait Until Dark
Take Over at Midnight
Light Up the Night
Bring On the Dusk
By Break of Day
WHITE HOUSE HOLIDAY
Daniel's Christmas
Frank's Independence Day
Peter's Christmas
Zachary's Christmas
Roy's Independence Day
Damien's Christmas
AND THE NAVY
Christmas at Steel Beach
Christmas at Peleliu Cove
5E
Target of the Heart
Target Lock on Love
Target of Mine

Firehawks
MAIN FLIGHT
Pure Heat
Full Blaze
Hot Point
Flash of Fire
Wild Fire
SMOKEJUMPERS
Wildfire at Dawn
Wildfire at Larch Creek
Wildfire on the Skagit

Delta Force
Target Engaged
Heart Strike
Wild Justice

White House Protection Force
Off the Leash
On Your Mark
In the Weeds

Where Dreams
Where Dreams are Born
Where Dreams Reside
Where Dreams Are of Christmas
Where Dreams Unfold
Where Dreams Are Written

Eagle Cove
Return to Eagle Cove
Recipe for Eagle Cove
Longing for Eagle Cove
Keepsake for Eagle Cove

Henderson's Ranch
Nathan's Big Sky
Big Sky, Loyal Heart

Love Abroad
Heart of the Cotswolds: England
Path of Love: Cinque Terre, Italy

Dead Chef Thrillers
Swap Out!
One Chef!
Two Chef!

Deities Anonymous
Cookbook from Hell: Reheated
Saviors 101

SF/F Titles
The Nara Reaction
Monk's Maze
the Me and Elsie Chronicles

Strategies for Success (NF)
Managing Your Inner Artist/Writer
Estate Planning for Authors

SIGN UP FOR M. L. BUCHMAN'S
NEWSLETTER TODAY

and receive:
Release News
Free Short Stories
a Free Book

Do it today. Do it now.
http://free-book.mlbuchman.com

SEP 3 0 2021

CPSIA information can be obtained
at www.ICGtesting.com
Printed in the USA
LVHW021532280821
696353LV00007B/500